Schwartzkopf

EX LIBRIS

ADVANCE PRAISE FOR GLASS HALO

"Eloquently bitter-sweet, *Glass Halo* takes you through a stained window into a world of shards. Colleen Smith has reached into the heart of her characters and found unlikely hope and redemption."
—NICK BANTOCK
International best-selling author of the *Griffin and Sabine* series

"*Glass Halo* is a beautifully written book about how two people find some hard-won personal peace through their vocations."
—JESUIT FATHER JOHN DEAR, the author of *A Persistent Peace*, was nominated by Archbishop Desmond Tutu for the Nobel Peace Prize.

"*Glass Halo* is a literary rarity; a first novel born fully formed. Evidencing both beautiful writing and remarkable plot, *Glass Halo* examines the fragile, tragic life of Nora Kelley, a glassmaker recovering from a brutal episode that shatters her psyche and causes her to question her entire wold. Colleen Smith has written a superb novel; understated, elegant, and moving. A powerful inaugural statement."
—JON CHANDLER
Award-winning author of the *Spanish Peaks* and *Wyoming Wind*

"The prose dazzled and humbled me."
—DAVID SCOTT, author of *A Revolution of Love: The Meaning of Mother Teresa*

"It is an indescribable joy to read a work of art. It's not just that this story transports you, it's the writing itself that compels and enriches you. In a world of fast-food fiction, I am grateful to read something that nourishes and delights my cells. I hope that Colleen Smith has more books in store for us!"
—TAMA J. KIEVES
Best-selling author of *This Time I Dance! Creating the Work You Love*

"...A great book, a beautifully told, image filled inspiring story that not only held my attention, it so brightened my every moment I didn't want the story to end; I hoped and prayed that I would hear more from the the author. That's just the truth."
—MONSIGNOR JOHN SHERIDAN
Pastor Emeritus, Our Lady of Malibu, California
Author of *Saints in Times of Turmoil* (Paulist Press, 1977), *Living the Psalms: Selections from the Psalms with Meditations* (Pauline Books & Media, 1996), and *Questions and Answers on the Catholic Faith* (Hawthorn Books, 1963)

"Colleen Smith's superb first novel, *Glass Halo,* shines as colorfully as cathedral stained glass in ever-changing moods of light. Smith's soulful characters, Nora Kelley—an artist glazier—and her spiritually vibrant companion—an inquisitive Catholic priest—wrestle with their experiences of life's mysterious forces that connect them and us while challenging our fragile sense of humanity."
—TODD SILER
Author of *Think Like A Genius*

"*Glass Halo* delivers excellent plot line, vibrant yet troubled characters and an authentic voice. The book sheds light on the secrets of the Catholic Church while maintaining a measured respect for that which is sacred. I wholeheartedly recommend this book.... A good read for anybody whose struggled with temptation."
—PAM COLBY
Executive Director, The Minneapolis Television Network

"Whether you read for a just a little while before bedtime or want to spend a weekend transporting yourself into lives that will interest and intrigue you, *Glass Halo* is a ride that you will enjoy."
—WILLIAM J. BANNON
Catholic Church Consultant

Advance praise for *Galo Halo* continued on next page.

ADVANCE PRAISE (Continued)

"*Glass Halo* holds a 'mirror up to nature' and reveals a very human love story set in the context of the Catholic Church's calendar year. One can follow this intensely moving story of Nora and Father Vin's powerful relationship and at the same time learn a great deal about how the Church looks at the tyranny of time. Anyone who shares a fascination for Catholicism and appreciates facing potent interior conflicts lived in the context of modern struggles will benefit from this read."
—DEACON DICK BOWLES

"*Glass Halo* reminds us that we are fragile, that none of us live above reproach."
—MILA GLODAVA
Co-author of *Making Stewardship a Way of Life*, and
Mail Order Brides: Women for Sale

GLASS HALO

GLASS HALO

By Colleen Smith

Denver, Colorado, U.S.A.
www.FridayJonesPublishing.com

First printing 2010.

www.fridayjonespublishing.com

Cover design by Colleen Smith and Nancy Benton
Cover images copyright © 2010 by Colleen Smith

Library of Congress Cataloging-in-Publication Data

Smith, Colleen
Glass Halo/Colleen Smith
Denver, CO: Friday Jones Publishing., 2010.

p. cm.
ISBN-13: 9780984428908
ISBN: 0984428909

Library of Congress Catalog Number: 2010924398

For the angels & the ancestors

"I believe in...
the forgiveness of sins."

—The Apostle's Creed

TABLE OF CONTENTS

AUTHOR'S NOTE

This is a work of fiction with fictitious characters. The liturgical year of the Universal Catholic Church provides the framework for this novel, but the dates may be skewed slightly. The novel's setting draws heavily from the Cathedral Basilica of the Immaculate Conception in Denver, Colorado; though the name has been changed in reverence to the actual basilica.

Prologue

lass is born of pedestrian materials: sand and potash. Typically, near a glass factory a river runs, a source of sand banks. Countless trees are felled and turned to charcoal and ash. Glass endures extreme temperatures. Without the crucible, no beauty. Without the fire, only a handful of dust.

Given a source of light, stained glass holds not only a saturation of color, but also the edges of emotion—sharp, fragile. Like the river, the glass is never the same twice. The slant of illumination varies. A bank of clouds filters the sun before it hits the stain of the window. A branch waves and brushes a shadow across the glass, deepening hues, if only momentarily.

Nora Kelley had cut herself so much she no longer bled. A

glazier from a long line of glaziers, she'd grown up surrounded by panes of colored light. Glass from France and Germany, Italy and South Africa. Mouth-blown glass with striations of rainbow trout, opal, deep space nebula. Wavy antique glass riddled with bubbles. Glass polished or dull, smooth as ponds or rough as pebbled leather. Factory glass of lapis lazuli blue, pomegranate seed red, amber the color of owl eyes. Beveled glass and leaded prisms that tossed quivering spectrums around a room. Weighty glass jewels like gigantic chunks of hard candy. Cathedral glass.

Nora had crafted countless windows. Dozens of leaded glass works went out of her studio each year.

Until the accident. Some cuts run deeper than others.

GLASS HALO

In the name of the Father ⊠ and of the Son ⊠ and of the Holy Spirit. ⊠

Father in heaven,

You know me as even I cannot know myself, so you recognize the hol— lowness of my prayer. ⊠ ⊠ Where has my hope gone, dear God? ⊠ What of the joy I once knew in your vineyard? ⊠

My soul cries out for you. ⊠ ⊠ I kneel barren and burdened. ⊠ Where is my anchor? ⊠ ⊠ ⊠

You refuse to reveal yourself in the Scriptures. ⊠ ⊠ ⊠ You lurk on a side road, around the corner. ⊠ And I cannot recognize you now, Lord—forgive me— even in the breaking of the bread. ⊠ ⊠ ⊠

Lord, look kindly upon me, your priest. Send a sign. ⊠ Bless me with a sign, O God, a signal from on high. ⊠ ⊠ ⊠

In the name of the Father and of the Son and of the Holy Spirit. ⊠ AMEN. ⊠

CHAPTER ONE

Whitsun Eve

DENVER, COLORADO
THE EVE OF PENTECOST (30 *May*)

he miller moths arrived in swarms that spring. Their dusty wings marred surfaces. Their bodies slimed windowpanes, bumped into any source of light. Miller moths startled Nora as they lumbered out of the silverware drawer or flew from the porch awning, her jewelry box, the medicine cabinet lined with rows of translucent orange prescription bottles that had not facilitated healing.

That May day, Nora had taken to her bed. The wind chimes on the porch keened frantically, waking her from a bankrupt sleep. A moth divebombed her forehead. She cringed under the rumpled covers in her darkened bedroom. The clock on her night stand read 4:40 p.m. Calculating, Nora realized she had slept 14 hours straight.

Her tongue was flannel. A peacock-blue wave shimmered in the corner of her vision. Migraine manifestation.

Her stomach growled. Desperately hungry, it wasn't so much that Nora wanted to eat, she *needed* to eat, yet nothing sounded appetizing. She made her way down the stairs from the loft to the small, sunny kitchen. The glare of light spangling the toaster made her wince. Nora closed the blinds and gulped a glass of tap water.

Smelly dishes filled the sink. Kitchen cupboards yawned bare. The refrigerator held only stone-ground mustard, cheesecake grown moldy, rusty ribs of celery, broccoli on its way to a liquid state and a reserve bottle of Champagne. Nora kept a split on hand to christen every completed stained-glass window that went out of her studio. That bottle had been chilling forlornly for nearly two years.

Her stomach gripped in pangs. She picked up the telephone, dialed.

"This is Nora Kelley," she said. "I'm calling for a prescription refill." She kneaded the back of her neck. "I need it today. Can you deliver?" She sighed. "No, I don't have anybody who can pick it up for me."

Dropping the cordless phone on the window seat, her blurred vision cast a confusing spell. ✍ Delirious, she tiptoed around the carriage house rounding up wrinkled clothes, worn sandals, her wallet.

Stepping onto the small porch, she looked up at a confluence of rowdy clouds. As she locked the door, the winds changed, whipping up dust devils. A gauzy veil draped from Mount Evans to Longs Peak and drifted toward the city.

"Nora! Nora!" Her name sailed on a gust of wind. She looked across the expanse of lawn. Mrs. Quincy poked her head out the ornate wrought-iron door. "Yoo-hoo," she called and waved.

Her landlady was the sole person Nora spoke to regularly—the old woman's choice more than hers. Nora could not shun Mrs. Quincy's warmhearted ways, her wisdom from the hip. Plus, Nora's disability benefits were soon to cease, so she tolerated Mrs. Quincy's nosiness knowing that one day soon, when her rent was late, she may need to grovel to the grandmotherly matriarch.

Nora waved, her wrist limp.

Mrs. Quincy motioned her to the imposing front porch. The wind tousled her wispy, bluish hair, styled weekly.

Nora's arrangement with Mrs. Quincy included yardwork, running errands and looking in on her from time to time. Nora could only hope she didn't have something planned for her now. The old lady held her hands to her low back.

"We're in for a gully washer," Mrs. Quincy said. "I can feel it in my old barometer bones." In the clutch of her migraine, Nora saw an indigo glow throb around the woman and seep out to fill the grand foyer. The old woman handed Nora a plaid umbrella.

"Where are you heading, dear?" The tiny polka dots on Mrs. Quincy's apron made Nora swoon.

A couple of moths bumbled around the transom. "I have to go to the drugstore," Nora said.

"Oh, dear. Are you ill?" Mrs. Quincy asked, touching the back of her hand to Nora's forehead. Nora flinched, then squeezed her eyes shut at the slight pressure.

You don't know the half of it, Nora thought, but said, "A little under the weather." She looked outside at the low ceiling of conspiring clouds.

"Have you been getting enough sleep?" Mrs. Quincy asked.

Nora snorted and nodded. "I've had enough rapid eye movement for days."

Mrs. Quincy untied her apron. "I'm going over to the 5:15 Mass," she said. "I could drive you to the druggist. Or maybe you'd care to join me; and we could swing by the pharmacy afterwards."

"Thanks, Mrs. Quincy," said Nora, "but the walk might do me some good."

It wasn't the first time Mrs. Quincy had invited Nora to Mass. Nor the first time Nora had begged off.

Nora walked away as if on a high wire. No net. *Exercise will help,* she kept telling herself. *Movement is life. Breathe some fresh air.* ❧

But the air smacked of something like sulfur. Nora took step after calculated step.

On the parkway, old Dutch elms swayed. The bricks of stately homes shifted and settled ever so subtly. Cyclists made their way against the wind. Housewives battened down the hatches, folded up market umbrellas, set down hanging pots of flowers, ushered children and pets inside.

Nora's legs quickly grew heavy as if she were walking in hot tar. She stopped, leaned against the trunk of a linden almost halfway to the neighborhood pharmacy that stocked basic groceries, a rack of greeting cards and several aisles of spirits and wines. Nora walked into the wind. Change crackled through the mile-high air. From the east, huge cauliflower clouds rolled in, filling with power, billowing.

In the store, Nora slowly navigated the aisles. She avoided making eye contact with the neon beer signs and steered clear of the aisle of caustic cleaning products as she gathered a few items and set them gently in a red plastic shopping basket.

The clerk took his time ringing her up, sacking her purchases. In no hurry, he watched a game show on the little TV near his cash register. He asked, earnestly, "Anything else I can get you?" His voice sounded synthesized.

"Not today," Nora said.

She hugged the paper sack of groceries against her hip and left, fleeing the buzz of the fluorescent lights and the canned laughter from the television. All she wanted was her bed. Home. Sedation.

These days, Nora wanted most of all to forget. Time, they say, heals all wounds. But they never say how *much* time.

Outside the store, Nora's hair whipped her face. She surveyed the agitated atmosphere, looking from north to south, east to west. The cityscape drew clouds like magnets pull iron filings. Attraction. ✒ From all directions, cumulonimbus boiled in a fury overhead. Unable to decide whether to take cover or continue to walk, Nora considered calling a cab, but rejected the notion of filthy seats, smoke lingering on upholstery, an expectation to make small talk with the immigrant driver.

On the eastern horizon, funnel clouds jutted down like slender stalactites, like the hand of God pointing accusatory gray fingers. She adjusted the bag of groceries and wondered about waiting out the storm at the store. The sky appeared jaundiced. Rampaging clouds displayed hues of a bruise.

Nora knew she should stay put outside the store, but she couldn't bear the one-ended conversations of shoppers braying into cell phones. She needed to lie down. Starting for home, head bowed in determination, she gained little ground. ✒ The air grew suddenly cool and calm. A large drop of rain plopped sharply on her head, right in the part of her hair. Rain fell in drops so large they dotted the sidewalk with wet spots the size of half dollars. The snare drumming of rain increased steadily into monsoon sheets.

The wet and the cold, the atmospheric release, somewhat

revived Nora. Ducking under the eaves of the St. Raphael High School gymnasium, she tipped her chin up at the French Gothic cathedral spires. She glowered back at the openmouthed gargoyles regurgitating rain, steady streams rushing past their concrete fangs.

Nora set down the grocery sack and ripped open the small white paper bag holding her prescription. She tossed pills to the back of her tongue and swallowed them dry. Knowing it would be awhile before the headache faded, Nora waited. Wiggling her bare toes in her sandals, she allowed the down-pouring rain to mesmerize her. Soon, water flowed in little raging rivers along the curbs. Puddles flooded into miniature lakes on the lawns of brick bungalows lining the streets. ✺

Deciding the storm wasn't about to let up, Nora made a run for it. She tucked the bag against her gut like a soggy football and sprinted, best she could. Rain soaked her hair, turning honey blonde to mousy brown. She tugged her drenched shorts away from her legs.

Then the low note of the emergency warning siren sounded. Nora stopped in her tracks. She whirled around and spotted halfway down the block, next to the cathedral, a man waving his arms. Squinting, she saw that he held a black and tan shepherd straining at the leash. He lifted his elbow up against the slant of the rain.

The rain chilled to hail. Cold pearls accumulated on lawns, in the street and freshly planted flower beds. Hailstones like little ice moons. Just as suddenly, the hail ceased.

The man near the cathedral shouted something Nora could not decipher. He waved, seemingly in slow motion. Nora fought the fogginess of a dense dream. He pointed to the sky behind her. She turned around and saw the big funnel skip on the distant horizon, a dirty cloud corralling all the deviant forces of nature.

Astonished, Nora stared down the eye of the storm: a *tornado*. The cloud twisted and jerked, writhing.

Nora could say nothing. Do nothing. Utter terror replaced awe as every tale of twisters she'd ever heard verified itself. Randomly, the storm lit on houses and yards in the distance. The twister peeled off sections of roofs and dislodged street signs. Random objects—a tree branch, a wrought-iron yard lamp, a tire, cartwheeling lawn furniture, planters, a mountain bike, mailboxes, trash cans, *everything*—exploded into the air with demonic force. She stood paralyzed. Rain saturated her clothes and washed down her bare limbs. The hail hammered again, even harder.

"Oh, my God; oh, my God; oh, my God," she murmured. Into her mind popped the inscription on her headstone:

"Nora Kelley

Born 1977

Died 2010

Blown away"

Nora was 33 years old. She had buried both her parents. She had survived violence unspeakable. Nora had noted that the oven in her carriage house was gas. More than once, she had emptied the entire contents of a bottle of sleeping pills into her moist palm. Driving in the high country, she had trifled with mountain passes, treacherous curves and deadly ravines. She had resisted so-called easy ways out.

Nora clutched the wet paper sack of groceries and recalled her second-grade teacher, Sister Marie Pierre, who had repeatedly advised students to pray simply "My Lord and my God" if they ever sensed impending accidental death—for example, in a plane about to crash. "My Lord and my God." A password, of sorts, a code to crack open the kingdom of heaven, all trespasses forgiven and forgotten by way of that succinct incantation.

Again, the hail stopped. Nora looked left and right. The man with the dog stood on the cathedral's top step, maybe 15 paces from her. The rain had plastered his dark hair to his head. He rushed down the cathedral steps two by two and yanked Nora's arm. Her wet grocery sack gave way. The dog barked and barked, barely audible over the wind and the warning horns. As they dashed toward the cathedral, Nora looked back at the rolling jar of almond butter, the sesame bagels, the green plastic basket spilling red strawberries, bundled asparagus spears, the small white paper bag holding the migraine meds. She broke free of him and grabbed the soaked sack containing the prescription.

"Come on!" the man shouted above the wail of the emergency

sirens. The shepherd's eyes flashed wildly. The man tugged Nora's arm. "Follow me!"

She stood back on her heels. "I'm OK, I live nearby. I'm going home." She pictured the carriage house she rented. "I live with an elderly lady. I have to make sure she's OK," she hollered.

"There's no time!" He bolted for the cathedral. She took one more look at the debris swirling in the storm and followed him and the dog up the front stairs. The man wrestled with the winds for control of the heavy double doors. His broad back bent and strained.

Nora noticed the bas relief emerging from the brass door. A wizened man clasped a book, his other hand held high, finger pointing toward the heavens.

"*Heave!*" the man yelled; and like any crew member worth her salt, she did. Together, the man and Nora managed to pull open one of the doors. The dog ran inside the cathedral ahead of them. The man pulled Nora into the vestibule.

"Downstairs, Puccini! Down!" he yelled, his voice a deep boom. The dog led the way down the stairwell to the church basement.

The lights flickered. ✒ He led her to a door with a sign in calligraphic letters: Bride's Room. The room was windowless. A three-paneled mirror spanned one wall. Nora imagined brides adjusting their bustles, straightening their trains. She had attended a couple of weddings in the cathedral. A funeral, too. Liam's.

She had lived in the neighborhood since defecting from the

suburbs the week after that funeral, but she generally avoided setting foot inside St. Raphael Cathedral, wary of her ancestors' brand of piety. She had admired the stained-glass windows from Munich.

The dog's pointed ears folded back against his head. "Everything's going to be all right, Puccini," the man said in a somber baritone as he locked the door.

The lights flickered again, went out and stayed out. In the cathedral basement, the dark ran so deep Nora could not see the man or the dog but she could smell them, musky, masculine. Outside, sirens mixed with intensifying wind. Doom crowded and cramped the Bride's Room. The dog panted. Nora could hear herself panting, too. The rain ceased; the sirens did not.

"The calm before the storm," the man said.

Unwittingly, Nora let out a nervous laugh. She twirled a strand of hair around her finger and held her breath. The dog whimpered. The winds moaned. Old trees chanted dirges. Even the foundation stones of the cathedral seemed to groan in queasy anticipation.

🙨 The man prayed aloud, his voice penitent: "'Remember, O gracious Virgin Mary, that never was it known that anyone who fled to your protection, implored your help or sought your intercession was left unaided.'"

The words paralyzed Nora. Her mother's preferred prayer, *The Memorare*. Nora had not resorted to such invocations in years, and she knew her mother would be appalled at her lapse. Her mother could make Nora feel guilty even from the grave. Nora remembered the prayer, but she did not chime in. At least not aloud.

Then the man prayed the *Salve Regina*: "'To you do we cry, poor banished children of Eve. To you we send up our prayer, mourning and weeping in this vale of tears.'"

Ardent Catholics never ceased to amaze Nora, whipping out their prayers like abracadabras.

The locked door blew open. The lights flashed on. She looked up to see the man bury the jittery dog's head in his chest and form his body around the animal. Nora followed suit, tucking into a ball, her arms covering her head.

"This is it," he said. The lights darkened again.

All around, a rumble. Wood splintered, timbers creaked and crashing objects pelted the outside walls of the room. Nora registered the unmistakable sound of glass shattering. She bit the insides of her cheeks. Above the cacophony, she felt her pulse gallop through her temples.

Aware that she might die, her thoughts turned to Liam, as her thoughts too often did. *Maybe*, Nora thought, *my husband has conjured this tornado from beyond the grave to carry out his volatile revenge*. Nora still granted him so much clout.

Sister Marie Pierre also had taught her students that wickedness incarnates. Evil holds sway. Horrific things happen to good people. Should she die here and now, Nora knew that her staunch refusal to forgive her dead husband stood most in the way of her entering heaven's gates. Still, she could not absolve him. Would not. Not even in exchange for life eternal, should it exist.

Once upon a time, she and Liam had spurred one another on, tethered by creativity, painting side by side, his brush on canvas, hers on glass. They had eaten from one another's plates, slept beneath the same bedspread, shared a steamy shower every night. They had backpacked and bicycled in the mountains, camped and skied. They had listened to the same music, laughed at the same comics.

Nora cocked an ear as the sirens grew more distant. She heard the three-way mirror shake. She smelled something caustic, a worrisome odor like an electrical fire. Her heart pummeled her ribcage. She clenched her fists and wondered: *Will the building cave? Will the cathedral catch fire, a wildly tossing votive candle grown deadly?* She imagined herself brained by blowing debris. Pinned beneath an implosion. She braced herself against the most incendiary scare she'd faced since the night her husband died. She hoped it would be quick.

St. Francis of Assisi, Nora had learned in high school, wrote of Sister Death. Nora would welcome her now as a sibling. Anything to put an end to her pain, anything to quit, to start over. Eternal damnation or paradise. Reincarnation. Limbo. Purgatory. Anything would be an improvement over the nothingness she'd felt for so long. *Besides,* she reasoned with herself, *heaven turns away suicides, but the nacre gates open to those who die in natural disasters. Acts of God.*

The tornado passed in a matter of minutes; but curled into the fetal position, Nora felt each second wax into imagined hours. The world settled. They waited in the Bride's Room for several more long moments before the dog whined. They came out of their tucks.

"Dear God," the man said. She felt a smooth hand squeeze her arm. The heat from his palm traveled up toward her armpit. "Dear God in heaven," he said, coughing. "Are you all right?"

"Don't let go of me," Nora wheezed, finding his hand, fright diluting her usual inhibitions. "Please. Don't let go." Her voice shook, heavy accents falling on every syllable.

"I'm here," he said in an analgesic tone. "I'm right here with you. Are you hurt?"

Contemplating the question made Nora want to cry. The dog huffed and puffed. Her neck tensed. Dust coated the insides of her nostrils.

The dog danced and sneezed. In the distance, emergency vehicles wailed. Rushing screams of ambulances, fire trucks, police cars. Nora took a deep breath, almost gagged on panic. She remembered the sirens nearing that night Liam died.

In a calm voice, the man said, "Oh, Puccini. Good dog. What a good dog. Oh, yes, what a good dog." And then, to Nora, "We're fine. We're fine. 'The wind blows where it will. You hear the sound it makes but you do not know where it comes from, or where it goes.' John chapter three, verse eight."

Nora rolled her eyes. She detested the platitudes of the church, this scrambling for Scripture to explain away life's atrocities, the clutching at novenas and votive candles and prayer chains, incense, scapular medals, bone chips of martyrs. ✑ All that holding out for eternal afterlife at the right hand of the Father.

Nora wondered whether her dad would agree. Though he had spent his life painting holy images on glass, she was never sure if he had truly believed in them. Angels. Saints. The Trinity. To him, she assumed, they were no more real than unicorns and leprechauns. Eventually, she would have asked him. She had trusted her father would live to a ripe old age.

Her mother, of course, was another story. Nora's mother had prayed when the car stalled, when she planted tulips, when she jockeyed for a parking space downtown, before and after meals and, on her knees at the bedside of Nora, feigning sleep.

The dog barked, and Nora jumped. Suddenly, she worried about Mrs. Quincy. *Had she come to the cathedral for 5:15 Mass? Was she in the building? And her house? And all my things?*

To Nora's surprise, she worried most about her artwork. All her rolled-up, hand-drawn cartoons from her windows. Her portfolios of pen and ink drawings, charcoal sketches of red cedar trees, careful watercolor studies of alpine wildflowers, textural oils of mountain peaks and lakes, dawdling sunsets, silvery river bends, stands of golden aspen. ✒

The man released a wistful sigh into the dark. "I'm going now. For just a minute. I'll be back. OK?" He cleared his throat. "Are you all right?"

Nora nodded, then realized he couldn't see her in the dark. "I think so."

"Stay here," he said. "Puccini will stay with you."

Nora blinked, spooked into near hysteria. She had always considered darkness sinister, something to avoid. She habitually left the light on over the kitchen sink. All night. She dreaded small dark places. The walls snugged in against her. She considered screaming, asking herself, *Isn't that what frightened women do?* She smelled the wet dog.

"Puppy? Are you a nice puppy?" The dog sidled up to her. Nora wanted to sob. She considered praying, but was too frightened to wiggle her fingers, let alone fold her hands.

The dog licked her wrist. Nora listened. In the blackness, her ears filled with the sound of her heartbeat punctuated by the crash of things still falling outside layered with encroaching sirens. And after a few minutes, she couldn't take it anymore.

Nora groped her way out of the Bride's Room and through the hampering dimness of the cathedral basement, toward the light of the stairwell, up one flight, feeling her way along cracked walls.

Puccini followed closely behind her. Grayness dissipated in the vestibule, where shafts of storm light sliced the dusty air.

The storm had scattered Catholic paraphernalia from the gift shop. She stepped over bibles and hymnals and parish bulletins, prayer cards and St. Christopher medallions and choir robes, plastic bottles for holy water, beeswax candles, plaster statues, crystal rosary beads. All the accouterments of believers.

Peeking past a walnut door in the baptistery, the shapes of martyrs and saints suggested themselves in the whorls of the wood. There, in the subdued light, desecration. Nora's legs turned to gel as she took in varnished pews upended and marble statuary toppled by the tornado. The altar split and overturned. The sanctuary light extinguished. 🙢

She looked around slowly, turning a full circle, horror scraping up her spine as she forced herself to look at the stained-glass windows. Her stomach rolled.

Nora looked closer at the pillaged windows, portions of which hung in tatters, the lead drooping within the Gothic tracery. Glass hands and heads and sacred hearts littered pews and aisles. Through the gaps in the glass, rain fell.

Next to the massive altar, tipped on its side and cracked in three main pieces, the man who had sheltered her from the storm crouched over bits and shards of colored glass. The dog sniffed and whined, its hind legs shuddering. The man hurriedly gathered scattered

Communion wafers and dropped them into a dented chalice.

Nora slowly bent and picked up a piece of glass—a painted portion of a face, perhaps an angel eye, an evangelist's brow, the hollow of a saintly cheek painstakingly painted and fired half a century ago. She slipped the piece into her pocket.

As if collecting seashells, she spotted another piece she couldn't resist picking up, another painted fragment—a silver-stained curve of a halo with starry detail. Memory stirred. Nora dropped the piece of glass as if it were scalding hot. The fragment bounced on the marble tile, rebounded, fell again and made a tinkling sound before breaking into even smaller pieces in the center aisle.

Slowly, the man turned around. He uprighted the crimson sanctuary light. The red glass candle holder was cracked and chipped. From his pants pocket the man withdrew a lighter. He ceremoniously lit the wick. The sanctuary light glimmered and glowed again, tremulously. The man held up his hands, palms open, fingers together, thumbs to fingers. He muttered a blessing over the candle.

He must be, Nora concluded, *a priest.* ❧

FATHER VINCENT DiMARCO

In the name of the Father ⊠ and of the Son ⊠ and of the Holy Spirit. ⊠

O God, God of my youth, God of my innocent belief, you walk in my garden no more. ⊠ ⊠ ⊠ I once believed you omniscient, and now I wonder. ⊠ I once felt you omnipresent, saw your "superabundant light" everywhere, in everyone, but now I find you nowhere except the dim depths of my glass. ⊠ ⊠ ⊠

Lord, I asked for a sign, I prayed for a parcel of your grace to bolster my disbelief. Is this then your message from on high? You destroy your own cathedral? ⊠ What now, God? You abandon me in the rubble of your divine will? ⊠ ⊠ ⊠

Father, I am your priest forever, according to the order of Melchizedek, but my faith falters. You know I cannot pretend. You who supposedly know me even as I cannot know myself, You know I have a problem. ⊠ You know I need your help, Hosanna in the highest, your grace. ⊠ ⊠ Please. I petition you. ⊠ ⊠ ⊠

In the name of the Father and of the Son and of the Holy Spirit. ⊠ AMEN. ⊠

CHAPTER TWO

Ordinary Time

TRINITY SUNDAY (6 June)

A week after the storm, streets and yards were still strewn with displaced property, detritus, and broken tree limbs stripped of their bark, the air still redolent with the scent of sap. Roofing teams and insurance adjusters converged on the neighborhood.

Nora, in a radical departure from self-pity, counted her blessings. The tornado had barely touched her place. She'd left the windows open and the storm had blown through, rustling papers, tilting paintings on their wall hooks, leaving wet floors but causing no substantial damage.

For once, she felt spared. Protected.

From the window seat, she looked at a large branch dangling from the tall Dutch elm just above Mrs. Quincy's entryway.

The phone rang, startling her. Nobody called anymore; her few friends had all given up on her and, to her occasional chagrin, respected her reclusive ways. She cursed Liam, who had isolated her. Jealous of everyone—male or female—he promoted only the implosion of the two of them, alone together.

She paced, then huddled in the rocking chair her mother had handed down to her. The oak chair was one of the few pieces of furniture not in storage since Nora fled from her old house and her old life. ✒

"*Get down,*" she still heard Liam say almost every day; and between stretches of insomnia, in nightmares.

The phone rang insistently. Nora noticed a brown plant she'd forgotten to water. Another ring. Another. Eight rings. Nine. The caller I.D. read "caller unknown." She grabbed the receiver, expecting a telemarketer.

"Hello?" she said, her voice rising with annoyance. She cradled the receiver like a fiddle against her chin, wrinkled up her nose as she listened to a resonant male voice. A voice of authority, vaguely familiar. ✒

"This is Father Vincent DiMarco."

Automatically, Nora corrected her slouched posture. "Who?" she asked, though she'd heard him perfectly well. Probably a new evangelization campaign for lapsed Catholics, she assumed. Or a fund-raising drive.

"Father Vin DiMarco. I'm the rector at the cathedral. The Catholic cathedral downtown?"

She placed the voice. *Ah, my savior.* The image of the cathedral's tattered windows flashed in her mind's eye. Nora knew why he was phoning her. Nonetheless, she was not about to let on who she was for fear he might call in a returned favor in exchange for the shelter he had given her in the storm. Her voice sharp, she said, "I don't do any business with telemarketers; please take me off your list."

"No. No," he chuckled. "I'm not a phone solicitor. I'm looking for a Nora Kelley."

"Right," she said, cautiously. "This is Nora."

"I understand you're a stained-glass artist," the priest said.

"No," she answered abruptly. Guilt clutched her throat. Lying to a priest. A priest who had sheltered her in a storm, no less.

"You mean you *are* Nora Kelley, but you're *not* a stained-glass artist?"

"Right."

"Oh." The priest paused. "Sorry." He cleared his throat. "Well. Maybe I have the wrong one. I was told that a Nora Kelley designed and installed the windows in the central public library and handled the repair of the glass at the state Capitol after the vandalism, and—"

"She did. I did." Nora's ears turned hot. "I don't do glass now," she managed to say.

"But you *did* do those windows?"

"I did, but I don't work in glass any longer."

"You've taken a sabbatical?" he asked.

"Something like that," she said. "Sorry. I need to go."

"Wait," he said. "Please. Don't hang up. Please. I need you."

Nora remembered the warmth of his palm on her arm. *Sick,* she told herself. *He's a priest!* She tore at a hangnail until it bled.

"Nora?"

The sound of her name on his voice made her hug herself. "Father, I—" but she did not know where to begin.

"Those cathedral windows are almost 90 years old," he said. "They were fabricated in Germany; the studios were bombed in the Second World War and—"

With a rolled-up magazine, Nora swatted a miller moth, pulverizing it on her coffee table. She said, "I know the windows."

Father DiMarco said, "I need to arrange for their restoration. It's a priority of the parish and the archdiocese."

Nora said, "I don't know anybody who could touch those windows. You're talking about a scale that's out of reach. And to match that glass… it's impossible."

"Aaaah," the priest said. "We have an old saying: 'Nothing is impossible with God,' Luke, chapter one, verse 37."

"All right," said Nora, rolling her eyes. "Maybe not *impossible*. You might try contacting one of the cathedrals in Europe, find out who does their repairs. That's my best advice. And stay away from hobbyists. You need somebody who knows what they're doing."

"Don't you?" he asked. Nora looked at her hands. The priest added, "I should think you'd want this job."

"I can't do it, Father," Nora said.

He said, "I'm told you're from a clan of distinguished glass painters."

Nora thought of her father and her grandfather and his father before him. How they would leap at the honor to work on the cathedral's windows.

"Listen," Father DiMarco said. "Maybe the painting won't be precisely accurate. Maybe the colors won't match perfectly. But I can't very well leave the glass in ruins. I'm not looking for perfection—not in this world. I know the windows will never be the same, but my research indicates that you're the one person around here who could take this on."

Nora's ego momentarily came out of hibernation. She puffed her chest, then slouched. "Father," she said, "trust me. I'm *not* the person you want repairing damages to your church. Really. There are studios back East specializing in this sort of thing."

"They're way out of our league—both in cost and in time," he said. "They said they couldn't even start on them for almost a year. And we'd have to ship everything both ways or pay the expenses of artisans to work on-site." He exhaled so heavily Nora could almost feel his breath in her ear. "Nora, listen: Saint Mother Frances Xavier Cabrini worshipped in this cathedral. Buffalo Bill was baptized here. The Unsinkable Molly Brown was a parishioner. This cathedral is the Mother Church for all the Catholics of the province. And, at least as far as the interior goes, the glass is the cathedral," the priest said, his voice softening. "Surely you can't just turn your back on us. You have a gift."

"Believe me, Father, I have my reasons, too. Sorry," she said, twisting into her emotional bulletproof vest.

But the priest was persistent. "Please," he said, "these windows are a part of our patrimony. As cathedral rector, I'm the steward of them." ✌

"That sounds like your problem, not mine." Silence. Nora's resistance did not buckle.

His tone shifted several octaves toward the demanding. "Those windows are a link to divinity."

"It's colored glass and lead, Father. Good luck with it all. I'm sure you'll find the right person for the job. Good-bye." Nora hung up. And as she did, she realized she had just passed on the project of a lifetime. And hung up on a priest.

She stretched out on the window seat. In her mind, a design suspended in glass: a dove descending into wind. ✌ Shapes and patterns introduced themselves. By force of habit, Nora looked for her sketchbook and a drawing pencil, but then let the image evaporate, shaking free of her muse.

Before colored glass, she contemplated, windows were covered with thinly sliced pieces of alabaster, horn or bone. Humanity had for so long attempted to let the light in, but keep the elements out.

As if human nature had any reliable defense against Mother Nature. ✍

✍ ✍ ✍

Nora poured water from a dented copper watering can onto the window box of withered beefsteak begonias. A cloud of miller moths burst out of the flowers, and Nora dropped the can, watching the water spill.

Mrs. Quincy pulled up in her vintage Mercedes. Across the yard, her landlady waved like the queen, then headed toward her across the cobbled driveway. Nora stuffed her fists in her empty pockets.

"Morning," Nora said, looking down at the puddle and the scuffed watering can.

"Hello, dear." Mrs. Quincy untied the silk scarf over her hair, smoothed her scalloped collar. The old woman's words seemed sweet, but her tone and timbre said something else entirely.

"I guess you're wondering about my rent money," Nora said.

"Are you a little short?"

"A little," Nora admitted, though it was more than a little. She picked up the watering can.

"Father DiMarco told me he offered you a job today."

Nora shook her head, her straight hair swinging. "Those windows were done by people who painted glass day after day, year after year. They specialized. Some did nothing but garments. Others, the really accomplished painters, did nothing but faces. I don't have that kind of skill."

The old woman's pursed mouth pulled back into a grimace. "*Some*body has to fix them."

Nora closed her eyes and saw the inexhaustible detail of the glass. "Have you ever looked at those windows? I mean really looked at them?"

"Since I was a girl," said Mrs. Quincy.

Nora looked up to the fluttering leaves of the oak that presided over the driveway. Her eyes were wide as the sky and just as cloudy.

"I've never had to evict anybody," Mrs. Quincy said. She was not smiling.

"I do have money. It's not liquid. Yet," Nora said, rejecting the idea of using Liam's insurance benefit—a compromise that would capitalize on all that went wrong. Nora wanted nothing to do with her dead husband. "I'll pay, I assure you. With interest."

"Fiddlesticks," Mrs. Quincy said. "It's not interest I'm interested in; and you know it." The old woman's bony hands flew to her heart. "If you should take this job, I trust you'd find Father DiMarco an...unusual man," she said.

Nora caught Mrs. Quincy's pause. The old woman turned on her spectator pumps and tottered toward her house.

All day, in the recesses of Nora's mind, the echo of the priest's voice lingered. Even just before fading into sleep, bits of their telephone conversation wriggled into her consciousness. Oddly, the preoccupation softened her forehead, eased her perpetual ache. She slept through the night, dreaming innocuously, nightmares corralled. At least for one night.

MEMORIAL OF ST. BARNABAS (11 *June*)

Nora faced another day, another pot of coffee. She tied on her ratty bathrobe, ground some beans, the fragrance cheering her somewhat. While the joe brewed, she did sun salutations, stretching and bending, reaching and folding over into herself. Practicing yoga had helped as much as anything. Hedging her bets, she had resorted to psychiatry and psychopharmaceuticals, grief counseling, hydrotherapy, Reiki, tarot cards, aromatherapy, herbs, energy work and, finally, yoga. Somehow, she had survived. Barely. Not that she really wanted to. ✆ She wished she could have just perished with Liam, that somebody else could have cleaned up their mess.

Standing on her head, her world turned upside-down, Nora noticed dirty clothes strewn about her apartment, dust bunnies hunkered in the corners, stacks of old newspapers, the table mounded with unopened mail, the fat telephone directory falling off a disorderly bookshelf, the overflowing trash can. She came out of her headstand and gathered newspapers, hauled them to the empty recycling tub on her porch. Grabbing a laundry basket, she picked up clothes.

With her coffee mug in one hand, she hoisted the wicker laundry hamper and trudged to the basement, realm of albino spiders. A ghostly one scurried up the exposed brick wall as she cranked up the washer, dumped the laundry in the machine. Though Nora didn't like spiders, she did admire their webs.

Nora couldn't stave off remorse, knowing how disappointed her dad would be, her grandfather, her great-grandfather. She had gleaned all their glass knowledge only to shuck it. She had broken the legacy.

If only Dad had lived longer, he could've done the windows and I could've assisted him, she thought. *If only he hadn't smoked. If only he'd been more careful around the lead and the chemicals.* But lung cancer had seized him before he was able to walk his only child down the aisle—not that he would have approved of Liam. She wondered whether the destiny of their marriage would have been different had she and Liam married in the Church and received the sacrament of matrimony.

Nora hugged a woven pillow and closed the splintered shutters of the bay window, turning back the light so as not to notice the dust bunnies on the floor. All the while, the priest's voice wandered in and out, snatches of their contentious conversation. Nora remembered Father Schmidt, the priest who had distributed her First Communion and heard her First Confession. A German man, tall, he wore a crew cut and carried himself with a militant sense of self-importance. He commanded fear of God. She remembered the effeminate and ebullient Father Brady, the priest who had led a retreat when she prepared for her Confirmation. Nothing sexually stirring about him. Something about Father DiMarco felt different. Nora tried to pinpoint his allure, then berated herself for obsessing about a Catholic priest.

She poured another cup of coffee and sat staring at her journal. On a page Nora wrote one two-word sentence: "I'm pathetic." The bell on the washing machine rang, and Nora slipped into an old nightshirt and flip-flops, reluctantly went downstairs, tossed the clean laundry in a hamper. Balancing the basket on her head with one hand and gripping her mug of coffee with the other, she headed out to her small courtyard.

Hanging out laundry ranked as Nora's favorite char duty, the lesser of the infinite evils of housework. The Colorado sunshine and the gusty breeze combined for a perfect drying day. Nora offered her face to the sun and basked in the warming morning light. As she leaned her head to the side, hot light filled the whorls of her ear.

She pretended the sounds from passing cars on Chamberlain Avenue were lullaby waves breaking on a mythical beach. She imagined the ocean large and lush, shells washed smooth, salt air, sea spray, beach glass with sharp edges modeled into harmlessness.

Hanging her clothes, she saw out of the corner of her eye and through the iron arbor, a man down the block. Nora paid scant attention, rummaging through the damp wad of her whites.

As the fellow approached, Nora picked up his lavish whistling of *Jesu, Joy of Man's Desiring*, a song her grandfather used to play on his fiddle. And when Nora saw the whistling man outside her gate, she froze, holding in midair her cotton panties. She stood for a minute, underpants flapping from one hand, the index finger of her other pressed to her lips. 🖋 As soon as she recognized him, she made a move to hide behind the junipers.

But the priest called to her. "Nora?" And then he grinned, nodding slowly. "Are you kidding me? *You're* Nora Kelley?" He leaned into the wrought-iron gate. He looked at a piece of paper. "Is this 404 Maple?"

She took in his husky frame, olive skin, dark hair and lots of it—all over, she guessed from the looks of him. With his clerics, he wore black cowboy boots. And despite his aviator sunglasses, she caught him stealing a glance at her laundry basket.

Mortified, she realized she was still holding her underwear. A blush spread over her chest and she quickly balled them into her cupped hand.

"You're the woman from the storm."

"I am. I have to thank you. For the—" She trailed off. *What was the word?*

"Sanctuary." He went back to whistling fluidly, effortlessly. He swayed slightly to the music. Nora almost smiled, enjoying his performance, but then, to her horror, realized she was, as habit dictated, still dressed in only her nightshirt, which she gathered about her torso. She thought about darting into the house and locking the door, yet something about his presence held her.

During the tornado, they had not even exchanged names. They had spoken only a few words, and most of those in shouts rather than regular voices that would have been swallowed whole by the 200 miles per hour winds.

"So," Nora said, at a loss for more than words. "You're tenacious."

"Father Vin DiMarco," he said. Gallantly, he extended both of his hands. Nora slipped her hand into his, warm and smooth and impeccably manicured. The priest's hands clasped around hers. Slowly, Nora withdrew.

"Nora Kelley, you live in my parish."

She wiped her perspiring palm on her nightshirt.

For an edgy, long moment, the priest just looked at her, bemused. Nora noticed the lines on his swarthy face.

"When we spoke on the phone, I had no idea."

Nora shook her head. "As I told you, I don't work in glass any more." She bent down and stretched up to hang her threadbare sheets splashed with faded cabbage roses and her cabana striped bath towels that had seen better days.

"My parishioners and I are prepared to raise the money to pay you whatever fee you name," he said, "if you will fix our windows."

She waved him off. "You don't know what you're saying. You're talking about big bucks."

"The Lord provides," he said.

"Meaning you don't have the money," she said. "Father, let's not waste one another's time."

Father DiMarco put a hand on the gate. Nora caught her reflection in his sunglasses, his eyes and therefore his soul safely concealed behind the shield of his lenses. "Name your price."

"You can't be serious. Stained glass costs a lot. Materials and labor add up." Nora drew her shoulders up to her ears. "Besides, I'm not available. Now, if you'll excuse me, I'm about down to my skivs. So, unless you want us both embarrassed..."

"Oh," he said. "Sorry."

She narrowed her eyes at him. "Look," Nora said. "I'm flattered that you went to the trouble of finding me."

"Were you lost?" He grinned.

"No. I mean to find out about my work. I appreciate the offer. It's just that I'm in a different line of work now."

"Which is?"

"Gardening," she fibbed.

"Vegetables or flowers?"

She faltered. "More like landscaping."

"These lilacs," he said, nodding to the shrubs. "They must be as old as this house." Nora looked at the lilac bushes as if she'd never seen them before; and actually, she hadn't. "So you quit glass for gardening?" ✍

Nora picked up her hamper with damp bras and panties still clumped at the bottom. "Change is good, don't you agree, Father?"

"Sometimes," the priest said. "Your husband is an artist, too?"

"I'm not married. "

"Divorced?"

"Widowed," she said, vulnerable as a bug on its back. Nora was taken aback by his assertiveness, but didn't want to let on.

"I'm sorry."

"I'm not," she said, trying on a hang-dog face as she braced herself, waiting for a line of questioning. This, in part, was why she had quit talking to people. She had grown tired of telling the tragic tale. But the priest asked nothing more.

Instead, he looked away, toward the steps where a jar of sun tea brewed on Nora's stoop.

Grateful for company, regretful that she had first hung up on him and then lied to him, Nora asked, "I could offer you a glass of tea?" ✍

"You could."

"I am," Nora said. She had never invited a man into her

carriage house. In fact, she had never invited anybody there. *But,* she reasoned, *he is a priest.* In Nora's family, refusing hospitality to a man of the cloth would have constituted cardinal sin. She shifted from foot to foot, willing herself to stop acting like a Catholic school girl. "You want to come in?" He nodded; and on the way inside Nora snatched sprigs of lemon balm and spearmint from Mrs. Quincy's herb border filling in along the fence.

He lugged the gallon of tea and set it on the counter. He looked around Nora's kitchen. She wished the sink were not so grimy, the countertop not so riddled with crumbs. On the stove, instead of pans, were salt-stained pots of Italian parsley, lemon thyme, rosemary. And half a dozen miller moth corpses.

"You grow your own herbs," he said.

"I'm getting ready to harden those off outside," she said, trying to sound like her mother, who had known her way around the garden. She bruised mint leaves for the tea. "Plants, I find, are easier to get along with than people."

He said, "Ah, but people are meant to be in relationship."

Nora raised her eyebrows at him.

"I suppose that does sound odd, coming from a celibate. But I didn't define the nature of the relationship. People need people. Otherwise, why would prisons use solitary confinement as an ultimate punishment? Because it *hurts* to feel alone."

The expression on his face told Nora that he was no stranger to loneliness. She locked her knees. "We're *all* alone. We come into this world alone. We leave it alone. And while we're here, some of us are introverted."

"Fair enough," Father DiMarco said, canting his head, his ear nearly touching his shoulder.

"Here you are." Nora presented him with a plastic tumbler of tea. Father DiMarco drew a long drink. "Mmm. This is... different."

"Raspberry. With fresh lemon balm and mint."

"How gourmet. Do you cook?"

"No. Sun tea is about the only recipe I can manage."

"So. You don't cook. And you don't work with glass. You do garden. What else do you do?"

"Why do you ask?"

The priest tugged at his Roman collar. He shook his tumbler and downed the rest of his tea, crunched an ice cube, said, simply, "Just curious."

Nora sensed a sermon coming on. "Would you like more?"

"No, thanks," he said, covering his drink with his hand. "Join me outside while I smoke?"

They moved to her front porch. He pulled out a pipe. "Better to smoke in this life than in the next." He filled the bowl and fired up the aromatic tobacco using, Nora noticed, the same silver lighter he had used to light the sanctuary lamp the evening of the tornado. A wispy halo of smoke formed around his head. Nora almost enjoyed the smell of his pipe.

"Plants love carbon monoxide," she said, an intruder in her own home. "Sometimes, when I notice plants under siege by fungus gnats, I make a nasty solution of my landlady's cigarette ashes and tobacco and water. Keeps the pests away."

"Hmmmm," he said. "And what's keeping you away?"

"From what?"

"From your craft, your talent," he said.

"Nothing in particular. Everything in general," said Nora.

"Why would an accomplished young artist such as yourself walk away from such a sterling reputation?"

"You *are* direct," she said, giving him a sideways glance.

Father DiMarco drummed his fingers on the porch railing. "You must miss your work."

"No," Nora lied again. "I enjoy gardening. Immensely. I like working outside. Besides, flowers are infinitely more beautiful than anything I ever created. Nature, after all, is the most accomplished artist."

"The artist," said the priest, "creates nothing without the hand of God."

"Father, with all due respect, I don't need to hear a homily."

"And I don't mean to preach one. I apologize." He sucked the pipe, looked down at the rickety table on Nora's porch, picked up a glass art magazine. "I see you still keep up on the trade publications."

"My subscription hasn't run out yet."

"So your departure from your field is recent."

Suddenly, Nora desperately wanted him to leave. She turned her face away from him, ran a hand through her hair.

"Will you think about it, Nora?" He stood. He held out his hand. They shook hands formally, but the priest held hers for an extra moment until Nora almost squirmed. Somehow she sensed that Father DiMarco recognized her for who she really was: not so much a believer as somebody who wanted to believe.

"Thank you," he said. "For the tea."

Nora said, "I wish I could help you."

"Me, too," said the priest.

"It's a long... it's a complicated story."

"I see," he said. "Maybe you'd care to tell me more sometime."

"Maybe." *He's already seen my laundry aired,* she thought.

"'Deep calls unto deep,'" the priest said. "Psalm 42, verse eight." As he walked away, she noticed black rosary beads dangling from his fist. He turned and said, "You can always find me at the cathedral or along Cherry Creek path—Puccini and I walk every morning before 8 o'clock mass."

Nora went to her bedroom and closed the old armoire door and inspected her reflection in the foxed mirror. She hardly recognized her own image. A glaze had dissolved from her eyes. A sadness had lifted. A bit of color returned to her cheekbones. Her lips parted.

Glass conducts light. Stained glass filters rays, but silvered glass throws back truth.

SOLEMNITY OF THE SACRED HEART OF JESUS (18 *June*)

That somebody had acknowledged her talent energized Nora. She had forgotten how affirming she'd always found the strokes from clients thrilled with her commissions or restorations. Boosted by Father DiMarco's acknowledgement, Nora gathered enough energy to overcome inertia. Having been so still for so long, she craved movement. ✨ She wanted to feel her body again. She dug through her closet and found her in-line skates. As she regained her balance, she regained confidence. Her muscles ached, but her heart lightened. *Maybe,* she had begun to think, instead of *no way.*

Rollerblading along Cherry Creek, taking in the contrast of the mall's frenetic bustle and the effortless flow of the water, Nora spotted Father DiMarco. He was hard to miss: His black clerics distinguished him from colorfully dressed bikers, runners, walkers and skaters. The dog that weathered the storm with them in the cathedral basement accompanied him. The dog's tail wagged as he sniffed his way along the path.

Nora's chemistry fluxed; her dopamine system engaged. She

watched the priest kicking loose stones back into the boundaries of the landscaping. He picked up errant cobbles on the sidewalk and tossed them back among the others.

Wearing shorts and a tank top, she skated toward him, show-boating a little, sucking in her belly. Repressing jubilation, Nora considered stopping, turning around and avoiding him. He hadn't, far as she could tell, seen her yet. She wanted to talk to him, though. His sharp wit seemed a whet stone for her own. She wanted to think on her feet, enter a repartee. She wanted him to pile praise about her work at her feet again so that she might remember who she was. She wanted him to make her laugh.

"Hi," she said with a surplus of nervous energy. A tingle. A hum. Her sentiment deflated when he gave her a puzzled look and she realized that he didn't even recognize her. She took off her sunglasses. "It's me, Nora. The stained-glass woman?"

"*Retired* stained-glass woman," he said, and kept walking. The corners of his mouth resisted a grin.

"How are you?" she asked, skating slowly along his side, her heart beating faster.

"I'm well, thanks," the priest said. "And you? You look fantastic."

She devoured his compliment. Simultaneously self-conscious and flattered, Nora chewed her lips. "Fine," she said, "I'm fine."

"Maybe it's providential I should run into you," he said.

"Maybe." Nora braked, turned toward him, "About your windows—"

"I think we've found somebody to do the job," he said.

Her ego clobbered, Nora gulped, crushed. "Oh?"

"A fellow from Minneapolis, actually. He apprenticed with an Austrian." He took out his pipe. "He's arriving the end of next week to have a look. He's enormously talented," the priest said.

Nora looked down at her skates. "Not as talented as I am," she said.

He smirked, stoked his pipe.

"Actually," she said, surprising herself and, based on his face, him. "I need a job. My rent is past due. If it's not too late, maybe this would be a good thing for both of us. Is there any chance you'd reconsider?"

"Maybe," the priest said, pulling his pipe close to his chest. "Tell you what, Nora, why don't you come by tomorrow at 9: 45 and look the place over; and then you can give us a bid. Will you do that? No commitment on either end—just consideration."

FEAST OF THE IMMACULATE HEART OF MARY (19 *June*)

Nora, that next morning, paced her apartment. She picked up scattered pillows, arranged and rearranged them on the window seat. She emptied the sink of vile dishes, stuffing them in the dishwasher. She showered, distractedly shampooing her hair twice. ✨

She rifled through her closet. *What to wear?* She pulled out a hanger with a white linen poet's shirt and rejected it, recalling that she'd worn it to a reggae concert with Liam. She touched the nubby weave of one of her mother's skirts, and the silk of her father's neckties she sometimes wore as belts.

Nora changed clothes seven times—finding many of the waistbands too tight—and finally settled on the simplicity of jeans and a white t-shirt, both a little snug. Nora looked down at the scars on her arms and changed one more time into a long-sleeved tunic.

In the bathroom mirror, she regarded herself, regretfully assessing the ways in which life had aged her. 〰 If she were to paint a self-portrait, she would render her eyes a flat Wedgwood blue, their edges down-turned. She would have to depict the disappointment in the slump of her shoulders. Nora lifted her chin and brushed her thick hair. She had chopped off her ponytail after Liam's interment and had not gotten a haircut since. Nor had she bothered with makeup or even shaving her legs.

Her face flushed. To grind down her mounting anxiety, Nora rode her bike to the cathedral rectory, wondering what, precisely, she was getting herself into. She knew she needed work, yet hated the prospects of the job. She needed money, but also freedom. Nora wanted to feel productive and worthwhile again, but could barely stand the thought of breaking glass. She welcomed the challenge and shunned it. She was attracted to the priest and repelled by her attraction. For Nora, life's decisions rarely rang clearly as bells pealing.

But when she pedaled down the parkway that day, Nora did hear bells. Ten bells. And she pedaled faster, realizing she was late.

When she arrived, breathless, Father DiMarco stood waiting on the porch. By his side sat the dog, tail wagging enthusiastically. The dog gave three loud barks.

"There she is, Puccini," Nora heard the priest say as she locked her bike. ✍ He opened his arms to her as he opened the gate. "Welcome," he almost whispered. And as if they'd hugged many times before, Nora and Father DiMarco embraced easily, warmly and without awkwardness. Nora rested in the envelope of his hospitable hug; and as they parted she caught a glimpse of a gray-haired woman peeking out the front door. The dog sniffed Nora's knees. Nora glanced down, but paid the dog no heed.

"I'm glad you're here," the priest said.

"I'm glad to be here, Father."

"I wish you'd call me Vin."

Nora scowled.

"Call me whatever's comfortable," he said. "Come on; let's have a look."

Together, they walked around the corner to the cathedral with Puccini prancing ahead of them. The dog's plume of a tail swayed. The priest took a bone-shaped biscuit from his pocket. "Puccini, preach!" The dog woofed on command, took his treat, then dashed toward the side door. The priest smiled widely. Nora did, too, unable to stop a desperate giggle.

The smooth gray stone cathedral was still surrounded by yellow police tape and orange cones. Here and there, construction workers tackled tasks. Even from outside, Nora blanched at the sight of the ruined windows. He led her past a prayer garden with a scented privet hedge. The gargoyles crouched high above them, guarding the corners of the cathedral's green tile roof. She recalled the rain running from their jaws during the storm.

Inside, Nora staggered under the majesty of proportion. The cathedral was quiet, demure. The windows drew her eye heavenward. She assessed the overall damage: gaping gashes in the vast curtains of colorful imagery, lead poking every which way, cracked glass. She cringed. The damage made the tornado real again. She looked at the priest, weighing the odds of seeing him again.

"Well?" he asked. "What do you think?"

Nora pondered the fragmentary survival: *Why this piece and not that?* She looked up at the pastoral scenery filling in the backgrounds, the medallions, the intricate canopy work ornamenting the clerestory windows, the spokes of the rose window. ✺ She noted the abundance of silver stain—expensive and always tricky, fickle.

Nora bit her lip. "I have to be blunt, Father," she said, humbled by the painting—the faces and hands of the figures and, above all, the silver-stained haloes. She tucked her hair behind her ears. "I don't think you can expect to restore these windows to their original condition." His face fell. "I know I can't do them justice. It's pretty much impossible."

"Nothing," the priest said, "is impossible with God."

"Yeah, you mentioned that," Nora said. She looked up at the bowed, broken windows.

"How do you feel about trying?" he asked.

His question was a skeleton key opening a vault of asps and adders. Memory washed over Nora when she allowed herself to really look at the broken glass. She asked herself another question: "*If I can't do glass, what can I do?*" Her breath damped down in her belly. The columns of the cathedral seemed to undulate.

"I need some air," Nora said rushing out of the nave and walking fast away from the cathedral and its shattered glass. She followed the path to a prayer garden. He led her to a marble bench.

They sat in silence, a transcendent tenderness. She watched a robin drink from a bird bath. The bird dipped his orange breast and fluttered.

"I love a garden," the priest said. He stood and the bird flew off. The priest walked toward a nearby flower bed of pale blue and ivory trumpets. "Do you know the significance of the columbine?" Father DiMarco asked, pointing to the flowers.

"Is this a test?"

He nodded. "Perhaps." He pulled a coil of bindweed from the bed.

"I know the columbine is Colorado's state flower."

"But," he said, striking an orator's pose, "did you know that the columbine is an ancient iconographic symbol of the Holy Spirit? 'Aquilea' is the Latin. 'Little doves.'"

"Yeah?" Nora smiled. "Of the Trinity, the one I could always relate to best was Holy Spirit. The Holy Ghost. Not that I give it much thought these days, but I'd once worked out a personal theology with God the Father as the Creator, the provider, protector. Jesus as my brother and Holy Spirit as sort of like my favorite uncle." ✒

"Or aunt. Holy Spirit hasn't been assigned a specific, doctrinal sex, as far as I know," he said. He leaned close. "Nora Kelley. I might have known. You're Catholic." He grinned.

"I'm sure the pope wouldn't think so."

"Father Vin? Father Vin?" she heard his name called. The priest waved to the man, who was pointing to his watch. "Be right there, Deacon."

"Come on," the priest said. ✒ "I want to show you my vegetable patch."

Her interest sparked, they strolled past an open area near the parking lot. A lone shrub grew in the space. "I should get the groundskeeper to hack this out of here," the pastor said. "I'm not sure why it's out here in the middle of nothing."

"Might be a place where fairies meet," Nora said, tease in her tone.

"Fairies?" he asked, his smile broadening. "And leprechauns? Garden gnomes? Water sprites?"

Nora found herself tittering inside, like any prepubescent Catholic girl swooning over the affections of her pastor. ✍ "Well, that's what the Irish believe. My mother would never allow any lone bush to be disturbed."

"Interesting." He looked over the lines of plants and vines in his vegetable garden. "It's been triage since the hail," he said, "but it's coming along."

Nora marveled at the shipshape rows of his garden, the frilly lettuces and spinach, Swiss chard with dark green leaves and magenta veins. Peas snaked up trellises. Chives with their round purple flowers bordered the entire bed. He handed her a few sugar snap peas. "Try these," he said.

She opened her hands as if receiving communion. She ate the bright green peas whole. "They taste like spring," she said.

"Precisely." He took out his pipe and a pouch of tobacco.

"Can you get me your estimate by this afternoon?" the priest asked. ✍

"This afternoon?"

"We have a finance council meeting. I'm supposed to have more than one bid, anyway," he said. "But the job's yours if you want it. It'll be more economical not to have to pay the expenses of the man from Minneapolis."

Nora looked toward the bed of columbines and pondered the iconographer's blind leaping to give form to the formless, to see doves in flower petals.

"Nora?"

"There's one small detail: I don't have a studio," she said. The admission saddened her. And the sadness, in turn, surprised her. She wanted the job. She wanted work. Meaning.

"We could make room in the garage."

"That might do," Nora said, pushing her sleeves up to her elbows, then tugging them down again. "But I sold all my stuff: my kiln, my bench, my tools. Everything."

Which was not altogether true. Nora had kept a box full of tools that had been her grandfather's and her father's, unable to part entirely with her heritage. The rest she'd taken to a friend's stained-glass shop.

"You sold the tools of your trade?"

"I needed the money," she said, "and at the time, I was pretty positive that I was leaving glass for good."

"But why?" he asked. He touched her hand softly, momentarily.

"I acted rashly," Nora said. "But I could start over. If I had an advance, I could replace everything. What you can't replace are these windows."

Much the way the tongue investigates something foreign in the mouth—like a recently chipped tooth—Nora's eyes involuntarily darted from the boards over the broken stained-glass windows to the windows untouched and awesome. She shuddered in the winds of doubt, wondering how she could make it work. She reached for a prophet's poetic utterance, something to galvanize herself.

"I thought you said it couldn't be done," he said.

"I thought you said nothing was impossible with God."

The cathedral's bells rang, and Nora counted 11 tolls. They exchanged a business-like handshake, and Nora surrendered into an extravagant hope. Father DiMarco, she knew from years of Catholic schooling, would label her feeling *grace*.

MEMORIAL OF ST. ALOYSIUS GONZAGA (*20 June*)

The night before Nora was to start her job at the cathedral, she tossed, tangled in sheets and apprehension about the task and uncertainty about whether her bid came in too low. The priest had acted so swiftly, calling her as soon as she submitted her estimate, hiring her over the telephone.

Nora rolled over in bed and watched the midnight hour arrive. All night, sleep evaded her. Between the hours of 3 and 6 a.m., she awoke every 30 minutes, anxious, afraid she hadn't set the alarm clock correctly. In the last two years, she'd had few reasons to get up at any particular time. On a good day, she rose with the sun.

Other days, nothing could prod her out of bed.

The day dawned differently, hopeful rays sliding in between the blinds, striping her bed. For the first time in a long time, Nora enjoyed the tickle of open-ended anticipation a new project brings. As she dressed and packed her lunch, she picked up a golden apple and couldn't help but think of Eve.

She strapped on her backpack and boarded her bicycle. She pedaled the mile or so to the rectory, breathing deeply through her nose, relishing the pine-scented morning air along the parkway.

Catching sight of the cathedral's stone spires, Nora slowed. Her stomach fluttered. She anticipated the job—from commission to sketch, sketch to cartoon, cartoon to cut glass, cut glass to paint, paint to the fire of the kiln, fired glass to lead, and leaded windows to openings in architecture. Nora could not imagine how she would endure the daunting process. She coasted down to the parking lot and into the rectory driveway where she parked her bike. Puccini barked. *♪*

A cadre of workmen cleaned and repaired the cathedral inside and out. Nora dragged her feet to the imposing front door of the rectory, wavered a minute, licked her lips, tossed her hair with her fingertips. She rang the buzzer.

Over an intercom, Father DiMarco's voice came through, "Hello?" *♪*

"It's Nora Kelley," she said into the speaker box.

A minute later he was there, opening the door. "Good morning, Glory." 🍩

"Morning." She regressed to a bashful second-grader on the first day of school, the girl in blonde braids and a plaid, pleated jumper.

"Puccini, you remember Ms. Nora Kelley," he said, patting the fuzzy dog.

"Um, I wasn't sure if I needed to see you first? Or what."

The priest said, "I'm not much for micromanagement. I won't interfere. But," he nodded rapidly, "you do need to see our parish administrator and sign our letter of intent. We always have coffee on. Would you like some now? Coffee? Fresh, albeit on the weak side. Millie thinks I drink too much. Which I do."

"Thanks, but I've had my fix." She watched him fold and unfold his hands and gathered that he was as nervous as she. "For me, it's a fine line. With the caffeine, I mean. My nerves. A little jangly, you know?" Nora felt tossed, but it had nothing to do with coffee.

He nodded. "Juan will be in soon. He's our parish business manager; and he'll get you set up with whatever paperwork you need," Father DiMarco grinned. "Now, if you'll excuse me, I need to get to the sandwich line. My volunteers will be showing up."

A gray-haired woman in a brown apron stuck her head into the office. She was the woman Nora had seen at the door the other day. Her hair was cropped short. She wore no makeup, no jewelry, no smile. "The students are here, Father," she said.

"Nora, meet Millie. Millie, Nora. Millie makes the most extraordinary comfort food," the priest said. "Macaroni and cheese. Tuna noodle casserole. Sloppy Joes."

"I'm also the sacristan," the woman said.

The priest said, "Did I mention she's also the sacristan?"

"And past-secretary of the Altar and Rosary Society." Millie looked down at her dingy Keds.

"Millie covers a lot of holy ground," the priest said, giving Nora a clandestine wink.

Millie beamed at him.

"Nice to meet you," Nora said, but Millie did not so much as look her way. She wiped her hands on her grease-splotched apron. "I've got something on the stove," she said.

"And I've got a crowd of hungry people in the alley. Nora, let Millie know if you need anything."

"I guess I'll get started then," Nora said, mostly to herself.

And she began. Stained glass had ornamented churches for more than a millennium, and the process Nora used had not varied much since medieval times. From her worn canvas backpack, Nora pulled a clipboard and a drawing pencil and binoculars. The indescribable beauty of the glass hit more than one color note at a time. Visual harmonics. Instantly, she knew a measure of purpose again as she paced the cathedral, studying the monumental windows. Nora softened her gaze, then focused with ferocity, as if she could look right through the Indiana stone foundation of the cathedral. She sat in a pew, her elbows braced on the back of the pew ahead of her. Magnified through the binocular lenses, the details in the glass dazzled her. ✍

Rapt observation is a practice. Maybe one careful observer in a thousand would notice the details of the Assumption window, for example, the Virgin Mary's pink fingernails or the flowers bursting from her tomb; but there in the focus of Nora's lenses were roses and lilies, anemones and hyacinths.

Nora calculated the ruffled edges of feathers on the wings of the angels who dwelled up in the stone canopy, imprisoned in the glass between heaven and earth. She noticed for the first time that an angel stood vigil in every single window in the cathedral. Angels with wings of purple and rose, green and gold. Angels with hands sheltering the shoulders of saints, catching the blood pouring from the side of the crucified Christ, deposing the dead body of the Son of Man, angels gathering around the Risen Christ. Angels hovering in places she hadn't thought to look.

Each window, Nora saw, stood on its own. Even the various elements within—a figure here, an urn there—could be the focal point of lesser windows. Such was the mastery. She focused on an iridescent orchid and marbleized violet glass, an opalescent white dove flying out of a fiery triangle of ember orange and translucent mussel-blue drapery glass. Sluices of light seeped through the colors, enlivening the silver stain, the precious metals in the glass, the pictures telling stories.

She admired the austerity evident in the rest of the cathedral, architecture with a willingness to take a back seat to the splendor of the glass and the mystery of light. Aside from the jeweled glow of the glass, an economy of color governed the rest of the church. Hushed whites and ivories. Touches of gold leaf. A ripple of earth tones in the marble.

Ironically, the window depicting the storm at sea escaped the brunt of the tornado. Only a minimal portion of the window was covered with plywood. She stood in awe of the power of wind strong enough to bend iron armature. She remembered the look of the sky that day. Nora asked herself, *Where was Jesus when that storm needed calming?*

Turning her binoculars on that window, she scanned the precision of the apostles in the troubled boat. Their faces showed fear. Their bodies were almost sculptural with muscles straining beneath the skin of their forearms. Veins bulged on the backs of their hands. Wood grain textured the oars. Nora admired the twist of the waves that gave motion to the chop of the ocean, or rather, the sea. Sea of Galilee. The glazier, Nora noted on her clipboard, had chosen precisely the right translucent sea green glass and precisely the right white to suggest the froth on waves. Like real water, the curling waves held light. A gust caught the hem of Christ's robe. From a gray cloud above, a wedge of light escaped. The sunlight's rays were rendered with silver stain in flourishes even her grandfather would have envied.

Nora's forehead released its lines.

The cathedral doors remained open. Workmen trudged in and out, carrying buckets and ladders and power tools. Through an open door off one of the side altars, Nora saw people lined up in the alley behind the cathedral. 🙶 Steadily, in line, they made their way to Father DiMarco and his volunteers—retired people and uniformed high school students—distributing sack lunches and styrofoam cups of steaming coffee.

Nora engrossed herself in the glass and started making color studies with felt-tipped pens, interpreting what she could see, trying to describe on paper the lacy haloes, intricate tapestries, faces in two dimensions suggesting three. Nora's eye preferred patterns, visual adventures.

Church art, any glazier would tell you, poses extra hindrance. The best windows exploit light and bend the waves into joy, sorrow, mystery. Whatever one's belief system, there is the terror of spirituality. The pomposity. The grandeur. The paradox of lending image to the ineffable Godhead. Did the earliest glaziers fear for their very lives? The eternal destiny of their immortal souls? Did they dare curse a cobalt blue streak on the occasions of cut fingers? It's a risky, risky business, accessorizing blind faith with pigment.

✒ ✒ ✒

Later that afternoon, Nora went to the Archdiocese of Denver archives. She nearly fell off the stool when the Sister who served as archivist hauled out a file thick as the metro Denver phone book. The file contained precious little written documentation, but lots of photographs of the windows.

"I'm Sister Mary. I'm happy to copy the articles, should you need them. You're welcome to check out photographs to take home, if that would assist you," the Sister said, her voice a cup of hot cocoa with marshmallows. She smiled ever so slightly, folded her doughy hands tidily. "Stay as long as you like."

"Thank you, Sister." Nora remembered the kindly nuns who had taught her in elementary school.

Sister Mary bowed and floated back to her desk.

Nora pulled out her clipboard. She knew the details gave her reason to converse with her client. She noted that F.X. Zettler, a chemical engineer, oversaw the crafting of the windows in Munich at the Royal Bavarian Art Institute. Herr Zettler, also a chemist, was known for his cunning coloration, dyes and glazes.

Zettler had hired 50 artisans to work on the windows. A final invoice showed that the price, in 1912, for all 75 windows was $34,000. She had no idea what that figure would be today. What she *did* know was that no dollar amount could buy windows of that quality today. They simply were not being created. The artisans had long since retired, died, taking their mastery with them. She'd admired contemporary windows and glass art of all stripes, but the Munich windows were, literally, a lost art.

Nora rifled through documents, finding a yellowed newspaper clipping from *The Denver Post*. Father DiMarco was right: Bombs destroyed the studio in World War II.

For the rest of the afternoon, she opened envelope after envelope, sorting photos. Intimidated by the scope of the project, she tried to imagine the studio in Germany, the 50 glaziers, Zettler and his formulae. ❧

Sister Mary brought her a paper cup of cool water. *She shall inherit the earth*, Nora thought.

"I'll be leaving now, but the chancery is open until 9 since there's a meeting on the second floor," she said, her face luminous as backlit alabaster. "Just pull the office door closed when you leave, won't you? And feel free to borrow whatever you need. Just leave a note in the file with your phone number and the date. We're all attached to those windows." The Sister put a hand to Nora's shoulder. "I'll be praying for you."

Nora checked out 40 photos, and back at home stayed up into the wee hours looking through a loupe at the images. In photographs, the windows guarded their mysteries. She couldn't get the big picture, nor could she find Zettler's studio signature in the glass.

The stained-glass canon does not exist. Though Matisse and Chagall did glorious works in glass, few galleries or museums collect glass. Stained glass holds court in religious and municipal buildings, homes, restaurants. Truly public art, its audience is vast and varied. The art itself tends to remain in anonymity, scarcely ever labeled. Some, a few, are signed with a cipher. But most glass artists remain unknown. As her great-grandfather, grandfather and father before her had done, Nora always added her studio cipher to her original works.

Through her magnifying glass, she studied the elongated cypress trees, the crusts on bread loaves and the scales on fish, the eyelashes of the Blessed Mother, Hebrew writing on tablets, the shine of Roman soldiers' helmets. Nora made notes, created lists, tried to absorb as much as possible. ✍ She imagined the masters in Munich scratching their beards over the intricacies of the iconography. *How to portray the adolescent face of Jesus in the temple? How to delineate a miracle?*

SUMMER SOLSTICE (*21 June*)

Eager to make her mark on the windows, yet avoid the heat, Nora arrived at the cathedral around 6 o'clock in the morning. On her way to work, she noticed homeless people, mostly men, near the cathedral. Some slept under the bus stop benches and rummaged through dumpsters, adding items to their carts or sacks. Some puffed cigarettes with blank looks and smoke clouding their faces. Others gathered, passing a brown paper-bagged bottle, passing a joint, passing time. They never made eye contact with Nora. Part of her feared them. Part of her feared becoming one of them.

She was glad she had a job. But everything seemed new to Nora, as if she'd never before worked with glass. At her workbench, she lurched, an impostor.

She gazed at the Sea of Galilee in one of the windows. Like water, glass can take liquid or solid form. Glass best depicts water because in many ways glass resembles water. Once pulled from the crucible, rolled and cooled, the thick fluid slackens into its solid state. Hardened glass, like ice, lacks grain and lamination. Like ice, glass splinters, shatters, cracks—oftentimes in unpredictable ways.

As a chorale group rehearsed their Latin hymns and four-part harmonies, Nora sketched the windows, the tracery, the positions of iron saddle bars and mullions holding the panels together. She marveled at the way their harsh lines established pattern but imposed no bedeviling distraction. The lead work resembled loose black lace. She focused on the clever counterpoints between the graphic lines of the mullions and the curvilinear lead lines surrounding color and image, underscoring the formal compositions, suggesting modeling. The delicate painting sharpened the image, clarifying intimations made by color shapes and lead. The glass held the light, remembering its genesis in fire hot as the sun.

Light, a vibration, directly strikes the retina, signaling from eye to cortex. Nora's brain felt divided between her client and her commission. Millie came and went throughout the cathedral, swishing a feather duster along the seats of the pews, stacking hymnals and missals, keeping an eye on the tabernacle. Nora tried to ignore her and instead concern herself with the otherworldly figures that peopled the windows. The silver stain haloes designated sanctity. Each halo differed, individual as souls. The silver nitrate penetrated the glass. The alchemy of paint fired onto colored glass stained the haloes from the palest yellow to rich amber, and created star bursts, swirls, concentric rings.

❧ ❧ ❧

On the way home from the cathedral, Nora stopped at the storage unit she rented and rummaged through boxes until she found her work boots and overalls, her gloves and goggles and the few antique tools that had belonged to her great-grandfather. Nora grabbed the box and hustled out before noticing too many other things crammed in the space — furnishings and belongings that served only to remind her of a past she attempted to forget. Liam's cross-country skis. His easel. The head board of their bed.

At night, Nora practiced painting the faces in watercolors and tried to find a thread of confidence. Her facility for design kicked in, but the technical difficulties daunted her, namely the size of the transcept windows. She couldn't yet persuade herself to take up her tools, so she went through the motions, hoping her process eventually would catch so she could bring herself to break a piece of glass.

※ ※ ※

Attending to first things first, Nora sorted and cleaned salvaged glass. She was dumbfounded, but absorbed. Ideas germinated in her mind, and the days took on a shape and rhythm.

She ate her lunch in the prayer garden, and Puccini often joined her. She shared a piece of her peanut butter sandwich with him or a slice of avocado. He even liked watermelon. With one hand, she stroked the dog, and with the other, she turned pages of trade catalogs, bending pages to mark materials she would need.

She went home at night tired and dirty. At the end of the day, a shower seemed a sacrament. Ambition took hold.

Nora awoke each morning achy from bending over the buckets of remnant glass, her shoulders stiff from craning her neck up at the impossibly delicate canopy work of the cathedral windows. But she hadn't felt so well in a long time.

Nora hadn't seen Father DiMarco all week, and she noticed she didn't care. Instead, she turned her energies to glass and color and light, shape and texture and hand-painted detail.

On afternoons when the sun scarcely shone she fell most deeply into the windows. Dull skies outside meant fair weather within the cathedral. On days of full sun, with rays blazing directly behind the glass, the windows poured out an unendurable radiance. The colors grew violent, too intense to behold, preventing the seer from seeing.

To make up for lost time Nora worked tirelessly. She moved to the beat blaring in her headphones. ✣ As she turned over pieces of glass in her hands, she turned daydreams in her mind. She imagined the studio. Fifty German glaziers filing in each morning, bent in Teutonic intent over their laying-out tables.

She wondered, too, about the glass blowers. ✣ *Plunging the blowpipe into the crucible, did their own sweat mix with the copper oxide in the blob of molten glass? Directing his breath into the gather of glass at the end of his blowpipe, as the knob began to inflate, did the glassblower possibly think of God the Creator breathing life into Adam?* ✣

Not likely. Blowing glass was merely a trade and not a particularly admired one. The men in the glass guilds, those who designed the windows, those who painted them probably lacked spiritual aspirations altogether.

Nora was lost in thought when the priest popped in, draped in yards of green fabric over white. The dog followed on his heels.

The vestments emphasized the breadth of his shoulders.

"Nice outfit," she said.

"I had a baptism in the chapel. People like us vested for their photos." ❧

"You look like one of *those* guys," she pointed at the row of saints portrayed in the lancets beneath the transept windows.

"Doctors of the Church. Defenders of the doctrinal proclamations of the Immaculate Conception and the dogma of Mary, Mother of God." He pointed from window to window, catechizing her. "The large transept windows depict Marian milestones. The other windows depict the Joyful, Sorrowful and Glorious Mysteries of the Rosary."

"Hmmmm," was all she said, realizing that to him the windows served as religious picture books. Catholic propaganda. He was ignorant of the engineering difficulties.

The priest pulled the green vestment over his head, folded it over his arm. "I must run. I'm celebrating Mass at the county jail."

"Really? Mass in jail? That must be grim."

"Quite the contrary," he said. "It's the bright spot of the week for a handful of guys."

"I'm always suspicious of people who find Jesus in a cell. I mean, I realize it looks good when they come up for parole."

"Are you putting a limit on God's mercy?"

"I have no idea about God's mercy," Nora said as she looked at the crucifix in the sanctuary.

The priest paused for her to say more, but she did not. He pointed up at windows covered with plywood as he slowly turned a complete circle. "I must say, with the windows boarded up, it feels so different in here."

"That's because glass defines space, yet extends it."

"Fascinating," he said and made her feel so. "It's so dark in here; I miss the sun."

"Glass needs light," Nora said, "but glaziers worry about the sun. Especially at this altitude, intense sun can damage windows. The heat can warm up the lead until it's soft, and the glass bows. You'd think the UV would alter the colors, too," Nora held a piece of ruby-glass up to the light, "but glass never fades."

"At least she has faith in something," the priest said to the dog. They traded playful smiles.

"I'm off," he said. And she thought, *So am I.*

ᕦ ᕦ ᕦ

Nora worked the rest of the day with diligence. She wanted desperately to impress him. ᕦ At day's end, she wrapped up, disappointed that he had not dropped in again. *He's busy*, she told herself. *Everybody wants a piece of him.*

Nora imagined Herr Zettler leaving late at night, stopping, perhaps, at a bierstube to wolf a wurst and hoist a stein. *Did he look into his* ale and say, "This! This is the color of gold of the crown of Christ the King!" Did he look into the eyes of his daughter in the clear north light and say, "This! This is the blue of the virgin's mantle!" Did he ever spot a carafe of wine and say, "This! This is the claret of the blood flowing from the crown of thorns!"

SOLEMNITY OF THE BIRTH OF ST. JOHN THE BAPTIST
(24 June)

Nora began to feel at home in the studio she'd set up in a portion of the rectory's three-stall garage. At the end of the work day, as Nora was getting to the bottom of one of the plastic pails of broken glass, she watched through the open garage door as the priest let the dog out. Puccini piddled, raced about the yard for a couple of laps and then ran into the garage.

Father DiMarco followed. Puccini barked and seemed to smile at Nora.

"How's it coming?" the priest asked, leaning toward her.

"Glaziers, glaciers, we're all the same," she said.

He tilted his head, puzzled.

"Slow," she said. He nodded. "It's the faces that throw me. And there are so many of them. I can't just repaint them. I have to paint the missing parts on a second piece of glass and glue that behind, double glaze it to the original." The dog leaned on her leg, and Nora bent over to scratch his fuzzy neck.

"Sometimes it seems nothing is easy," the priest said. "Can I offer you something cold to drink? Millie keeps a pitcher of iced tea in the refrigerator. Or I have some cold beers."

"Beers? I'd drink a cold beer."

"I'll be right back."

Nora's arms dangled at her sides, her wrists leaden. She was uncertain whether she should have accepted the offer of alcohol from her boss, a priest.

Father DiMarco returned with two green bottles. He twisted the top off one and handed it to her.

"Thanks," she said, pulling off her gloves. She looked around to see whether Millie or anyone else was watching. They sipped the beers in awkward silence.

He looked at his watch. "Actually, I need to get going. I'm late for a meeting."

Just then the door from the sacristy opened and Juan leaned out. "Father?" he called. Nora noticed the priest put the beer behind his back. She wondered whether she should hide hers, too. "We're waiting on you."

"Be right there, Juan."

Juan pointed at his watch before letting the sacristy door close. The priest finished his beer, set down the empty bottle, and popped a breath mint. "Come in for just a minute. I want to introduce you to the finance council." He offered her a mint.

She followed him to the cathedral's side entrance. He held the door open for her. She watched him walk up the marble steps, brace himself on the communion rail, genuflect.

"You know," the priest said to Juan, "this would be a good time to get the rest of the windows cleaned, too, while we're at it."

"*While we're at it,*" Juan said. "That's an expensive phrase I keep hearing. 'While we're at it, why don't we update the plumbing?' 'While we're at it, why don't we lay down new carpeting?' 'While we're at it, why not retile the entire roof?' Father, you know good and well there's no money in this parish. We can barely afford to turn on the lights. And what the parish really needs is more staff. Another priest, at least. And now we have the unbudgeted expense of restoring these windows."

"People need beauty almost as much as sandwiches," the priest said, looking at Nora. "Art feeds people."

"That's easy to say when you're getting three squares a day," Juan said. "I'm sure your pals in the alley would rather we spend the money on their lunches."

"Art is a link to the divine. These windows are worth every dime."

"The question is, how do we come up with all those dimes?"

"You could round up some volunteers for some of the clean-up work," Nora said. "When the panels are finished and sealed, somebody could clean them. And maybe they could clean the other glass before I reset it, too. It'd save me a lot of time."

"Not a bad idea," Juan said.

And the priest said, "I'll see who I can find."

FIRST MARTYRS OF THE CHURCH (30 *June*)

The job overwhelmed Nora on every front. Time and again, she got stuck before even starting. She couldn't summon her dogged resolve. She wanted to dash across the parking lot, never to return. She knew she couldn't.

At her bench, she could almost hear her dad say, "You have to start some place." She pivoted. She positioned her cutter and began. The sizzle of the score was a touchstone. ✒ Nora carved a compound curve. With the metal ball at the end of her glass cutter, she tapped the underside of the glass. She made her first thumb break; and as the glass snapped, something inside her—like the first crack in the ice that instigates the spring thaw—gave way. With her hand grindstone, she softened the edges of the glass shape.

But Nora floundered again as she began to cut more glass to match her patterns. The tools did not fit into her hands. The glass mocked her with fragility, refused to yield pure color. The surface was slippery, without bite. In the cathedral, the windows hung like tattered jigsaw puzzles. And she was missing many, many pieces.

Moreover, the sound of glass against glass grated her nerves. So she kept her music cranked up. As she studied the strata on a piece of variegated glass, singing along to a favorite song, she felt a tap on her shoulder and almost jumped out of her jeans.

"I apologize," Father DiMarco said. "I didn't mean to startle you." He looked over her shoulder. "How's it coming?"

"Fine," she took off her headphones. "I was just going to take some measurements," she said, grabbing her tape measure.

He asked, "May I join you?"

The voluminous cathedral both welcomed her and browbeat her. At the door, he dipped his hand in the holy water fount. Nora did not. He greeted the workers: painters, plasterers, carpenters—many of whom he knew by name.

"I can't believe these windows are older than I am," he said.

"This one time? My dad took me to the Philadelphia Museum of Art and we saw some *medieval* glass."

"I didn't know glass went back that far."

For the first time in a long time, Nora felt talkative. "Actually, ancient Egyptians had glass, but this was *stained* glass. It blows my mind to think that people had actually developed this craft way back then. They colored the glass with metallic oxides while it was still in a molten state. They blew the glass into tube shapes, then cut off the ends to make cylinders. Then they slit the cylinders lengthwise and rolled them into sheets while still hot and pliable. And voila!"

"They had what they needed to illustrate the Bible in glass. Humanity giving form to divinity," he said.

Nora nodded eagerly. "Early church glass was done mosaic style, fairly crude, but we're talking sixth century. The Church of St. Sophie in Constantinople, I think, was the first. Then some churches in Rome followed suit."

"Ah," he said. "There's no place like Rome."

"There was a monk in 12th century Germany who wrote about making stained-glass. Theophilus was his pseudonym," she said, elated to be the one giving the lesson, for a change. "He got the process documented—and it's basically what I'm doing here today."

He scratched his head. "You mean to tell me that with all the technology today, glass is still stained the way it was nine centuries ago?"

She ate up his interest. "Technically speaking, glass isn't really stained. The color is frozen *in* the glass," Nora said. "That's why glass won't fade. 'Stained' refers to silver stain, which wasn't discovered until the 14th century." She hesitated, wondering if her rambling bored him.

"Go on," he said. "Edify me. I'm intrigued."

"Well, the black and brown vitreous paints add details and tones and suggest dimension. Artistically speaking, stained-glass hit its stride in the 12th and 14th centuries. They weren't using any enamel paint on glass then. I don't think anything done now could surpass the stuff from that era. But this," she said, looking at a piece of painted glass, "comes close." She set about measuring, noting numbers on her clipboard.

He turned around, looking at the windows. "I'm jaded. I celebrate the Eucharist here day in and day out and seldom notice the glory of the glass or the architecture." He sat in a pew, his arms stretched wide. "But once in a while, when the sun hits one of the windows at just such an angle, the Scripture is revealed to me. ✍ And I remember that God incarnated to bring light, and that God, mysteriously, is the source of light and therefore, perhaps, given form via these windows."

She nodded. "Watch the first-time visitors respond to the glass when they come in. Notice the children—infants, even. They're captivated when they look up. Maybe it's because the glass has a life of its own: It's constantly in flux with the light."

"As we are in flux with the light," he said.

"I definitely lean more toward the dark," she said. A burst of nervous laughter escaped her. "Right. Well. I'd better get back to work." ✍

He followed her back to the garage. She singled out a bit of glass with exquisite painting—the brocade on a shoe. Nora handed the glass to him. "This is a vitreous enamel that's fused to the glass by firing. Paint and fire, paint and fire. Over and over. I'm going to have to go look for this absinthe green and this sort of hydrangea blue. I know a place that stocks out-of-the-ordinary glass."

"I'd like to accompany you," he said.

"Why?"

"Because I'm interested." He handed the piece of painted glass back to her. "Because I've taken a proprietary interest in these glorious allegories of light."

"To tell the truth, I've never worked with glass like this. Nothing quite this elaborate. I hope I'm your woman."

"Trust me," he said. "You're my woman."

His declaration rang in her head. She pressed her lips together. "We've got a lot of damage. More than I initially thought."

"Whatever it takes, I'm grateful," the priest said with a humble bow. "Tremendously, terrifically grateful."

She smiled. "Oh, I meant to tell you, I was working in the church this morning, and that homeless man wandered in. That black guy who hangs out here a lot."

"Two-Wheel Rich."

"Is he…OK?" she asked. "I mean, I can see he's not, but he kind of creeps me out." Nora didn't tell the priest that the guy's eyes reminded her of her late husband's. "He's on something."

"He's a recovering addict."

"And you just let him camp out in the cathedral?"

"It's as much his as mine," the priest said. "It's the one place he can be exposed to beauty and art, to quiet and calm. He needs that cathedral more than you or I."

The priest's largesse put her to shame. She buckled beneath his authority, his piety. When he wanted to, he projected a trenchant force that threatened to siphon all the oxygen out of the room.

"You know the Church has a long-standing preferential option for the poor. If we forget the poor, we've forgotten the Gospel. Rich is harmless. He shows up every weekday to make the coffee for the lunch line; and that lunch line is where the rubber meets the road. I became a priest to serve people like Rich—not the pious old ladies in their fur coats and family diamonds. Jesus came for the sinners." The priest smiled. "Besides which, they're inherently more intriguing."

Nora took off her gloves. She crossed her arms, uncrossed them. "I can't imagine being a priest."

"You wouldn't really want to. It's gotten worse after all these sexual misconduct scandals. It's very disquieting. I feel like people look at me and assume I'm a pedophile." He shook his head. "I often wonder what I would have done with my life if I hadn't been ordained."

She held her breath, wanting him to speak his heart.

But he made light again and said, "But you know the old cliché: A priest's retirement package is out of this world."

BLESSED JUNIPERO SERRA (1 *July*)

When she worked in the cathedral, oftentimes the organist practiced, filling the space with blasts of Mozart and Fauré. Choirs rehearsed, perched like songbirds on the risers. The vibrations of color from the windows and notes from the choir filled the cathedral, pushing up against the barrel vaults.

At the same time, workers conducted repairs: Painters and plasterers, electricians and woodworkers came and went. Nora nodded politely to them, but stayed behind the isolated safety of her head-phones.

She caught glimpses of the priest as he directed wedding rehearsals, baptized babies and occasionally led groups of school children on tours. Informally in the aisles and pews, he counseled parishioners before and after Mass. He graciously received loaves of bread, pies, hot dishes, garden produce and adulation from the women of the parish. Frequently, he took money from his wallet and stealthily slipped rolled-up bills into the grimy hands of street people who slept in the cathedral during the day. Much to Nora's discomfort, he operated casually, unintimidated by odors or raggedy clothes or crazed eyes of the men who approached him. His light shone on everyone he met.

Before she knew it, Nora was ready to seal the first finished pane—one of the angels at the top of a trefoil. The angel wasn't in terrible shape from the storm; and the section was small. Nora looked down at the finished piece on her bench. Every joint was fluxed and soldered on both sides. The angel's hair was mustard-yellow seedy glass. Her flowing gown was rouge wispy glass. Her wings were opalescent.

Mixing water, linseed oil, whiting and a pinch of lampblack to darken the pewter-colored lead, she found the right creamy consistency. With a paintbrush, she spread the paste, taking care to cover the spaces between glass and lead. The putty weatherproofed and strengthened the windows.

She poured sawdust liberally onto the glass and rubbed the piece with her hand, to allow the sawdust to absorb the sealing paste. With a soft fingernail brush, she swept away the excess dust. Then, she turned the panel over and did the same on the other side. She heard the garage door open and close. She held up the panel. "Ta-da," she sang. She couldn't help but smile ever so slightly.

"One window down," Juan said. With his tired face and cheap haircut, he appeared older than his age, Nora guessed. He handed Nora her paycheck.

"Correction: One *panel* down," she said.

"It's a start," Juan said, leaning closer to look at the glass.

"Barely," said Nora.

"Looks good," he said.

"To the pedestrian eye, I suppose," she said. "No offense." Nora realized that nobody would know the innumerable times she'd wiped down the glass, erased errant lines. Nobody was privy to the fissures in bowed windows she dismantled and reassembled, leaded. "This one's ready to be washed. We'll need to get lime and burlap rags. You mentioned you could get some volunteers?"

"Actually," Juan said, scratching the back of his balding head, "Father thought you might need somebody to assist you on a more regular basis."

Nora looked from the panel to Juan.

Juan pushed his glasses up the bridge of his nose. "He hired Two-Wheel Rich."

Nora found the priest in the alley. His sandwich line crew cleaned up the last of the used coffee cups and empty sugar packets from a card table.

"Two-Wheel Rich?" she asked the priest. "I'm over there busting my hump to get these windows right, and you hire a homeless addict to do clean-up on them?"

"Rich, as I explained, is a *recovering* addict," he said, folding a plastic tablecloth.

"Once an addict, always an addict."

"He goes to meetings. He's working his program." The priest started to walk away.

She scoffed. "Yeah. I know how well that works." He spun around, looked her in the eye. "Father, my husband was an addict."

"I'm sorry."

"I'm not looking for an apology."

"What *are* you looking for, Nora?"

The pit of her stomach hardened. "You have no idea the *magnitude* of what you've asked me to do."

"You accepted the job. Do you want out of your commitment?"

Nora paused. "No. But I want to pick the person who assists me."

"No," he said in her face. She took a step back. "I do the hiring around here. Rich gets a chance. I've already told him." He paused. "Look, if *we* lack charity, who will ever give him a break? He's very conscientious. He's taking his meds. I would not assign this to just anybody. He won't bother you."

"He already does," she said, hands on her hips.

"Get over it," the priest said.

Nora shrank, swallowed hard. "Anything happens, don't expect me to start over. I've got more than enough to handle as it is."

"I assure you," the priest said as he turned toward the rectory. "Nothing will happen."

�� �� ��

A heat wave crested in Denver. Nora worked in the stuffy garage, cleaning and piecing together bits of rescued glass through which the windows revealed their endless icons: an anchor, a thick-maned lion, a pink pelican, the eye of God centered within a triangle. She studied the patina on a wine jug, the hinges of an open door.

She banished thoughts of the priest. *Just because I'm attracted to him doesn't mean he's attracted to me*, she lectured herself.

She sketched the tracery, noting in her journal the schedule of the summer sun's passing. Nora catalogued which windows included enamel, which relied on silver stain. The glass never showed the same face twice. Like a sentient being, the windows changed moment by moment. While there was light to gather, the glass never grew stagnant.

Two-Wheel Rich stayed out of her way, but each morning she returned to find carefully washed and wiped glass.

Nora headed for the garage studio to scissor the cardboard shapes that dictated the glass cuts. Just as she picked up her pattern shears, Puccini ran up to her, followed by Father DiMarco. ✎ He wore a Colorado Rockies hat and T-shirt, shorts and running shoes.

"Hey, Puccini!" she said. The dog nudged her with his nose.

"How're you getting along?" the priest asked her. "Rich doing his job?" ✎

Nora sighed. "Yeah," she said. "He is."

"Everything OK, then?"

"I'll need to get some more materials," Nora said.

"I'll go with you," he replied. "Puccini, do you want to go?"

The dog woofed and scurried to the door.

"I didn't mean this very minute. But eventually."

"No time like the present."

"I'm in the middle of something," she said, toppled by his insistence. Still upset from his new hire, she popped in her ear buds, turned up her tunes.

"Too hot to work this afternoon," he said. "Besides which, it's my day off. Are you free for lunch?"

Nora turned down the volume and, even though she had heard every word, she feigned indifference, "Pardon?"

He lowered his alluring voice. "I said, are you free for lunch? Or at least relatively inexpensive?"

Her heart palpitated. *❧* She realized this was his attempt at an apology for imposing Two-Wheel Rich on her. She looked at her filthy hands and her shabby overalls and faded shirt. Ash-smudged Cinderella had nothing on her. Nora pictured herself in a crisp white linen sailor dress and a straw cloche with a silk gardenia, pearl earrings—real pearls—and jute espadrilles, white cotton crocheted gloves—all whisked with the airy scent of lavender and lime *l'eau du toilet. ❧*

"I'm a mess," she protested.

"Not to worry. We'll go someplace very casual. Come on," he gestured to the rectory, "you can wash up a bit; and we'll be off."

Inside, Nora changed out of her overalls and work boots and

into the shorts and top and sandals she'd worn to work. Puccini made off with one of her socks. "Hey!" she watched him prance down the hall, his hind end high in the air, so proud of himself. She chased him down in the kitchen, retrieved her sock, gave him a treat and a pat on the head.

Outside, the priest put the top down on his British racing green MGB. He opened the door for her.

"Fun car!" she said. "Isn't it kind of fancy for a priest?"

"I'm a diocesan priest. We don't take the vow of poverty like the Franciscans, for example. Besides which, I inherited it from my father," he said. A white rosary swung from the rearview mirror.

"My father would never drive an English car," she said.

"Oh?" Father DiMarco said. "Why not?"

"Well, he was Irish, so not a lot of love for merry old England," she said.

"You're—what?—the fourth generation to go into glass? He must have been glad you continued the legacy. Did he want you to follow in his artisan footsteps?"

"No," she said, pulling her hair back into a ponytail. "Maybe if I had been a boy. But he wanted me to marry well, which I did not. He wanted me to go to college. Which I did, as an art major. But I got bored with all the theory," she said. "I've been painting glass since I was a tyke. Some kids had coloring books, I had a studio. I used to stand on a milk crate so I could reach the top of the bench.

My grandfather was still alive; and he was the one who first stuck a badger in my hand and showed me just one stroke, which I would practice for weeks and perfect before he'd show me another."

"He'd be proud of you," the priest said.

Nora was glad his eyes were on the road so he couldn't see her blush. "Well, I didn't just do it because of my lineage. I always knew I wanted to do something creative. And I knew I had to support myself. So I considered all the applied arts and took a shine to glass when I realized that it's sort of a hybrid art."

"How so?" he asked.

"It combines drawing, painting a fresco, illuminating a manuscript, firing enamel work and designing architecture all at once," she said, trying to shut herself up.

"Aaaah, I never thought about it that way. You must have grown up around lots of beautiful windows."

"My grandparents' house had a wonderful bay window that my grandfather's father had done. ✺ He was a master glazier, my great-granddad; and Ireland was churning out some first-rate stuff. He worked a lot with beveled glass—very unusual in his time—and nuggets and multifaceted jewels and what we call rondels—mouth-blown disks. His work was very 3-D. It made an imprint on me." Nora closed her eyes and pictured the bay window. "Somebody somehow managed to bring some panels over on a ship. Can you imagine?" ✺

She almost blabbed that she met her husband in art school, but stopped herself before pulling on that thread.

He hummed along to the opera on the radio as they drove.

They arrived at the Emerald Isle—a bar and grill overlooking Cherry Creek Reservoir. Out of the way. Way out of the way. They followed the gangly and bubbly hostess to a table on the sun deck. Boats sailed on the calm water. ✺ The Front Range provided a dramatic backdrop.

"Good place to take an Irish girl, right?" he asked. "'Tis a grand view. Leprechauns in the landscape," he said in a decent facsimile of a brogue. Then to the waitress, "Pale ale. Two cold ones."

Nora had never had a man order for her without consulting her first. She was too anxious to protest. *Besides which,* she reasoned, *maybe a beer will settle me down.* Ale arrived in heavy, frosted mugs. ✺ Cold and bitter, the beer jarred her. They deliberated over the menu, ordered. When their food arrived, Nora was too nervous to eat. He gobbled a juicy cheeseburger and curly fries while she self-consciously dabbed her napkin at her mouth and stabbed at an Oriental chicken salad. Gawky silences weighed down the lunch. They made teeny-tiny talk.

"The cherries are reddening on the tree outside the sacristy," Nora said. ✺

"I know. So do the robins." He ordered another beer. "I always associate Independence Day with ripe cherries. Fresh cherry pie on the Fourth of July. The pits make me a little nervous, though. They're scattered all over the sidewalk; and I'm always afraid somebody will slip coming or going from Mass."

"Who's the patron saint of broken bones and cherry stones?"

He chuckled. "There probably is one. ✍ The patron saint of bakers is Elizabeth of Hungary. Isn't that amusing? Here's another one: The patron saint of short-order cooks is St. Lawrence, who was martyred on a grill."

She opened her mouth wide. "Serious?"

"God's truth."

"That's sick."

He swigged his beer. "I like to cook. I make a mean marinara," he said, punctuating his statement with a Mephistophelian grin. "Cooking is an act of love."

Over the tops of their mugs, they looked at one another from behind their sunglasses. "I love fruit pie for breakfast."

"What else do you love, Nora Kelley?"

His stare seared her.

She decided to take him up on his earlier offer: "I'd love to have you look at some glass with me."

"We can do that." He signaled for the check, plunked down cash, anchored it with his empty beer mug.

And then he was behind her, pulling her chair out for her as she stood, exhilarated and dizzy from the beer. The oxytocin. The serotonin.

❦ ❦ ❦

"Great Panes," he said, groaning at the sign at the glass supply shop. "Clever."

"We're not exactly dressed for glass shopping."

"You have to dress for it?"

"Sandals and shorts can be dangerous around glass," she said. "So be careful."

He opened the door for her. A brass bell jingled. "Be right with you," a familiar voice called.

"Hey, Harry?" Nora called.

The proprietor lumbered out, tucking his T-shirt into his Levis. He tugged his salt-and-pepper ponytail, then let out a whoop. "Nora Kelley?" He swooped upon her and landed a kiss on the top of her head. "It's been... what? A year? Two? Too long, anyway." And then his bemused smile disappeared. "I heard about..." his voice trailed off. He hunched his shoulders beneath the awkward moment.

"Bad deal," Harry said.

The priest looked from Harry to Nora, then wandered off discreetly.

Harry took a toothpick from the pocket of his shirt and worked it around his canines. "It's good you're dating again."

"He's my client," she whispered.

Harry raised an eyebrow. "Don't get your honey where you make your money," he muttered.

"Don't worry," she said softly. "He's a Catholic priest."

"No shit?" Harry mumbled. "Don't they wear those funny collars?"

"They're supposed to," she whispered.

"So you're working again? Your dad would be happy."

The priest re-joined them.

"She's the best," Harry said to Father DiMarco.

"That's what I hear," he extended his hand. "Vin DiMarco."

"Father DiMarco is the rector at the cathedral," Nora said as the men shook hands, sizing up one another, chests inflated.

"Girl," Harry said, scratching his beard. "Don't tell me you're tackling those big old church lights."

"Trying. OK if I leave this materials list?"

"You got it," Harry said. The phone rang and he vanished.

"He certainly thinks highly of you," the priest said to her.

"He doesn't know everything."

"God forbid you should accept a compliment."

"Harry really loved my dad. He apprenticed with him. He's brilliant, actually. Harry, I mean."

"Good Lord!" He eyed the aisles of bins holding glass, samples displayed above each slot. "There's a veritable rainbow in here."

"Handmade Euro glass comes in about 3,000 colors," Harry said, reappearing. ✍

From her backpack, Nora pulled a bit of broken glass wrapped in newspaper. "I'm trying to match this Virgin Mary blue, Harry," she handed him the sublime glass.

He held the glass to the light. "Don't got it in stock. Looks French. I could custom order it. Might have something close."

"I can't use 'close.'"

"You sound just like your old man," Harry said. He moved from bin to bin, setting squares of sample glass in racks to view. The phone rang again. Harry handed Nora's bit of glass back to her. As she reached for it, Harry noticed the scars on her arms, winced and shook his head. "'Scuse me," he headed for the telephone.

Nora looked to the priest, who had observed their interaction. To his credit, he said nothing. She held the bit of broken glass up to the light. The subtle differences would have escaped the less discerning eye. She sighed.

"That's a lot of blues," Father DiMarco said.

"Blues are my specialty," she said, squinting at the glass, comparing texture and opacity, advancing and recessing color. "I once heard about laws imposed against using too much cobalt blue glass in churches because of the extreme emotional impact."

"So, the blues cause the blues?"

Nora shrugged. "When there's no perfect match."

"I'm not demanding perfection, Nora."

"I am."

"Nobody will know if this piece or that isn't original."

"I'll know," Nora said. "And everything is interconnected. It's not just disparate elements. This lead line leads to the next. Each color and shape needs to flow organically into its neighbors." Her eyes flooded with frustration. "It's not just manufacturing. It's art."

"But isn't that the beauty of stained-glass? Can't you patch it in?"

"You don't get it," she snapped, turning back to the bins of glass.

"I don't get *you*. Is that what you mean?"

She flinched at his abruptness, regretting her testy tone.

"Look," he said, pointing to a sign. "Cathedral glass."

"Machine made," she said.

"And that's bad?"

"It's not the best. It's uninspired, but affordable. Mouth-blown glass is five times as expensive."

"And visually?" he asked.

"No comparison. Top-drawer materials are crucial for windows," she said. Pulling a sample of seedy glass, she held the square up to the light. "You see this? You see all those bubbles? You know how they got there?" He knit his brow. "When the glass is molten, they throw a potato into it. The potato vaporizes. The chemical reaction causes all those bubbles. And those bubbles give the glass an interior life."

Nora overheard Harry winding down his phone call.

She set two pieces of glass on either side of the original in the rack and considered the contrasts. "Do you want to go darker? Or lighter?" she asked the priest.

"I want whatever you want," he said. "You're the artist."

Nora wanted to believe him.

And as she reached toward a bin labeled "Lagoon," he touched her hand. Then he gently turned her wrist over and looked closer at the undersides of her forearm. He touched a scar. Her spindly self-confidence caved. "What happened here?" he whispered.

She withdrew her arm, hugged herself. "Nothing."

"Doesn't look like nothing."

"Car crash. A long time ago."

"Is this what Harry was referring to earlier? Was he talking about your husband?"

"I don't discuss it."

The priest retreated. "Didn't mean to pry."

"It's OK," Nora said with a flip of her hands.

His brow furrowed.

She walked to the cash register. He followed. Mutely, they waited as Harry packaged the tools she'd purchased: a ball-tipped cutter, an India stone, drafting tape, drawing pencils.

The priest started to take a credit card from his wallet. Nora bristled, held up her hand like a traffic cop. "These are my tools," she said. "I'll pay for them. I'll use them again after this job." *Will I?* she wondered.

Harry grinned, "I'll take care of this." He waved her list of materials. ✇

"Good luck, girl."

"I'll need more than luck," she said. "And I'm going to need some major equipment, too. I'm wondering if maybe I can rent a kiln?"

Harry lit up. "I've got some stuff you might be interested in. Come on back," he motioned to her. "You, too, Padre." Harry led them through the back hallway into a cluttered storage area and back to the far corner, where Nora saw all her equipment with a poster board in Harry's draftsman's hand that read: "This belongs to Nora Kelley. Not for sale."

"Harry!" She smiled, mouth wide open, astonished at her good fortune. "You never sold this stuff?" She rushed into his arms, hugging him hard.

"That light table was your daddy's," he said. "That easel was your grand-daddy's. You think they'd let me into heaven if I let that go to strangers?"

She hugged him again. "Can I count on you and your crew to help with the installation?"

"Of course," said Harry. "You're not in this alone."

∾ ∾ ∾

In the car, almost shoulder to shoulder in the roadster's bucket seats, Father DiMarco said, "Somebody was looking out for you."

"Yeah," she said. "Harry."

The priest said nothing. She braced herself, expecting him to question her, but he didn't. The strained quiet unnerved her. Nora wanted small talk, talk radio, anything to defrost the air between them.

On the road again, tooling along, shifting smoothly, he said, "It's so hot. Why don't you take the afternoon off?"

"Good idea, I think I will." She realized he was letting her off the hook. ✍

"I'll drop you at home."

"Great," she said. Nora would have stopped just short of voodoo to cause that afternoon in his company never to end. Wind in her hair, his hand on the steering wheel, the relaxed planes of his profile — everything seemed all right.

They pulled up to her place and he shifted the car into neutral in the shade cast by the leafy branches of the old elm. She looked blankly at him, yearning. Then she recoiled. "Um, thanks for lunch," she rushed past her infernal embarrassment, as if he could read her mind.

"Nice neighborhood. Lived here long?"

"I have a pretty good arrangement. I take care of the grounds, do some errands for my landlady, so my rent is manageable. You might know her. Mrs. Quincy?"

"Vera comes to daily Mass," he said. "She's not exactly salt of the earth. More like allspice of the earth."

Nora grinned. "I hope I'm that spry if I live to be 83. She gets up every morning and puts on a housedress, hose and heels, even if she's just staying in for the day. She drinks a glass of wine every evening with dinner. And she smokes a cigarette if I'm around to watch her. She doesn't trust herself to smoke alone. She's afraid she'll burn down the house if she has a stroke." Nora reddened, irritated at herself for rambling. "Would you like to come in? It's small and a mess, but—"

"Nora," the priest said. "You're forgetting something."

"Oh, oh," she stammered, feeling rejected. "I didn't mean to insinuate anything."

"No, no, not that," he said. "I've been inside before. Remember?"

"Oh, of course! I forgot." Her stomach back-flipped and she fumbled with the car door handle.

"Do I make you nervous?" he asked softly.

Nora could not answer. She could not look at him. "I guess I should go," she said through her welling anxiety. "Thanks again for lunch." ✍

"My pleasure. Someday we'll have a real meal, prepared by me."

She wasn't sure what he was implying. She felt so gratified, so consumed, so lighthearted and lightheaded that she just said, "I'd like that." She recalled what he'd said earlier: *Cooking is an act of love*. "Father?" He turned to look at her. "It's not that I don't want to tell you about my scars, but..." He adjusted the volume on the car's stereo, turned down the aria.

"I know," he said. "I absolve you," he half teasingly and half reverently blessed her with the Sign of the Cross. "You had an injurious experience that involved glass." He phrased it as a statement, not a question. He sounded as clinical as the shrink that she used to see weekly. ✍

"Yes, there was an accident," she said.

"Some people claim there *are* no accidents," the priest replied.

"I seriously doubt that."

"I won't press," he said. And as Father DiMarco reached across and opened the door for her, his forearm ever so slightly— unintentionally?—brushed first his rearview mirror rosary and then—was she imagining it?—her breast.

Swooning and mortified, she practically jigged to her front door. Then she noticed Mrs. Quincy looking out her living room window, watching the green MG pull away.

FEAST OF ST. THOMAS THE APOSTLE (3 *July*)

The record-breaking temperatures marched on; and the fever sacked the city. Father DiMarco had enlisted the help of a few of the guys from his food line to help deliver Nora's kiln to the garage. Two-Wheel Rich was among them, directing the others. Grunting and sweating, they scraped the box along the concrete floor while she held her breath.

The priest gave them cash and extra sack lunches. He judged not.

"I feel guilty," she said, "having them do all that heavy work."

"Nothing wrong with hard work," the priest said. "People need work. We all need to contribute. You know that." He turned to the men and shook their dirty hands. "Thanks, guys. Thanks, Rich." Rich saluted the priest. And for the first time, Nora saw Rich smile, gaps between his teeth white in contrast with his ebony skin.

The priest returned the salute. "You know, Rich was a Vietnam vet," he said to Nora under his breath. "Worked in a hospital that was bombed. Can't stand to be indoors. Hardworking. Honest. Good man. ✒ Not a lot of places in the world for a guy like Two-Wheel Rich."

"Hey, how did he get that name, anyway?"

"The guys call him that to distinguish him from Four-Wheel Rich. Their carts: One has two wheels, one has—"

"I get it," she said, interrupting.

"Look, Nora," he said, and she felt a sermon coming on. His voice went soft and mellow. "I don't know what happened with your husband, but you can't go around casting aspersions." His tone did not condemn her. "Rich looks a little rough, but he's a gentle soul. I'm about the only person he'll talk to. He told me a chaplain in Nam saved his life. He was 18 years old. I think he might confuse me with that priest. The heroic one."

"*You're* heroic," she blurted. The priest shook his head. "I'm sure you're a savior to those guys," she insisted. "And to *lots* of your parishioners. I see the way they kowtow to you."

He loosened his Roman collar. He wore a pale blue clerical shirt instead of the standard-issue black. Renegade. He wound himself up and belted out a song—"It's me, it's me, O' Lord, standing in the need of prayer"—as he walked away from her and toward the cathedral, taking his rosary from his pocket.

His scattershot affection infuriated her. Nora turned up the music in her headphones and went back to work. She considered the ruby-red glass on her bench. With vinegar, she diluted her tracing paint. She couldn't seem to get the consistency right. She berated herself for taking on such an arduous job. There was a reason that only large studios typically handled these sorts of restorations. She resented the glass, her compulsion. She told herself that she should've just taken the insurance money and run.

Memories of Liam seeped in. *"Get down!"*

The temperature had already climbed to 100 degrees. It wasn't even noon. The whole city sweated. She began the daunting task of painting the face of Christ as he was taken down from his cross.

She held her brush, loaded with pigment. 🖌 Facing the blank surface of the glass, her brush hovered.

She looked across the garage at another window waiting for repair. In the background of the cracked and broken window, a round red sun sank. Traditionally, 3 o'clock marks the hour of the death of Jesus Christ, the moment when the earth had heaved. The sun had disappeared, obscured by an eclipse: Darkness had fallen over the land. Boulders had split. The sanctuary curtain had been torn in two. To this day, millennia later, even banks close at 3 o'clock on Good Friday. The window's sky resembled the sky that day of the tornado.

And then, mustering aplomb, with a sure hand, Nora made her first stroke. Then another. Another. She was in! A sweep of brown paint here—the curve of the jaw of the dead Jesus on the crucifix. A stroke there, a curl of his beard. Nora was possessed, inexplicably. The brush, as if of its own accord, lifted, parting ways with the glass, paused, dropped and swerved again. She did her best to keep breathing, wondering how the drawing would read in the light.

But to her chagrin the strokes she had executed would not do. Pinched and paltry, the face looked nothing like the enlarged photo of the original detail. As she had from time to time in her life, she rued what she had started.

Even with a fan blowing on her, Nora's head ached from the heat and infatuation's fever. Her tongue cottoned to the roof of her mouth. She fled the hellish studio. Resting on the bench in the relatively cool shade of the globe willow outside the garage, she gulped water and scratched brown paint spatters off her forearms.

Looking up to the rectory's second-floor window, she saw him in profile, hunched over the computer at his desk. *Was she so drawn to him because he was so attractive,* she wondered, *or was he so attractive because she was so drawn to him?* Nora wished she were able to read what he was writing. ✎ Unwittingly, she stared.

He turned his head, as if to read a thought on a cloud. He saw her. Leaning into the pane he waved. She waved back, exalted beneath her tight skin. She indulged a romance-novel reverie in which he led her to a gazebo where a crystal tumbler of iced tea waited, sweating. She itched to drink inches of sweet tea and kiss him with a cold, wet mouth.

"*Oh, God!*" she said aloud, appalled at herself. She panted in the heat of the day. Her brain felt like a lava lamp. A bead of sweat threaded its way down her sternum. Heat waves rippled above the parking lot, teasing with their fluid illusion of water. Normally, Nora wore long-sleeved shirts to protect her arms and hide her scars, but she couldn't take the heat, so she stripped down to her sports bra.

Humming, Nora plodded back to the garage, determined to find the angles of the Lord's face. Her ponytail had loosened; strands of hair spilled out. Just as she wiped down the paint to start over, she heard the jangle of keys, and a shadow fell over her.

"Don't paint yourself into a corner." Father DiMarco stood in front of her, his pipe between his teeth. He wore a black suit. *That has to be uncomfortable,* she thought, *wearing all black in summer.* His eyes lit on her torso.

Nonchalantly, Nora looked around to see where she'd left her shirt. She didn't want to appear the strumpet. Nor too modest. She looked through the open garage and saw her shirt near the flower bed behind him. Zinnias wilted.

"You'd better give those flowers a drink." She resented that he held so much power by merely standing close. She stared at his shoes. Black wingtips. Not knowing what to say, she stated the obvious: "Painting is very physical work."

"And mental, as well, I should think."

"And spiritual," she added, regaining some of her composure, glad he was there, terrified, too.

"Oh?" Father DiMarco said. "Spiritual?"

"At least the subject matter."

She walked toward her shirt. Just then, a Jeep crammed with teenage boys drove by. They honked, wolf-whistled.

Humiliated by her own exhibitionism, she muttered, "Knuckle-draggers."

Father DiMarco howled. He picked up her top, tossed it to her. "Better put this on," he said. "Not that I..." He paused.

She glared at him and pulled the shirt over her head.

He tried not to smile. "Heckling attractive women is a male form of compliment," he said, "unevolved as that is."

She wiped her face with the back of her forearm and felt a smudge of wet paint on her cheek. "Great," she said. "Did I just do what I think I did?"

He grinned. She groaned. He pushed his sunglasses up on his head. She took off her shades, hooking them on the front of her shirt so that they dangled down her chest. Her eyes sparred with his, the slightest, most subtle movement of focusing on one eye, then the other.

"You look like you could use a break," he said, nodding toward the rectory. "Inside," he said. "Let's wipe that paint off before it dries." 🙦

On one hand, his parental tone outraged her. On the other, she welcomed it. Besides, the heat had made her malleable.

"It's hot as hell in there with that kiln," she said, as they headed for the rectory. "I was just cooling off."

"It's just that I'm not accustomed to looking out from my office window to see a gorgeous, half-naked nymph."

Her ego ballooned. And, in that moment, despite her sweat and dusty skin, Nora *felt* gorgeous. Vanity, vanity.

Inside, at the kitchen sink, Father DiMarco tore off and moistened a paper towel. He walked toward her. She leaned backwards. For all the attraction, being so close to him repelled her.

"I don't bite," he said softly. Part of her wished he would. He gently, slowly wiped at the smudge on her cheek, exercising the same care as if he were washing out the chalice after consecrating wine. Nora closed her eyes. Her face twitched under his touch. He whistled languorously, a lovely melody, lucid as a song bird's, the refrain of a familiar old hymn she couldn't quite name.

Her cheekbones relaxed. The touch of his fingers on her face and the sound of his whistle velvety in her ears triggered the twang of libido. ✍

The phone rang. Nora jumped.

He gave her a look of concern. "It's just the phone," he said. "Be right back."

He headed into the hallway to take the call. She eavesdropped, heard him launch into his pastoral persona.

Under the guise of going to the bathroom, Nora tiptoed upstairs and into his study. Her nosy instincts surfaced when she stepped into his personal space. She noticed snapshots held by magnets on the filing cabinet: pictures of the priest holding babies at baptisms, standing between brides and grooms, posed with little girls in white First Communion dresses, surrounded by smiling families in church clothes. Nora looked at the stacked mail spread on the credenza. His guitar case with the Greenpeace sticker. Copper etchings of Jerusalem. Diplomas on the wall.

Juan cleared his throat, scaring the bejesus out of her.

"Excuse me." His glasses slipped down his nose; he looked at her over the tops of the frames. He wore a short-sleeved shirt, a foulard tie. He held a stack of manila file folders. "Are you surviving out there?"

"Yes, thanks," Nora said.

Juan took out a pocket watch. ✑ "Is Father here? We were supposed to have a meeting with the insurance adjusters."

"He just took a call down in the kitchen, I think. I was just going to leave this glass catalog," she said, but she had no catalog in her hand. She couldn't look Juan in the face. Shame fogged her head, as if Juan could read her lascivious thoughts about the pastor. Juan shuffled his loafers—low in the heel, but well polished.

"I was just going back downstairs," she said. Juan followed her to the kitchen.

Father DiMarco pulled two bottles of Coors from the refrigerator. Nora tried not to show her surprise. "Join us for a libation, Juan?" the priest asked.

Juan looked at his pocket watch again. "Thanks, but no thanks." Disapproval weighed down his words. "I have the budget for your review." He set down the stack of folders.

"I'll get to it soon as possible," the priest said. He took his rosary from his shirt pocket, dropped it near the sink.

"We're behind schedule already." Juan fidgeted with a mechanical pencil. The hair at his temples was shot with gray. "Maybe you could get to it this evening?" Juan looked at Nora. She looked at the pastor. ✑

"Soon as possible," the priest said again. "*Muchas gracias*, Juan. I won't let you down."

"Thanks, Father," Juan said and stepped out.

Father DiMarco twisted off one beer's top for Nora, then did the same for himself, and they clinked brown glass bottles. He took a swallow. "How rude of me. *Mea culpa*. Would you like a glass?"

"Na," she said, wondering whether a modicum of innocence remained in either one of their imaginations. She'd barely touched her beer when he opened another for himself. On the counter, she noticed a foil-wrapped platter. Attached, a recipe card written in feminine penmanship that read, "Lemon bars. Baked with love."

"Hungry?" he asked.

She shook her head. "You sure get a lot of baked goods."

"The guys in the lunch line end up with most of it," he said. "Are you sure you're not hungry? I made lasagna last night. I could heat some up for you."

"No, thanks."

"Focaccia? I have some blood orange olive oil that somebody brought back from Sonoma." He pointed to a plate with the bread. She declined. Again whistling the hymn she couldn't place, the priest tugged the chain of the ceiling fan. A stirring breeze from the rotating blades chilled the sweat on her face.

He reached out to her. "Your hair," he said, touching her bangs. "It's turning all different colors from the sun."

She ducked ever so slightly, Father DiMarco's whistle wandered off key to strained, high notes. Discordant.

INDEPENDENCE DAY (*4 July*)

Fourth of July weekend: unofficially midsummer. The sign outside the cathedral read "Under God." The offices closed for the Independence Day holiday, but Nora worked anyway, aware of and shamed by her hope that she might catch Father DiMarco alone, away from the baleful peering of Millie, the watchdog housekeeper. She allowed herself to glide into a racy fantasy about the priest showing up with a picnic basket and a blanket, inviting her to the fireworks, then finding her flashy red toenails irresistible.

But after a long day in the garage under the midsummer sun, with not even a glimpse of the pastor and no time for a pedicure anyhow, she scowled at the American flag flapping by the rectory door. She went home alone feeling rejected, sorry for herself and stupid, stupid, stupid. She showered and waited for dark, dreaming he might call. Wishing he would. All but praying. She knew she was a nut job. Certifiable. She'd gone off the deep end, off her rocker, half a bubble off plumb.

At twilight, the telephone rang. She begged to hear the sound of his voice.

"Hello?"

"Nora?"

Her expectation withered. "Hi, Mrs. Quincy," she said, forcing the words from her constricted throat with a phony carefree tone.

"Hi, dear," the old lady said in her slightly shaky voice. "I saw your lights on. Are you home alone?"

"Aren't I always?" Nora asked, annoyed. "Do you need something, Mrs. Quincy?"

"No, no, no. But the parish seniors group has a bus out to the fireworks at the fairgrounds. If you aren't previously engaged, you might like to come along with us old farts. I'm bringing a wineskin, too." ✺

Nora grinned, in spite of herself. "Thanks, Mrs. Quincy, but I'm going to pass."

"Suit yourself. You can see the Denver Country Club fireworks if you get on top of your roof, you know. Why, Mr. Quincy and I used to climb up there with the kids when they were small."

Nora was silent, wishing she could mourn her husband the way Mrs. Quincy did hers. Wishing she were not pining after the impossible. ✺

"Are you there, Nora?"

"I have plans, actually," she fibbed.

"Oh, good. I'll be going then. Happy Independence Day," Mrs. Quincy said.

"Happy Independence Day," Nora mumbled and hung up.

She sat in the porch swing listening to the radio. Not even John Philips Sousa marches could cheer her. Nora swung and swung, craving comfort. For lack of anything better to do, she painted her toenails. But the polish was old and tacky. Nothing like in her fantasy.

Twilight thickened at the end of the lonesome day. She hauled a ladder out from Mrs. Quincy's garage and scrambled onto the carriage house roof. She wondered what Father DiMarco was doing.

In the distance, Nora heard hollow M-80 booms, heralding fireworks displays. In the summer sky, the glittery sparks rained down like so many blue stars of Bethlehem. She couldn't help but ooh and aah at the shapes: weeping willows of neon green, turbo-charged tad poles, incandescent alliums bursting into bloom, red hearts exploding within white asterisks, their reports echoing. Giant ghostly smoke spiders drifting off, disappearing.

Nora asked herself, *If it's Independence Day, why do I feel so needy?* ✍

The fireworks displays ended; and the neighborhood grew quiet except for an occasional burst of firecrackers and the incessant fiddling of crickets.

✍ ✍ ✍

Shuffling into the rectory kitchen for coffee the next morning, Nora choked down Millie's watery brew, inhaling the bitter steam, wishing she had stopped for espresso. She had slept even more fitfully than usual. His rosary beads formed a clump near the sink.

"He's off on a week's fishing vacation," Millie crowed, stirring something in a stainless-steel bowl. Her skin looked gray as her hair.

"Who's that?" Nora asked, crossing her legs.

"Who, indeed," said Millie, still wearing her anachronistic chapel veil from morning Mass. She pared and sliced a fresh peach, pushed a plate with the fragrant fruit toward Nora.

"Thanks," Nora said.

Millie peeled bright orange carrots, said not a word.

Nora topped off her coffee and sat at the kitchen table for a few minutes. "I didn't know he was a fisherman," she said.

Millie snorted as if to say,  "There's a lot you don't know about him."

Nora ate the peach, stretching her legs under the table. Millie looked at Nora's feet, the bumpy red polish on her toenails bright as stoplights against her yellow flip-flops. Nora tried to curl her toes under without seeming self-conscious. Millie looked from Nora's feet to her eyes, her eyes to her feet. "I'm not stupid," Millie said.

And, without thinking, Nora said, "Neither am I."

Without Father DiMarco around, even the short week dragged. Nora sulked, irritated that he didn't even mention that he'd be leaving. She suffered a bout of heart sickness as debilitating as influenza. She didn't eat. Couldn't sleep. She woke up several times each night, mentally flailing herself for her fruitless longing.

Roofers and painters and sundry repairmen milled about the cathedral. ✍ They smiled, waved, greeted her, but she kept her distance, nodded politely, protecting her bubble. Toward them, she could keep her temperament cool as the marble altar. If only she could stay so staunch with the priest.

MEMORIAL OF ST. WITHBURGA (8 *July*)

Arriving home after a swim at the recreation center, hair dripping onto her backpack, Nora wheeled her bicycle to the carriage house and noticed Mrs. Quincy walking toward her gazebo. Nora waved.

"How's everything?" Nora called. She joined Mrs. Quincy in the gazebo festooned with Concord grape vines.

"Well, I'm still here. I guess the good Lord wants me around for some reason. You've been over to the pool again, I see. Sometime, I'll tag along." The age spots on her hands looked like miniature Rorschach tests. She fingered the rhinestone buttons of her cardigan, a cornflower blue that reminded Nora of the color of the Virgin's robe in the Visitation window. Mrs. Quincy always seemed to wear a sweater, even in the heat of July. "How's the job?" she asked.

"Demanding," Nora said. "I'm wiped out by the end of the day, but satisfied. And Father DiMarco is getting interested in the glass.

And we have these stimulating talks."

"Stimulating?"

"You know—engaging. ✍ He's always taking care of me with lemonade and iced chai, this and that."

"You've taken quite a fancy to Father DiMarco," Mrs. Quincy said.

"I suppose." Nora considered admitting to Mrs. Quincy that she was coiled in a preposterous infatuation. She wanted to unburden herself, but, more so, she wanted this decent *grande dame* to go on thinking of her as a nice girl, a good girl, a girl with any amount of morals. ✍

"I must say, he's sure more chipper since you entered the picture." The dowager pulled out her red leather cigarette case. "Just... watch yourself," she said. Mrs. Quincy handed Nora her lighter and put a cigarette between her thin, wrinkled lips. Then the old lady pulled the cigarette out of her mouth, shook it at Nora. Lipstick stained the filter. ✍ "Father DiMarco has a gift for acknowledging people and making them feel special, but I hope you know by now that he's got more charm than sense."

Her blatant statement slayed Nora. "Why would you say that?" she asked.

"He fawns over you," Mrs. Quincy said. "And parishioners are beginning to talk."

"Fawns?" Nora clasped her hands, pressed the pads of her fingers down hard. "Well, it's not like there's anything going on."

"I've seen a lot of priests come and go, Nora; and they always *do* go. I know a thing or two about these matters." She wagged the unlit cigarette in Nora's face. Her wrist was white and dry as garlic skin. "You're not doing him any favors."

"I'm not sure what you're getting at," Nora spurted.

"There's a lot at stake here," Mrs. Quincy said. "*Souls*. Not only his. And not only yours. If he leaves active ministry, that leaves a big hole. *Lots* of souls. We'd never know how many."

"It won't come to that," Nora said, slammed by Mrs. Quincy's assertiveness, then regretting admitting there was an "it" at all.

"See that it doesn't," Mrs. Quincy said, shooting her a look, penciled eyebrow arched. Nora stood up and turned to leave, chin on her chest. Mrs. Quincy said, "One fine day, Holy Mother Church will have to decide which is more important: the God-given institution of the Eucharist or the man-made institution of celibacy. But until then, priests can't have it both ways, and unless you want him shipped off, you'd better back off. Nowadays especially, the bishop isn't going to tolerate any monkey business."

"There *is* no monkey business." Nora pressed her lips together. "We're friends," she said with flimsy defiance.

"Fiddlesticks. Not that men and women can't find higher love."

Nora spun around, looking straight at Mrs. Quincy. "Higher love?" She took her seat again.

"Light my cigarette, won't you?"

Mrs. Quincy blew a puff of smoke into the tense air. They sat quietly for a while as she smoked, gathered her thoughts. "Maybe it's more of a grace than a discovery. Happened to me several times. Men I loved, but not in the physical sense. Men who became rather like brothers to me, but better, without all the family ties and shared history and sibling rivalry and such and so. That's a blessing, Nora. A gift. To have a man as a friend allows you to see the world in a different way. But you can't see it through the eyes of a man whose arms hold you. You don't get the same view from a relationship with a husband. Or a suitor. Don't ask me why."

They did not look at one another. ✺ Mrs. Quincy smoked. Nora fumed. "I'm trying to solve a problem, not cause one. I'm just restoring the glass."

"Celibates are an inch deep and a mile wide," Mrs. Quincy said. "Married people are an inch wide and a mile deep. People don't trust what they don't understand. Tongues wag. 'That loose artist woman,' I heard you called in my bridge club the other day. Some people feed on gossip, you know."

"Whatever. They want their precious windows repaired, but meanwhile these holy people are happy to cast stones at me? How very Christian." Nora bit the inside of her cheek.

Mrs. Quincy stubbed her cigarette out in the crystal ashtray. She said, "Trust your moral compass. Let your conscience be your guide. But just remember this: Priests are not as black and white as their cassocks."

FEAST OF ST. BENEDICT (11 *July*)

Father DiMarco had been gone for days that seemed like weeks. While working in the cathedral, Nora watched the retired priest who covered the Mass and sacrament schedule. The man was so old he seemed embalmed. Nora had worked herself into a foul, sucking mire of despair. She missed the dog, too.

So when she saw the little green car in the rectory driveway, Nora perked up. She just wanted to see him. Hear his voice. So as not to appear too obvious, she went about her business. Coy. An organist practiced Mozart.

Nora waited for him to come outside to the garage studio to see her, but she couldn't stall much longer. She decided to arrange a welcome-back bouquet. On a shelf in the corner of the garage, she found a row of empty wine carafes. ✎ She also found, under a tarp, several boxes filled with empty liquor bottles: beer and wine, spirits, aperitifs. More than several recycling bins would hold. Nora didn't give them much thought; she was too eager to see the priest.

Outside at the spigot, she held the carafe under the rushing cold water, rinsing off a film of dust, peeling off the label, scratching at the wet glue with her thumbnails, half filling it. ✎ With her pocketknife, she cut daisies and snapdragons and bachelor buttons perfect for a man married to the Church. Before going into the rectory, Nora stole a glance at herself in a side mirror on one of the workmen's pickup trucks parked in the cathedral lot. She wished she had some lipstick.

Nora walked into the kitchen, homecoming bouquet behind her back, heart on her rolled-up sleeve. *Blessed are the bold.*

Sadness snagged his face, but when he saw her, he lit up. "Hello!" he said. She weighed his considerable enthusiasm.

"Hi. Welcome back," she chirped, hesitantly presenting him with the flowers. 🖋 He offered his hand; but without much thought and because it seemed only natural, she quickly hugged him. Foolhardy.

"Oh, how nice," he said, setting the flowers down without really looking at them. "Maybe I should go away and return more often."

"Did you have any luck?"

"Luck?" His mood shifted.

"I thought you went fishing."

He shook his head. "That's what I told Millie." He rubbed the back of his neck. "I wish it were so pleasant, but no. A priest friend of mine. We were seminarians lo these many years ago. He's living in Boston. He has some...legal problems." The priest sat down and put his head in his hands.

"What?" Nora asked, ecstatic that he'd come clean to her and not to Millie. "What's the matter?"

Father DiMarco mumbled something unintelligible.

"Is everything OK?"

He groaned. "That, my dear, is what we're all wondering, isn't it?" He lowered his gaze. "Red toenails," he said. "Red, you know, is the liturgical color for martyrs."

Nora folded her arms behind her back. "Got any coffee?"

"I'll brew some." His eyes lacked luster. His mouth held no joy. "Millie's out sick."

As he measured coffee beans, she asked, "Are *you* OK?"

"I got in late last night. Then I got a call before dawn and went to anoint a man early this morning. The father of five. Grandfather of 14. The whole family was there. It's never easy."

"He was dead?"

"Almost. We never anoint a dead body. We pray over a dead body, but the sacraments are for the living. "

"Have you been with a lot of people when they died?"

"Only a handful," he said.

"Must be eerie."

"Can be," he said. "But it's ambiguous: The people left are so sad, and at the same time, relieved. People tend to think of death and dying as ethereal, but I've found it a very human experience. It's gut-wrenching when somebody gurgles through their last breaths or coughs up blood. And there's nothing to do but get a towel and wipe up the mess," he said. "It's humans. It's messy."

"My parents both died suddenly. There was no praying over them. No deathbed," she said. "My dad had lung cancer, but the doctor said he died of an aneurysm. Keeled over right on his bench.

He would have liked that he died working."

"And your mother?" He inquired with genuine interest, which touched Nora.

"Her heart attacked her," Nora said.

"Interesting way to phrase it," the priest said.

"I miss them."

"That's how we know we love people: We miss them."

Tell me about it, Nora thought.

"No siblings?" he asked.

"I'm the one and only. ✺ I always wanted to have a brother and a sister. I used to pretend I did." He smiled. "I made up names for them. I even made them birthday cards." She laughed, then grew serious. She shook a packet of sugar. And even as she pictured him anointing the near dead, Nora imagined a life in which he came home to her, his hands lingering on the sensuous banks of her hips. She would give him succor. Snapping out of it, she asked, "Does it leave you depressed? All the death and dying?"

"You know what leaves me depressed?" he asked. "One of the morticians told me that some people don't even bother to pick up the cremains. ✺ They don't even want to go through the ritual of burial or interment. He said he has ashes from people cremated five years ago." The priest fell silent.

"Father?"

"I'm fine," he said. "I evidently need to catch my spiritual breath."

In the kitchen, coffee brewed. Around the world, Catholics fingered their beads, prayed novenas, blessed themselves with holy water, buried their dead.

FEAST OF THE TRANSFIGURATION (6 August)

By the first week of August, the crab apples in the cathedral courtyard had prematurely ripened into red; and Nora had moved on to the windows on the east wall of the cathedral. The eastern windows had bore the brunt of the tornado.

Above the cathedral ceiling and below the tiled roof, a catwalk ran the length of the nave. ✺ The narrow metal bridge spanned the cathedral's upper innards. The space resembled the underside of a great ship.

To get a closer look at the condition of the top of one of the windows, Nora made her way down the ribs of the ceiling to the porthole opening that allowed access to change the light bulb.

Tentatively, Nora put her eye to the round opening. She peered out. Only inches away, filling the whole of her vision, the blazing face of an angel with purple wings stared back at her. Nora met the angel's celestial gaze. The glass was intact. "You're fine," she said gently. "I thought you were broken."

Heat rose. On the catwalk, Nora felt like one of Millie's loaves of bread baking.

Back in the garage studio a headache set in. The day heated up. The metal of her straight edge grew warm to the touch. The glass would not yield to her diamond cutter. She fractured one piece after another. ✺

"Damn!"

She was so hot. So tired. She took off her work shirt, stripped down to a cotton camisole. Her head pounded. She needed to recline.

Outside, even the shaded grass felt warm. Nora's mouth was dry as the Mojave. She rooted through her backpack, hoping for another bottle of water. No such luck. She had drained the other liter an hour ago. Dehydration set in, but she didn't want to intrude on Millie's kitchen, so she shuffled outside and over to the garden hose limply coiled in the direct sun. ✺ She licked her lips. So thirsty she couldn't wait for the water to run cold, she drank from the hose gushing sun-warmed water, tepid as a tired bath, slightly metallic tasting. She spit it out.

The throbbing headache and the heat stifled her. Running water was too much to resist. Nora pulled off her work boots, peeled off her socks, rolled up her pant legs. She bent to turn on the hose full force. She sprayed her feet, first startled and then energized by the clear water. Gasping in the reprieve from the dirt and the heat, she let the water run down her dusty calves, her shins, ankles, wrists, forearms, biceps, her shoulders and finally the tensed nape of her neck. The water ran colder, invigorating and crisp. She couldn't help but squeal when she directed the water down the crevice of her spine as she arched her back. ❧ Water dripped off the knobs of her ankles. Sanctified rivers ran down, initiating her arches, tickling. Her hair follicles tingled. Nora shot the stream down the gully between her breasts, shivering. With the palm of her hand, she washed her arms, rubbed dust off her shins. She splashed the cold water on her face. Baptism! Heaven!

Nora took a long drink from the hose and let the refreshing water trickle down her chin. She knelt and drank some more, feeling the cold tingle all the way down to her empty stomach. Nothing could taste as refreshing and quench so thoroughly as plain water. ❧

When she turned to shut off the spigot, she saw Father DiMarco standing at the window in the upstairs hallway. She dropped the hose in the grass beside her bare feet. They exchanged quicksilver looks of complicity, identifiable even from that distance. And then he was gone. Cold water gurgled at her twitching soles. A puddle collected in the grass. Squandered.

SOLEMNITY OF THE ASSUMPTION (15 *August*)

All summer Nora flirted with storms. Every morning before work, she rode her bike on a ridge just outside of town where she could watch the clouds dark as charcoal drawings. Lightning flashed—neon zippers between heaven and earth—but rain did not fall. Nora looked at the clouds, begging them to release.

The savage heat wave baked the earth and the cathedral upon it. Green lawns went brown. ✺ Plants wilted. The city implemented watering restrictions.

Nora stared at her clipboard. Her drawing skills had rusted. She decided to try her hand at paint on glass again. Aware of the cathedral bells counting the hours, she spent the morning wiping down glass paint, erasing strokes, starting over and starting over, full of envy at the rendering skills of long-dead Germans. She blocked in leaves, stars, scratching out fine details with the point of a stick. The distant pink stones walling off Jerusalem dropped off the end of her brush. ✺ Then Cana. Galilee. The Mount of Olives. Gethsemane. Calvary. Emmaus.

Nora looked up and spotted the pastor walking from the rectory to the cathedral. He did not look her way. They had not spoken in a week. A week and two days, to be precise, since the day he saw her take the pseudo-shower with the garden hose.

"Pray for rain," she shouted through her dust mask.

He stopped. Hung his head, then walked over, eyes downcast.

"Sorry?" He clasped his hands.

"I said, 'Pray for rain.'"

"Oh," he said. "Why don't you join me? You know, 'Whenever two or more...'" he quoted. "Today is a holy day of obligation."

"Obligation?"

"The Solemnity of the Assumption of the Blessed Virgin Mary," he said. "It's depicted in the window north of the nave. The mystical rose taken up to heaven."

"I know what Assumption means," Nora said.

"And you know that Catholics are required to attend Mass on Holy Days of Obligation. Maybe you could find an hour."

She scraped one piece of cut glass against another to smooth their sharp edges. "Can't I pray for rain without going to Mass?"

"Of course," he said. His gaze shifted and shadowed. "What are you doing?"

"Do you really want to know?"

"Very much."

She tossed him an extra dust mask. "Lead-poisoning prevention."

He pulled on the mask.

"Well," she said, "you see these H-shaped strips?" He stuck his neck out and peered at her workbench. "This is what we call 'came.' In England, it's called 'calm,' which strikes me as bizarre because this stuff makes me crazy, not calm. But it helps hold the glass together and provides the linear support for the design. And this," she held up a tool, "is a lathykin. I use it to pry open these grooves in the came. The lead is only semi-rigid. It moves. See? These German leads are so soft." She looked at him. He concentrated on her hands. She wished she'd had a manicure. "Using the lathykin, I widen the channel—called a heart line," she gulped, "to receive and hold the pieces of cut glass. ✍ And it's not an exact science. I have to make it up as I go. Sometimes the glass pieces don't fit the pattern exactly. Sometimes there's not enough room for the lead and you need to grind the glass. Other times, there's maybe too much, which makes soldering difficult. ✍ You have to consider the relationship between the edges. Straight edges seem to shrink. Curvilinear lines seem to expand." He was looking off into the distance. "I'm boring you."

"Hardly!"

She cleared her throat. "One time when I was little, I was watching my grandpa work. He had all the pieces laid out on the pattern, and he was soldering; and I told him the glass looked prettier without the lead. And he stopped working and picked me up and sat me down on the workbench and said, 'You need something to hold it all together. And if you get it just right, it's like a lovely spider web, and it almost disappears.'"

They stared at one another, not blinking. Nora felt her inhibitions unhinge. She leaned toward him.

He backed off. "It's marvelous to have a family trade. That's one thing about the priesthood: It's not as if I can have a son to follow in my footsteps."

"Did you want a son? Or a daughter? Did you want a family?"

He shrugged.

"You give up a lot to be a priest," she said.

"And gain a lot," he said. "Nora, I apologize if I... if I made you feel uncomfortable the other day, watching you."

She pinned him with her eyes. "You're the one who seems uncomfortable."

He mashed his lips together and nodded. "You're right," he said. "I need to go." His back bowed, the priest left her for the cathedral. Nora thought she caught a glimpse of gold light shining around him just as he crossed the threshold into the sacristy, leaving behind the secular, entering the sacred.

Nora did gamble on a prayer, wary whether God would listen to her—even if God could hear.

What if? Nora asked herself. *What if I prayed for* him? *What if I prayed for us to find a way to be together?* Examining her calloused hands, she prayed, simply, instead, for precipitation.

Almighty God, send rain. Please.

After her petition, Nora paused. Listened. Heard nothing. Went back to work. At her bench, doldrums set in. She regretted revealing the story about her grandfather. The day passed in slow increments between drinks of water and yogic breaks from the glass. She was running low on glazing nails. Without them, she was unable to hold the window together before soldering, so she stalled. She considered making a run for supplies, but she didn't want to miss the possibility of seeing the priest again. *Maybe*, she thought, *he'll come back for more conversation. Maybe he'll invite me to lunch again. Maybe after lunch we could go for a drive in the foothills. And then we could stop and take a hike. And then maybe he'd hold my hand. And then maybe he'd kiss me in the shady woods.*

He did not show his face.

In the evening, riding her bike home, Nora noticed an enormous, dazzling white thunderhead in the east. The wind came up. From her porch swing, she watched clouds tumble in and stack up.

In the middle of the night, a thunderclap awakened her. Outside her open window — by God — rain fell, a cloudburst that washed the choking dust from the world.

Nora peeked into the summer night. Even in the darkness, every surface and plane glistened, anointed by holy rain.

ST. HELEN (*18 August*)

"**A**nd you thought God didn't listen to your prayers," the priest said. He handed her a cup of coffee and on her workbench he set a plate with a pecan roll.

"For rain or sweet rolls?" she said, affecting detachment.

"Millie baked them this morning. She demanded that I bring you one." ✿

"Is this hemlock frosting?" she asked, taking off her gloves, dipping her finger into the sugary white.

"Arsenic." They shared a laugh.

"Thank you," she said, sweet as the pastry. Puccini stared at the pecan roll. "She hates me. Millie."

"Millie Mataloni does not hate anybody."

"Guess again," Nora said.

"You don't know anything about her."

"I know she has a strong sense of rusty piety," she said. "Chapel veils? Didn't those get thrown out in the '60s?"

"Millie was abandoned as a child, raised at Mother Cabrini's orphanage. Her husband came back from Korea missing both legs. Committed suicide about 20 years ago. Shot himself. She's had breast cancer. Twice."

"That gives her the right to treat me like dirt?"

"No," he said. "That gives you the information to forgive her." Nora's eye twitched. She pouted, duly chastised. She rubbed the bridge of her nose. She needed a sign of reciprocation. Something more than a sweet roll. "You must think I'm terrible. Mean-spirited and petty and judgmental."

"You must think that about yourself" he said.

"Sometimes." The way he looked at her made her feel naked. On her bench, she looked at the next panel to repair. "I'm working on the Latin for the east vestibule. The one with Jesus at the door," she reported. ✒

"'*Pulsate et aperitur vobis,*'" he said, rolling the R. "'Knock and the door shall be opened.'" He walked over to her bench and leaned close enough that she could smell him. The back of her neck went hot. "You did pray the other day, didn't you?" he asked. His face filled with unsettling earnestness. "For rain," he said.

Nora suppressed a smirk. "I did, actually."

"But tell me this: When you prayed for rain, did you carry an umbrella?" ✒

OUR LADY OF SORROWS (15 September)

The nightly chorus of crickets had slowed from summer's frenetic mirth to a languid pulse. ✒ The shifting of seasons always dampened Nora's spirit. September was one of Colorado's shining months—cerulean skies, flower beds bursting with blooms, autumnal leaves. Mornings bit with coolness. As Nora dressed for work, she put on the new fuchsia hoodie she had ordered from one of Mrs. Quincy's catalogs. The hoodie was the first new article of clothing Nora had bought since the death of her husband and she congratulated herself on selecting not her usual uniform black, but bright pink.

When she arrived, the priest was kneeling in his vegetable garden, tossing weeds helter-skelter over his shoulder. Nora dropped her backpack on her workbench, took out her sack lunch and her water bottle. She cleaned her goggles, then picked up her clipboard and flipped through her pages of lists.

The garage held a chill. It was that time of year when temperatures were colder inside than out. She decided to step back outside in the warming sunlight.

The priest sat on a bench in the prayer garden, a book open in his lap, his head bowed, his gardening gloves beside him. She considered ignoring him. She felt impelled to engage, so she plopped down next to him to gather any amount of affirmation from him. "What are you reading?"

"My breviary," he said in a monotone.

"What's that?"

"The Divine Office. Sacred Scripture." He wiped dirt from his hands.

Bees visited blossoming trumpet vines. "How does your garden grow?"

"Contrarily."

"How can you say that? Just look." She was not merely flattering him. Her eyes roved among the tethers of pumpkins writhing between hills of potatoes and rows of reddening chili peppers. Tomatoes like clenched red fists, the night purple of eggplant, the almost luminescent yellow squash, waxy cucumbers. Lacy carrot tops like delicate plumes draped over orange nubs bulging from the black dirt.

"The bugs are getting the best of it," he said.

"It's a little Eden," she countered.

"Bounty. Beauty. I suppose," he said, sullen. "I tend to notice only the weeds." He looked at his mug, stamped with a Latin phrase she tried to translate. "'*Illegitimate non carborundum,*'" he said, anticipating her question. "'Don't let the bastards grind you down.' Easier said than done, even in Latin."

"I'd better get to work," she said, rejecting his dour mood, wondering whether she'd caused it. She stood and walked back to the garage studio. He followed her. Picking up a paintbrush, she turned to the cartoon she was coloring, the full-size guide to the window of the Ascension.

"You paint so well." She felt his breath in her hair. "Why don't you work on canvas?"

"Because a window can be ten times brighter than a painting." The priest gave Nora an *Aha!* look. "A painting or a drawing or even sculpture depends on light reflected *off* the piece. With glass, the light moves *through* the work. And the windows alter and shape light and transform space unlike any other art."

"Must be gratifying, being so talented."

"Everybody thinks it's romantic to be an artist, but actually it's humdrum. It's tedious. And lonely. I enjoy my work, but I don't know why I end up feeling so antagonized."

"I could venture a guess," he said.

She looked straight at him. "Have at it."

"You really want my opinion?"

"I really do."

He spoke to the wall behind her. "You're so focused on your own life. You forget that you're not alone." His preachy tone offended her. "You don't realize that many, many other people suffer very real struggles every day. Hunger. Homelessness. Addiction. Abuse."

"Listen, Father," she said, hands on her hips. "I know a thing or two about pain."

The priest said, "If you ever want to talk…"

"You think I can just talk it out? You think I haven't *tried*? You don't know anything about it. Or me, really."

"I know that you have gifts. And I sense that you hold yourself back. You're young, intelligent and talented. Need I go on? You're also cynical and sarcastic. If you want to see people worse off than you, you don't have to look hard. Look at Two-Wheel Rich. Or can you? You think you've had hard luck? You've lost a husband. You don't know the half of it, kid."

"How dare you presume anything about me?" She looked straight at him, as if he were glass she could cut and break.

"I'm a priest. I know things," he said. "You feel sorry for yourself. Look around. You've got it made." He reached over, pointed at her temple and said, "You're telling yourself a wicked fairy tale over and over; and you know it's not true, but you scare yourself again and again. You want to see real ogres and wicked stepmothers? Talk to people out there in that food line, people suffering the inequities of poverty."

Nora closed her eyes, as if that would stymie his words. A rash of anger surfaced. She said, "Look, I've had some pretty dark days, myself."

He asked, "How dark?"

"Well, don't bother waltzing me around the mulberry bush, Father," she said, wishing she had not given him such emotional capital. ✀

"Why should I?" He leaned toward her. "We're just having a conversation."

"You want to know how dark? Well, let's just say I've never actually tasted the barrel of a gun, but I've cast some longing looks toward the gas oven."

He jerked his head back. "You've entertained suicidal thoughts?"

"Entertained them? ✀ Sounds like I'm having them over for tea and finger sandwiches."

"You know what I mean," he said.

"I have visited that valley if you must know," she admitted, unsure whether she wanted to shock him or stimulate his sympathy.

"All the more reason you need to spend some time around that sandwich line. When we walk with people who are poor, they convert us. ✺ They teach me gratitude every day. They're enormously grateful for what little they have. The fact that they're in need makes them appreciative of everything. And pretty soon my life starts looking pretty damned blessed."

"I'm sure you're right," she said, wanting to shut him up.

"We mope around thinking the Lord has abandoned us, that He doesn't give us what we want. ✺ God save us. We're like bratty, spoiled children. Some people know real want. Exposure to cold that claims fingers and toes. Mental illness with no medicine, no counseling, nothing. I know children traumatized out of their wits, old people too destitute to afford both heat and groceries, women who've been beaten to within inches of their lives."

She recoiled. She wanted to run. He let the silence stand. "So why doesn't your God do something?" Nora asked. "Why doesn't He perform miracles to fix the world?"

"The real miracles aren't when God does what we want *Him*—or Her—to do. Real miracles are when *we* do what God wants *us* to do."

FEAST OF THE ARCHANGELS (29 September)

Nora wasn't sure what God wanted her to do. Go to Mass, maybe. Receive the sacraments, probably. Lay the ghost of Liam to rest, assuredly.

As is, she had plenty to do by way of restoring the cathedral's windows. She prepared to cut the halo of Mary in the Annunciation window. To hold the complex curve, she needed a pliant sheet of golden glass that would resist fracturing. She took an informal inventory of the bins in the garage. Bright, thin sheets with heavy pigment, yellow as amber. Thick, translucent sheets with minimal pigment, pale as honey. Nothing she could use.

Nora considered making a run to Harry's, but she didn't want to lose momentum. She abandoned the plan and decided to work, instead, on the dove appearing above Mary and the foliage at the base of the vignette. But first, she wanted to measure the window one more time. The day was cool, overcast, so she put on her pink hoodie before she headed outside with her tape measure.

In the prayer garden, the pastor sat, his face in his hands, rosary beads dangling from one fist. She felt her temples pound upon sight of him. Nora resented him. She respected him. She adored him. She abhorred him. She ignored him. Puccini sniffed the shrubs and tree trunks. ✍

To triple-check the width of the outside sash, Nora scaled the extension ladder leaning against the cathedral exterior. She leaned toward the window and tugged a strand of ivy.

Then she spotted the papery and pocked nest stuck in a corner where the window met the mortar. Yellow jackets buzzed past her face. She scurried down the ladder, shooing the angry insects away from her. Before she reached the last rung, a sharp prick punctured the back of her neck. Another yellow jacket stung the web of her left hand. Another, the inside of her wrist.

"Goddamn!" she screamed, waving her arms.

She heard Puccini bark and bark and bark.

Another stung the side of her neck. She felt bites on her low back, her cheekbone, her bicep. Nora pitched and reeled. Utterly ungrounded. No *terra firma*. She saw Father DiMarco rushing toward her. Nora's throat closed in on itself. She felt her lungs implode.

She faltered into a hazel hedge as the priest ran to her. "Millie!" he shouted, "Call 911! 911! Now!"

He lifted Nora's head. Into his hands, she commended her spirit.

"Can't breathe," she mouthed, frantic. *Nora felt herself turn into a pillar of salt and heard the clang of cymbals as she slipped into another reality.

Word of the rebel rabbi buzzes through the narrow, cobbled streets. She catches snippets of rumor. He fishes with a few or—with meager provisions provided by a boy's good intention—feeds multitudes. At his hand, hemorrhages dry up. Friends rise from the dead. Storms calm.

Near a fountain surrounded by the sway of palms, she watches the muddy waters clear. From the pool rises the Messiah naked and wet, silvered, every bead of water a mercurial galaxy shed from his body. She recognizes him immediately. He looks just like the man painted in the glass.

With metered showmanship he shakes the water from his long and oily black hair. He looks over at her, knowing precisely where to find her stunned, confounded, struck dumb. And just before they kiss, she coos, "You are my most passionate, persistent, jealous lover."

She tastes his saliva tinged with olives, with wine, with the bread of life. Jesus says, "You shall be comforted. You shall be satisfied. You shall obtain mercy. You shall see God. Yours is the kingdom of heaven." ❧

Then the face of the Messiah became the face of the priest. "Nora!" Father DiMarco shouted, shaking her shoulders. "Nora, are you allergic to bee stings?"

"My Lord," Nora rasped, "and my God."

MEMORIAL OF ST. FRANCIS OF ASSISI (4 October)

Dogs and cats, rabbits in hutches, fish in bowls, gerbils and hamsters and ferrets in wire cages, even a parrot on a perch joined the assembly in the cathedral courtyard. Juan passed out sheets of paper printed with a prayer to St. Francis of Assisi and the Blessing of the Pets.

It was Nora's first day back at work since the yellow jacket attack and the anaphylactic shock that ensued. In the prayer garden, kids poked sticks into the pond water. Mothers showed their babies the pretty pansies blooming in the urns. Dogs sniffed at trees and corners. October roses bloomed.

Father DiMarco strode through the crowd. His costume—a brown Franciscan robe—flapped around his legs. Puccini bounced along at his side. The dog saw Nora first, barked and bolted toward her.

"Hey, honeydog," she said. Puccini stood on his hind legs and Nora bent so the dog could lick her face.

"Now that's what I call a how-do-you-do," Father DiMarco said. "Welcome back."

"Thanks," Nora said. "Good to be back." She meant it. Relief smoothed her forehead.

His face yielded a proud smile. "One day a year, I am a friar," he said, striking a pose in his robes.

"The doctor said you saved my life."

He switched his mask from comedy to drama. "Actually, Millie dialed 911."

"Father?" Juan shouted, waving him over to the crowd gathered.

The priest held up two fingers to Juan, and Juan nodded.

"Shall I include the bees in the blessing?" Father DiMarco asked Nora. "Or damn them for all eternity to the furnace of affliction?"

"It was a yellow jacket. Most yellow jacket stings happen this time of year, I found out; and the little devils are attracted to brightly colored clothing."

"Your pink sweatshirt. ✍ Aw, it probably thought you were a flower. Not a total misunderstanding."

"Go christen the critters."

"Will you keep an eye on Puccini?" he asked, handing her a leash.

"Puccini will keep an eye on me," she said, watching the priest part the crowd, touching the heads of pets and children as he went.

Nora hooked the leash onto Puccini's collar and felt just as tethered.

ALL SOULS' DAY (2 November)

As the weather cooled, so did things between Nora and Father DiMarco, as if the anaphylactic shock shocked him into realizing how deeply he cared for her. ✍ At least that was what Nora told herself to excuse his absence.

The last of the leaves showered crimson and amber orange. They whirled about the grounds like apprehension. Lawns went dormant. Nora knew just how they felt. The dark days were upon them—daylight savings time—a span, typically, during which Nora's winter blues calibrated.

Juan brought a space heater to the garage. He set it up for Nora, saying, "It's getting chilly."

You're telling me, she wanted to say, thinking of the priest's cool mood. ✎

"We'll move you indoors before too long," Juan said. "Father suggested we set you up in the sacristy."

"He did?" She wanted to ask Juan what else Father had said about her, but she didn't. She detested herself for feeling like a lovesick junior high kid, desperate.

Using her stopping knife, Nora pushed lead stripping tight against the glass. With restrained fury, she worked the short curved blade, forcing open the pliable lead, wishing she could force the priest to open to her as easily.

But the pastor grew distant as the winter sun. He came and went with a mere wave of his hand, sometimes passed looking only at his rosary. She pretended not to notice, not to care.

Gusts of wind denuded trees; and the trees stood naked and unrepentant. ✎

EMBER DAYS (*22-24 November*)

The day began inauspiciously. Nora overslept. She headed for work without a shower, without the benefit of coffee. Groggily, she put on her goggles and gloves. She picked up a sheet of costly flash glass—green layered on gold—careful to keep the sheet horizontal to the floor.

"That's the first rule of handling glass," she could still hear her grandfather's gruff teaching. "Otherwise, if the glass slips or cracks, your hands get shredded. The second rule is this: When a sheet of glass slips, never grab for it. All you can do is let it fall."

Which Nora did, jumping back even before the flash glass crashed on the garage floor. The sound of the breaking undid her. The green-on-gold glass pieces scattered every which way.

"*Jesus!*" she hissed.

Two-Wheel Rich, who happened to be outside raking leaves, heard the crash and came running. His dirty jacket hung from his wide shoulders. His dark eyes widened then searched the floor. He was the last person Nora wanted to see.

She brushed past him, walked around the block, arms pumping. The priest was under her skin; and she was under his thumb. She tried to reason with herself. *He can't just push me away after trying so hard to draw me out! He can't just act as if it's business as usual.*

Sadly, of course, she knew he could. And did. Unable to tolerate the frustration, Nora decided to force the issue. *I'll be an adult and discuss it with him,* she told herself. *He'll at least talk to me. Won't he?* She wasn't sure of anything except her amorous madness.

Nora went back to the studio and grabbed some sketches, inventing a reason to see the rector. Two-Wheel Rich continued sweeping, never looked up.

"I'll do that," she told Rich, the edge to her voice as sharp as the shards of glass he hastily cleaned up.

He nodded, then stopped sweeping. "You have to break some glass to make a window, right?" ✍ It was the first time he'd ever looked directly at Nora. Nora looked right at him, into his eyes, and saw that they were not menacing like Liam's after all. Wounded, yes, but not the brutish warrior eyes of Liam.

Nora reached for the broom.

Holding onto the broom handle, Rich said, "It's nice to be of use."

"I know," Nora said and released her grip on the broom. "Thanks." ✍

Nora rang the rectory bell. Millie answered from the intercom in the kitchen. "Yes?"

"It's Nora," she said.

A buzzer sounded. The lock on the door released.

"He's on retreat for a week," Millie said, scouring the sink.

Nora's cheeks flamed. She thought fast. "It's sort of important that I get in touch with him because I want to order some more materials, and we're running out of time."

"He's completely out of pocket," said Millie. 𝒮𝒪𝒜 "He's at the monastery in Snowmass."

"Do you have the phone number?" Nora asked, annoyance breaking down all her couth.

"There's no way to reach him." Millie crossed her arms in front of her low-slung breasts. "He goes up every year for Ember Days."

"Ember Days?"

"In thanksgiving for the harvest," she said, pulling a pan from the oven as the timer sounded. "I guess if he wanted you to know where he'd be, he would have told you."

Nora considered accidentally tipping the hot coffee cake onto the floor. Maybe, she thought, there was something indicated on the pastor's desk calendar. She crafted deception. "I'm just going to take this request list and some sketches to his office, anyway. He'll want them on his desk when he returns."

Millie gave her a suspicious look, but Nora barged past, shaking the papers. "I'll just leave these on his desk," she said, and headed up the stairs into the priest's study. She placed the bogus papers on his desk and spied a brochure on St. Benedict Monastery. She pocketed the pamphlet. ✵

In the garden, Nora read the brochure explaining the monks' regimen. The Cistercians begin each day with Vigils at 3:30 a.m. They pray, sing, meditate and study communally and individually throughout the day. To contribute to the community's economic self-sufficiency, they work around the 3,800-acre ranch or in the cookie bakery or the guest facilities. They vow poverty, chastity, obedience. And they keep something called the Great Silence.

Nora couldn't imagine living a life so ascetic. She couldn't quit thinking about the possibility of a life so contemplative. *What if he's leaving the parish to become a monk?* she asked herself. *Oh, my God,* she thought. *It would be just like him to bolt.* And then she panicked.

When Nora went back to the garage, the mess she made had been swept away, but craziness set in. Nora considered the possibility that the lead particles she had breathed her entire life had caused her to go psychotic. *Maybe my brain and bloodstream are poisoned, a biochemical wasteland.* ✵ She needed to speak to the priest right away. Impulse control flew out the door. And so did Nora. Back at her carriage house, she snatched some things—a sweater, a coat, hiking boots. She tossed her duffle bag in the car and set out for the high country. She had not been to the mountains since

Liam's death. Too many memories of summits and saddles.

On the long drive alone, she realized she had lost it. She felt as if she were watching herself blow up a balloon, larger and larger, larger, knowing that it would burst in her face. A panicky thought crossed her mind: *What if he lied to Millie again? What if he wasn't at the monastery?* But she was on the road, and there was no turning back. A pilgrimage, the priest might have called it. The police would have been more apt to label it stalking. She drove and drove, intent.

Past Idaho Springs, she passed the area where she and Liam often spotted the bighorn sheep alongside I-70. Near Vail, she saw a waterfall splashing out of the mountainside. Last time she passed by, the waterfall was frozen, a small glacier, silent and still.

Outside Snowmass, she wound her way up the lane lined with glowing golden yarrow and shadowed by snowcapped peaks. She turned into the entrance of the monastery—almost four thousand acres of the Creator's loveliest landscape. ✺ The quality of the light instantly inspired her.

"Well," she said to herself, breathing in the view, "maybe *here* I could find God."

Slowly, barely accelerating, she drove beyond a barn yard with a chalky white statue of the Blessed Mother, past a stone gate house under renovation. She pulled over, let the car idle. The pastoral mountain valley suspended her in such a quiet she could actually hear the Black Angus steers rip the grass from the earth and chew their cud. She noticed the chiaroscuro of the surrounding mountains; the amber meadows and the dark pine forests marching up to the tree line, the olive green of jack oaks, a few dried orange autumn wildflowers like jewelry decorating the short blonde grasses. Nora squinted and saw the landscape as if rendered in stained-glass. Here even white seemed more colorful.

She parked and wandered into the bookstore, where a monk in a hooded white robe greeted her almost immediately, unbidden. "Welcome. I am Brother Daniel, guest master."

"I—I was wondering if you had a room. For one?"

"The hermitages are booked a year in advance," he said. He had the soothing cadence of a golf announcer. "But by virtue of a cancellation, we do, in fact, have an opening—just for two nights."

She signed the guest book and rolled with his assumption that she had come solely as a retreatant, though her conscience told her she was dragging wickedness into this holy place. Brother Daniel toted her duffel to a small building made of river rock and timber. It was perfect.

Maybe here, she thought, *I can get a grip*.

"I work at the cathedral in Denver," she offered as an explanation though the monk had asked for none. Casually, she inquired: "I trust Father DiMarco arrived safely?"

"Father DiMarco," the monk said without expression, "was our cancellation."

She gulped, crestfallen. "I see," was all she could manage.

"We invite you to join us for prayer, Miss Kelley. You'll find a schedule posted inside. We welcome you and trust that your stay will give you what you need. If we might be of further assistance, please leave me a message in the basket on the bookstore counter. If there's nothing else you need now, I'll bid you good afternoon."

And with that, the monk took his leave. As he walked away, he folded his hands behind his back. Without a sound, he closed the door to her hermitage.

"What am I *doing* here?" she asked herself aloud. She wanted to cry. She wanted to scream and rage, throw things, but she looked out the window at the looming mountains and contained herself. She'd driven for hours in hope when none existed.

She wondered where the AWOL priest was, but then again—half mad with contradictions—didn't quite know where she was herself. Monk's Peak threw its cloak on the valley. Staying at the hermitage seemed less demanding than the drive back to Denver alone in the dark, for sure; so she opted to stay, hoping the holiness of the place would work its wonders on her.

In her room, the first thing she noticed on a night stand was a basket with a flashlight, a stocking cap, and a paperback book titled "The Cloud of Unknowing." She picked it up and started to read, but the concepts seemed dense. More like mud than clouds.

Besides, she couldn't stop wondering about Vin. Vin! She heard herself call him his first name for the very first time. Not *Father Vin*, but *Vin*. So he had his wish after all. They were on a first-name basis, at least in her warped mind.

The rarefied air slowed the pace of her thinking and pried open her sensory thresholds. Her head ached, yet there was something soothing about the luxury of simplicity in the spare but adequate room. She looked out a window at the enveloping view. She settled into a chair on the little stone patio. As the sun dropped behind the mountains, she listened to the cries of magpies and observed the scarves of light and hatch marks of umbra on Mount Sopris. She ached with disappointment, but sat still, hypnotized, until she heard the chapel bell invite her to Vespers.

Curious about the monks, Nora wanted to step into their world. She wanted to be one of them, sure of God, flush to His will. Flashlight in hand, she scuffed down the hill to evening prayer, the loudest sound the crunch of gravel beneath her hiking boots. The extended autumn reigned unseasonably warm, but snow shrouded the summits. ✍

In the chapel, Nora dipped her fingers into the crude ceramic pot of cool holy water—something she never bothered to do at the cathedral in Denver. Desperate for an old familiar faith, she blessed herself, making the sign of the cross with her wet fingertips. In the chapel was one predominant art glass window. The design was masterful, executed all in white and clear pieces suggesting snowy mountains, clouds, a cross, a dove.

She walked over to read a sign by the window. The plaque read, "The Trappists simplified church decoration, shunning boldly colored and pictorial windows. Yet St. Bernard of Clairvaux, A.D. 1153, Doctor of the Church who founded the Cistercian order openly praised the glorious glass of the Middle Ages; and the Cistercians subsequently designed windows using subtleties of colorless glass." ✖️

Nora saw that they had perfected minimalism, saying more with less. Backlit, the window appeared like a garden designed with only understated white blooms, restrained elegance.

The sing-song chant of the monks began to swell in her ears, softening her forehead. Together with the robed monks, Nora prayed, but her prayers had no words.

After evening prayer, as the waning moon rose and Nora walked back to her hermitage, coyotes sang, making a high-pitched cross between a yelp and a cry, an otherworldly noise simultaneously melancholy and menacing. Something like Nora's wordless prayer.

✖️ ✖️ ✖️

The alarm beeped at 3 a.m. For the monks, day dawns in darkness. Nora tried to match their monastic stride based on the 1,500-year-old continuum known as the Rule of St. Benedict.

Nora heaved herself out of bed, hastily dressed, opened the door. The dark night crept in. She chewed a fingernail, started to close the door.

She told herself, *You're at a monastery, for heaven's sake. There's no reason to be afraid. You have a car, a flashlight.*

But she didn't go down to Vigils. She went back to bed, but not back to sleep. She pulled the blanket up to her chin and imagined she could hear the monks' plainsong rising up the gravel road from the monastery chapel.

⚜ ⚜ ⚜

Later that morning, clouds shrouded the valley, lending a gossamer quality. Through the monastic lens, to Nora, the world appeared redeemed. ⚜

She went to morning Mass, which she had not done since Liam's funeral, when she was so shocked and medicated that she barely knew what was happening.

The monks entered the chapel, their long black tunics belted over white robes with large cowls. Nora swayed slightly to their soothing chant, tightly woven in its harmony, haunting in lyric. Their plainsong dialog with divinity rocked her gently, a buoyant ship on calm, open seas. As Nora deepened her breath, she smelled an evasive fragrance she couldn't quite label. Then she saw the table with the offertory gifts below her a couple of steps and off to her left several yards. Her eyes widened, nostrils flared. The wine! She could smell the wine.

Nora couldn't recall the last time she felt her senses so acutely. She hadn't even realized how shut down she'd been. But when the time came for Communion, she did not stand on line for the Bread of Life. She did not drink of the cup.

After Mass, Nora wandered the property, happening upon a solar greenhouse lush with vegetables. She pictured the priest's garden near the cathedral. She pictured the priest and wondered whether he'd be more attracted to her if she were a practicing Catholic again. She pushed him out of her mind.

Outside her room, she found an Adirondack chair and carried it beneath bare aspens. As she sat, looking at the pool of blue sky, she remembered a camping trip with Liam. He had set up his easel in an aspen grove, dappled light igniting golden leaves. But he had painted *en plain air* a canvas of autumn aspens with leaves not of amber, but black.

A bell rang. Nora watched the monks make their way to the refectory. She was too hungry to eat. Anyway, she knew nothing of this world would feed her.

She spent the afternoon mesmerized by the simple beauty of the mountainscape. The high-altitude air forced her to relax. She built castles in her mind. She'd forgotten why she came and remembered something of herself.

Again, she walked the road down to evening prayer, her ribcage seemingly filled with light. She whispered hello to the cattle.

In the chapel, the men in black and white hooded robes chanted their prayers, knelt and sat and stood, heads bowed.

As Nora walked out of the chapel, the good abbot sprinkled her with holy water. As the blessed drops hit her, she smiled, inside and out.

"Sanctity is work," the abbot softly said to her. "You work on it; it works on you."

❧ ❧ ❧

The alpine air downshifted her, and Nora tucked herself in early.

When the alarm sounded at 3 a.m., she rushed into clothes. As she opened the door, she wished she'd packed a heavier coat for the night mountain air. She grabbed the flashlight and a wool stocking cap provided by the monks—another small but huge trace of hospitality. ❧

Outside, the dark ran deep. The coyotes were mum, yet Nora imagined them skulking in the rocks and scrub oaks. She wanted to walk the half mile to prayer, as pilgrims ideally should, but she could not muster the courage. She swallowed considerable fear and stepped into the black and silent night—technically morning. Once outside, stars debuted. Or, rather, having grown accustomed to the dark, Nora found herself able to notice them. She called to mind the shimmery star of Bethlehem in the cathedral's Nativity window.

Again, she debated whether to walk. She turned on the flashlight, pointed its beam into the heavens, then across the landscape. Every rock seemed a carnivorous beast. Every tree a marauder. She could not let go of her fright; and her fear disarmed her as she realized she really did lack faith. Her disbelief was more than a pout or protest. *Believers*, she told herself, *trust. They trust in God and trust in His way and therefore fear nothing.* In the darkest hour, she looked up at the twinkling wrap of the Milky Way so distant.

Nora unlocked her car, got in, put on her seat belt, locked the doors and realized she had been living in the city too long.

"Yea even though I *drive* through the valley of darkness, I still fear evil," she said, strangling the steering wheel. "Where," she asked God, "did you go that dark night?"

She slowly drove down the winding gravel lane, disgusted with her wimpy self. 🖋

Inside, the monastery's quiet echoed louder than ever. Irritated that there wasn't so much as a night light, Nora inched her way along the long hall toward a subtle glow from the chapel. In the chapel, she settled onto one of the wood benches. The monks in their white cowls swept into the dark sanctuary. One brother lit a single white candle on a tall wrought-iron stand. Two votives beneath the icons near the door, the requisite red sanctuary light, a lamp by which to read Scriptures, and the soft glow from the single backlit grisaille window provided the only other sources of light.

In the duskiness, the simple chant was a lullaby. Nora battled sleep. Her head rocked to one side, the other. She empathized with the dozing disciples nodding off while the Master sweat blood. To fend off drowsiness, Nora straightened her spine, lifted her chest, moved her breath deep into her flesh, temple of the Holy Spirit. Her body, however, seemed secondary, tertiary. The monastery was a place of intellect, of spirit.

After Vigils, she joined the monks in silent meditation. Seated in stillness, she chased Father DiMarco out of her mind. She chased out Liam. The accident. The windows. And found, in the quiet, peace. A nothingness that contained everything.

ᴥ ᴥ ᴥ

Hearing the wispy rustle of robes as the monks began to leave, Nora's consciousness flowed more fully back into the chapel. She had no idea how much time had passed. The pearly window glowed; and so did she.

She walked down the dark hallway without hesitation. She entered the predawn outdoors. ᴥ She pressed the button to turn on the flashlight, but the beam faded and failed, either the battery or the bulb dead. Nora didn't mind. The stars hung thickly, draped over the valley, countless cosmic night lights. Nora traced the few winter sky constellations she recognized in the heavens.

She walked to the parking lot, then banked on her confidence and walked right past her car and up the gravel trail. On the path back to the hermitage, the soles of her hiking boots left no footprints.

Back in her room, Nora tugged off all her clothes and collapsed naked as a newborn into bed. And just before she surrendered to sleep, she heard a car door slam. She sat bolt upright, grabbed her nightshirt, pulled it on. Terrified, she heard the doorknob turn. She held her breath, not sure whether to scream or hide or pray or make a run for it. Her heart throbbed in her throat.

The door swung open. A light switched on. They looked at one another, their mouths open, their eyebrows drawn together.

"Nora?" he whispered. "Good Lord. What are you doing here?"

She almost sobbed with humiliation. She rubbed the bridge of her nose. ✆

Gently, barely wrinkling the linens, he sat on the edge of the bed, alcohol wafting off his breath.

"They said you'd—you'd canceled."

He shook his head. "They misunderstood."

Nora nodded. "I feel so stupid. Oh, God. I'm so sorry."

"Don't be," he said.

"I'm so dumb. I'm so pathetic," she moaned.

"Don't," he leaned over, hugged her. "It's all right." He rocked her slightly, left and right, which to Nora felt natural and damnable. He breathed in her ear, "Maybe this is God's will."

Nora pulled back from him. She shook her head as if she could toss off shame. "It's *my* will. It's *my* fault." She groaned, "I found out you were here. I had to see you. And then when I found out you weren't here, I decided to stay. I'd come all this way. And this place looked so appealing; and I was too tired to turn back; and then there was an opening for this room. And then I started wondering why you were here, if you were going to become a monk and leave the cathedral."

"Me? A monk?" He smiled at her, reached as if to touch her face, stroked her forearm instead. "I just came up to get away."

"From me?" Nora asked, afraid of the answer.

"From everything."

"You're not mad?"

"I'm exhausted," he said. "And this is where you belong. You were led here. Stay. I'll go down to the monastery and find a bunk."

A pause mushroomed. Nora's eyes darted back and forth between the priest and the door. "Stay," she blurted.

"Shhh," he said.

"No, stay," Nora said, again, vaguely aware of the bizarre circumstances, more aware of the fact that they both carried a freight of loneliness—a problem they could alleviate for one another.

He stood. "It's not for lack of desire." He took a step toward her, then a step away. He glanced over his shoulder at her just before he closed the door behind him. "Goodnight, Nora. God bless you."

The door clicked shut. Nora ground her teeth, clawed her fingernails into her forearms. She wanted to cry, to let go. She wanted to end the obsession.

And then, within a minute, she heard the faintest knock at the door that had no lock. He opened the door slightly. "Why can't I leave you?" he squeezed his eyes shut.

In a breath, she moved from despair to ecstasy. She knew what they were about to do was dead serious. He knelt at the side of the bed. She sat up and swung her legs over the edge, in front of him. He squeezed her ankles, one in each of his hands. He traced his fingertips up her calves. The deep touch of his hands on her thighs relaxed her. Her conscience scolded her. She did not want to feel bad because it felt so good to be touched and to touch, to fondle and be fondled. He held her hands in his. ✒ An image of the stigmata flashed through Nora's mind.

She withdrew her hands, turned his over, traced his palm with her pinkie finger. "Your holy hands," she said.

"No more so than your own."

"I don't turn bread and wine to the body and blood of Christ," she said. ✒

"So you believe?" he asked. "You believe in the Real Presence?"

"No, but *you* do," she said. "And I believe in *you*."
She picked up his hand, "Is it true that a priest missing a finger cannot be ordained? I heard that once."

"It's called a canonical digit," he said. "A priest has to have the index finger on each hand so he can use two fingers together to hold the Host. But it used to be that a man couldn't be ordained if he were blind in his left eye because that's the side you read the missal from. But then somebody suggested, 'Well, what if he turned his head just a little bit?' So rules do change—even in the Catholic Church."

He held her hips and rested his head in her lap. She worked her fingers through his hair lifting his head, he sat next to her on the bed. They inclined into one another until the muscles of their necks touched. Her limbs went limp. They stayed that way a long while. The air in the room eddied. Fire coursed through her inner thighs. Nora turned her face to his. He placed his fingertips on her cheekbones.

They exhaled into a kiss, but just as their lips touched, he stopped. He whispered, "I'm sorry, Nora; I can't do this."

"What if that was God's will that we came together in that tornado? What if all this is Providence?"

He stood.

"Don't go," she said, sickened by the desperation in her voice.

"God have mercy on us."

Mortification solidified as she heard him drive off. Disgraced, she stepped outside. ✍ Nora pressed her hands over her face, her fingertips partially covering her eyes as she watched his car's taillights snake away down the gravel road, out the monastery's gates. The firmament deepened. Nora could only hope the universe had interconnecting lead lines of its own, a web of cosmic order that prevented everything from falling apart.

ST. CATHERINE OF ALEXANDRIA (25 *November*)

By noon the next day Nora was back to work, not wanting him to dismiss her out of sheer shame. Unwilling to let on the sharp degree of her regret, she started right in where she'd left off. She trusted he'd backslide into denial, too. ✠ Nothing would be said. She knew the drill.

In her studio, vaporous Venice turpentine lingered. She picked up her palette and added dry black pigment and binding solution. With a palette knife, she ground the black grains into the liquid. From her bouquet of brushes, Nora plucked a turkey quill sharpened like a square-nubbed pen. She laid a piece of glass over the fluorescent light.

A face: the profile of Judas of Iscariot. At first, slavish to the original, she tried to copy the enlarged photograph precisely. Her strokes dragged. The paint pulled like molasses. The face appeared lifeless. She wiped it down, then, with an articulated stroke, gave the traitor apostle a brow and a nose and a chin just like Vin's.

FEAST OF CHRIST THE KING (28 *November*)

This much Nora understood: He would never open the conversation. And if she didn't broach the subject, she would always wonder. Now, she knew, or never. She went for broke. Assuming he'd have to be around on a Sunday, she headed to the cathedral, timing it so she'd bump into him as the last Mass let out.

Slants of late November light saturated the burnished red oaks near the rectory. Even in the brisk wind, the trees unremittingly hung on to their brittle leaves.

Incense hung in the cathedral air. Churchgoers milled about, lighting candles at the side altars, speaking softly in the aisles. The pastor stood near the baptistery, shaking hands, sharing pleasantries. She waited until most of the people cleared out before she approached him.

"Working on a Sunday?" he asked, not bothering to say hello.

"I have a lot to do." Her heart jiggled. "I finished painting the hand of God today. For the top of the west transept? And those eight lancets below are almost ready to be soldered. I have to double-check some measurements."

All he said was, "Fine."

"Listen," she said. "Are we going to go on not talking about what happened? Not talking at all?"

He shied, looking over her shoulder and then over his. "This is hardly the time or place."

"Then when? And where?"

"Nora," he dropped his rosary. "Please," he said, bending to retrieve the beads. "Please leave me alone."

Her breath caught in her throat. Her jaw dropped. She saw at the hem of his vestments the toes of his scuffed shoes. She looked into his face—ruddy, rubbery. His eyes closed and she watched him fade away. And when he opened his eyes again, his irises looked to Nora like clouded beach glass, like broken brown beer bottles whose sharp edges had been modeled smooth by the endless waves of the salty sea.

In the name of the Father ✠ and of the Son ✠ and of the Holy Spirit. ✠

Heavenly Lord, God of light, of mercy and love, hear my prayer. To you I lift my will, my worries, my worldliness. My anger. ✠ The cross of my temptation. ✠ I beseech you to steer me back to you. Show me, Father, your way; I wander lost and lonely in the desert. ✠ ✠ ✠

To let this woman go unnoticed is not in the realm of possibility for me. ✠ Why do you tempt me so, God? ✠ I pray your will be done, but how am I to recognize it? ✠ ✠ How, Holy Spirit, when she and I share so much so deeply? ✠ When she turns my mind, after all, to you, O Lord, as she personifies your love and all its legacy: the glory of your creation, O God, created anew in the ravine at the small of her back, darkness separated between the spires of her limbs. ✠ ✠ ✠

Forgive me, Lord, ✠ ✠ ✠ even in prayer she occupies the folds of my mind. What do you want from me, God? Did you not send her to me? Am I to attribute our connection to happenstance? The work of the dark one? ✠ ✠ I cannot think her evil, Lord. Not when she's resurrected so much

in me, so much of me. Please God! ⊠ Do we not come to know your love through one another? ⊠ I remember my vows. But you taught and I believe that You are love. ⊠ So how can she be anything less? In this time of awaiting the light, she reflects your light, O Lord. In her I see your glory. ⊠Help me, dear God. Sustain my resolve. Sustain my vocation. Sustain me. ⊠ But bless her. ⊠ Bless her and keep her safe. You put me to the test. Protect her from me. Look kindly upon me, your humble servant, that I might lead your people to your light, that I myself might shine with your holiness for the sake of your Kingdom. ⊠ Grant that I might uphold my vows of chastity and obedience not out of obligation but out of love.⊠

With my heart humble and contrite, I ask this in the name of Jesus Christ, who knew and loved women at the well, at the wedding, at the empty tomb. ⊠ ⊠ ⊠

In the name of the Father and of the Son and of the Holy Spirit. ⊠ AMEN.⊠

CHAPTER THREE

Advent

FIRST SUNDAY OF ADVENT

wags of flowing pink and purple silk festooned the cathedral's columns. Advent ushers in a season of waiting, expectation, preparation. Nora was waiting, all right. 🖋 She stood vigilant because, in her personal tradition, Advent ushered in the dark days prior to the Winter Solstice. Advent meant Seasonal Affective Disorder; and that meant wavering mental health. She hated being so jeopardized by externals, but alas she was a solar-powered unit.

And then there was the work—a mountain she couldn't climb. She lacked motivation. Nothing seemed easy. She couldn't seem to get anything right the first time. She slogged through the days.

Nora went back to the carriage house and ached, alone. She couldn't resist the gravitational pull of her flannel sheets. She slept too much, hovering somewhere between dreams and wakefulness, slowed to a slouch.

The rector never stopped by her studio. 🖋 She missed his company, his encouragement. Him.

On her bench was a portion of the window in which Christ's dead body was taken down from the cross. She waxed up the cut pieces of glass and assembled them on a sheet of plate glass propped on her easel. In the full light, she studied the relationships of the colors.

She dropped the hot wax on the corners of the cut glass that would configure Mary Magdalene at the foot of the cross. With the wax, she temporarily secured the pieces for painting. She laid on a thin coating. Applying tonal washes lent a somber mood to the panel. The paint decreased the light, modulated glare and flare.

Depression hooked her, dragged her deeper. She grappled with decisions large and small, deliberating to the point of exhaustion on her every choice—from salad dressing to moral-compass issues, let alone details of dealing with the windows.  Treading water in ambivalence, she simply couldn't decide. Nothing mattered. She hated that the same man who had helped lift her depression had caused it to return. Her melancholy locked her away in a safe with a code that refused to be cracked. Despite the merry-making of the season, her emotional numbness and glumness tranquilized her. Nora knew herself well enough to recognize a spawning breakdown. She could not face another Christmas alone. Without telling anyone she was leaving, she went home to fend off a migraine.

Nora helped Mrs. Quincy hang garland from the pillars on her porch. Or, more precisely, Nora hung garland and lights while Mrs. Quincy dragged on a cigarette. Wrapped in her fox coat, she looked like a wise old witch of the woods.

"I have lots of extra light strands if you want to put some on your place," she said. "Mr. Quincy used to outline the whole house. Overkill, I called it. But help yourself. Might cheer you up."

Nora sniffled in the cold, securing strands of lights and avoiding eye contact.

"Don't think I don't notice," Mrs. Quincy said. "You moping around, dragging your nose on the ground."

Nora lifted her chin, added an extra staple. "I'm fine."

"Pshaw," the old lady said, flicking an ash. "Lovesick cat."

Nora flinched.

"The Altar and Rosary Society is making a pilgrimage to Cabrini Shrine tomorrow," Mrs. Quincy said. "Why don't you come along? Might do you good."

Nora ignored the invitation. "Maybe I will put some lights up," she said. "All blue ones."

Mrs. Quincy gave Nora her snort of disgust. "Nora, dear, love is a choice. If we choose it, love—honest and decent love—is fine as it comes to us, in whatever way, shape or form. The inclination to love is never wrong," she snuffed her cigarette in a zinc planter containing a dwarf spruce. "But certain situations are wrong. I don't have to tell you that. You're a smart girl. A good girl. You'll do the right thing."

It wasn't that Nora didn't want to do the right thing. She didn't think of the priest as a friend, and she couldn't quite think of him as a lover.  He lingered somewhere in between, loitering in relationship Limbo.

He made himself scarce.

Nora listened to sappy love songs. She ranted to her journal. The pages wrinkled under her rancor and rhetoric.

The windows tormented her. When she realized that an almost complete section was too large—it wouldn't fit past the cusping and into the groove—she was ready to resign. The fragmented repair process broke her down. And the combination of loneliness and frustration eventually lowered her into Bedlam. She curled into a fetal position on her bed. She wrapped herself up in blankets, silent as the purple candles burning in the rectory window.

FEAST OF ST. NICHOLAS (6 December)

Nora woke up on her day off, but could not drag herself out of bed. She went back to sleep and woke even more groggy.

Slowly, she got out from under the covers and sat in a chair, doubled over, her head in her hands. She wished she had a dog she needed to walk. She wished she had parents she could call, somebody who would listen to her whining. She considered the friendships she had let grow cold.

Nora showered until she drained all the hot water. She stood under the spray, soaping and scrubbing, attempting to rinse off depression's dust. She flossed her teeth, slathered on lotion. Nora dressed carefully in wool trousers and her only cashmere sweater— clothes she did not wear at all last year, having so-called "lived" in yoga togs and pajamas. She put on her mother's pearl bracelet and earrings, gave her clogs a quick brush-off.

She walked to the Italian market Father DiMarco frequented on Saturday mornings. She shuffled along the path near Cherry Creek, hoping the priest might be walking Puccini. She drove past the cathedral, thinking she might catch the pastor outside, for some reason. She laid plans, a confirmed stalker. She even considered going to Mass, just to see him, to hear him.

Instead, she decided to call.

"Hello, cathedral rectory," he said, his voice fraught with fatigue.

"Hi," she said. "This is Nora."

"Oh, Nora," he said; and she detected a tinge of surprise and cheer. "Everything going all right? I understand you're making headway on the windows."

"Uh-huh," she said.

"If you need more supplies, you can go through Juan. I've told him you might need a purchase order."

"No, it's not that. I think I'm in good shape." The dead air boomed. She wasn't sure why she called. She couldn't just come out and say she missed him. "Um, the reason I'm calling, I'm thinking about having some friends over," she said capriciously. Thou shalt not bear false witness, she thought, but continued, "and I'm wondering if I can get your focaccia recipe." She grimaced. How lame!

"You're cooking? That's great."

"Well, I hate to serve Ants on a Log."

He laughed. And the sound of his laughter served as an elixir until Nora told herself the truth that she really had no friends to welcome. She had isolated herself long enough that nobody called anymore except telemarketers.

"My sisters perfected this recipe, actually," he said. "Our mother never wrote it down."

"Father?"

"Nora?"

"Um," she said, uncertain of how to continue. She pinched her earlobe. ❧

"Nora? Hello?"

"I'm here," she said. "Did you ever hear of Sarah Driscoll?"

"Doesn't ring a bell," he said. "She's a parishioner?"

"She worked in Tiffany's studios. There was a whole bunch of woman that worked there cutting glass. The Tiffany girls, they were called. Sarah Driscoll designed the butterfly lamps."

"Huh," he said.

Nora wanted to hang up, she felt so stupid, but instead asked, "Do you think the painters who did those windows had any inkling of their power? Do you think, when they were peering through their watch-maker's glass, they possessed even an iota of insight about the emotion and even faith their craft would inspire generation after generation?"

He laughed. "*You* sound inspired."

Disappointed by his lack of perception, Nora relaxed her shoulders. He had no clue what she was going through. Or did he? Over the phone, she heard the sound of ice cubes in a glass.

❧ ❧ ❧

In the cathedral, Millie directed the hanging of fir swags strewn with white lights and studded with coppery beads. Millie came into the sacristy, but the two women avoided each other. Millie brought in a stack of current Catholic periodicals, hauled out the old ones. In the sacristy, Nora worked on the Nativity window, scratching the Star of Bethlehem from the inky night sky. She pulled out an ox hair tracing brush and added a little cleft between the Christ child's upper lip and nose. Mary, she noticed from an enlarged photo, wore a gold wedding band. The look on the Blessed Mother's face was one of innocence and awe. The Madonna knew little of what had happened, nothing of what was to come.

Nora remembered her own mother, her reverence for priests. *Had she ever lusted after one?*

SOLEMNITY OF THE IMMACULATE CONCEPTION
(8 December)

Sorrow settled into her marrow. Nora picked up an antidepressant refill in the afternoon, but she didn't swallow a pill. She carried them like silver bullets, stashed them in her backpack in case the psychic werewolf actually sidled up to her during the dark days when the noon sun angled lower and lower.

She did everything she could to distract herself. At work, she waded deep into the process. She exacted revenge by insisting on perfection in every cut. As she broke away nubs of glass, she kept a tight grip on her grozier. Bits of glass dropped to the floor. Remnants of the manger, the shepherds, the lamb.

After work, she forced herself to do something creative. Anything. She cut a deal, allowing herself to do whatever she wanted before bedtime except sleep. She pulled down the vines from the Virginia Creeper growing on the carriage house and twisted up a wreath for her door and one for Mrs. Quincy's yard lamp. She popped popcorn and strung it with cranberries and put the garland and tiny twinkling lights on the dwarf conifer in her courtyard. She spread orange halves with peanut butter and hung them for the birds.

The next day, after work, she caved in and bought a small Christmas tree for the carriage house. ✍ On the way home, Nora stopped at the storage unit she rented. Quickly as possible, she pulled out the boxes marked in Liam's hand "Christmas Decorations," careful not to look too closely at other things: furniture, lamps, cartons of clothes and shoes, camping gear and ski equipment—vestiges of her past. She locked the door of the storage unit and wished all the stuff would vanish.

Then, she unlocked the door again, went inside and grabbed her Nordic ski equipment, untangling her skis and poles from Liam's. She reached into her downhill helmet and pulled out her goggles swaddled in a microfiber pouch. She took out the goggles and put them on, adjusting the strap. Liam had been an expert skier. He had pushed her and pushed her. Steeper runs. Deeper powder. The back bowls. Skiing, eventually, out of bounds.

That was Liam: no regard for boundaries.

Nora took off the goggles, put them back in the protective pouch, and tucked the pouch back into the cavity of the helmet covered with stickers from Vail and Beaver Creek, Winter Park and

Keystone, Monarch and Copper Mountain, Wolf Creek Pass and Steamboat Springs. She had no interest in skiing. She had, she realized, no confidence. Not enough to step into the fall line of a mountain. Not enough, even, to have a simple conversation with a man she loved.

Is there any way? she wanted to ask him. She wanted to inquire, *Is it just me? Or is it reciprocal?*

Nora looked around at the detritus of her yesterdays and then locked the storage unit again.

At home, Nora hummed carols and drank eggnog spiked with Grand Marnier. She unwrapped the antique ornaments that had been her grandmother's: clusters of glass grapes, birds with brush tails, squares of needlework, colorful globes fragile as Nora felt. Staving off dejection, she cut paper snowflakes and drizzled glittery glue on pinecones. She wrapped the tree in strands of lights. Carefully, she hung the ornaments on the boughs, then finished with tinsel icicles. She stepped back to look.

The enchanted tree chased away her gloom. She turned off the other lights in the room and admired the twinkle. Seated on the window seat, she sipped the fiery orange liqueur, wishing Vin were with her. And just then, a glass ball painted with herald angels fell off the Christmas tree. She saw it happen, watched the frail ornament bounce from limb to limb. Anticipating the inevitable sound of broken glass, she gasped as the heirloom ornament fell to the tile floor.

But did not break. Incredulous, she rushed over, bent down, picked up the blown glass ball. Not even cracked.

FEAST OF ST. LUCY (13 December)

Just when Nora had adjusted, just when priest-withdrawal symptoms waned, she brought in her mail after work; and out from between junk mail and bills fell a crisp maroon linen square envelope addressed in amateurish calligraphy. Metallic gold ink. She turned the toothy envelope slowly and did a double take at the return address: Cathedral of St. Raphael. The muscle of her heart flexed.

With fumbling fingers, she carefully opened the card. An invitation. The parish Christmas party. Below the typeset copy inside she saw Father DiMarco's handwritten postscript: "Love and joy come to you. Vin."

Nora grasped at innuendo.

The event was less than a week away. Her spirits sank when she realized he had invited her as a second thought. Letdown welled up, but then she turned over the envelope to check the postmark and found that the card went out a week earlier—plenty of time to please Emily Post.

Later that afternoon, while lying on the window seat, Nora saw Mrs. Quincy heading to the carriage house. She held a cigarette case in one hand, her cane in the other. When the doorbell rang, Nora did not answer.

WINTER SOLSTICE (21 December)

Nora couldn't remember the last time she wore high heels. She clicked around the carriage house, almost pulled a calf muscle. She spritzed on some perfume, wondering about its shelf life and even went so far as to dig out her makeup bag, but the mascara wand was flakey and the lipstick smelled like a rancid petroleum product. She tossed the makeup in the trash, not wanting to appear too vain, anyway.

She sat on the window seat, swinging her feet. She kicked off the absurd shoes. She'd always hated parties. But she did want to see the pastor. And she did want to feel more normal—somebody who can attend a party without a major production—so she rose to the occasion.

Slipping into the crowd as inconspicuously as possible, she shed her coat and handed it to a kid from the youth group running the cloak room. She adjusted her dress, which—without benefit of a slip—clung to her tights. The social hall was crammed with people. The children's choir sang carols.

She felt a tap on her shoulder. "Don't you look pretty!"

"Hi, Mrs. Quincy." The old woman wore a festive red tartan dress with a matching beret.

"Say, I forgot to schedule the shuttle service, and now they're booked. I hate to take a cab. Any chance you'd be able to run me to the airport in the morning?"

"I can do that. Sure. What time?"

"If we leave by 10, that should give us plenty of leeway."

Over her shoulder, Nora spotted Father DiMarco, busy holding court among his parishioners. He shook hands, kissed hands. She made her way to the refreshments and ladled a cup of wassail warming in chafing dishes. She hesitated. She hadn't eaten, and warm booze always intoxicated her quickly. But she needed to file the razor edge off her nerves, so she downed a generous portion of the punch.

Father DiMarco breezed past, squeezing her elbow as he ushered out some doyennes. He helped them slip on their fur coats. He returned. "Ah, Our Lady of Glass, enjoying yourself I see," he nodded to her cup. Nora couldn't help herself—she hugged him hard, sniffed musky whiskey.

He snuggled her back, harder, then bid another huddle of old women Merry Christmas, turning back to Nora. "Holy smoke," he said, holding her back at arm's length. He pulled mistletoe from his black suit coat, held it over her head, smooched her cheek, which surprised her, then didn't: *It's permissible,* she realized, *if he does this in front of everyone. As if we have nothing to hide.*

Over the din, he whispered into her ear, "I'm glad you're here."

"I have to tell you something," she said. ✍ And she related the story of the Christmas ornament that fell but did not break, assuming he would care.

He looked at her as if her story was inconsequential then shifted into pastor: "Wonderful!" he said. "'...He, the Dayspring, shall visit us in his mercy...' Luke chapter one, verse 78. You got your own visit. Your own sparkly and merciful Christmas miracle."

"Well, I don't know about miracle," she said, "but it got my attention." ✍

"George Bernard Shaw said, 'A miracle is an event which creates faith. That is the purpose and nature of miracles.'"

She sighed. "I didn't come for a Bartlett's quotations recitation."

"Why so hostile?" he asked. "'Tis the season to be jolly."

She rolled her tongue. "I'm not jolly."

"Wait right here," he said. "I'll be right back," and he left to show out more parishioners. He strutted, paraded with unabashed panache. Nora watched him work the crowd. He brandished his masculinity with the men—all sports statistics and fish tales. He buttered up the women with genial compliments. "What a lovely dress, Mrs. Dolski." "Don't you smell nice, Mrs. Corley." "Oh, Mrs. Burke, those emerald earrings are almost as beautiful as your eyes!"

Nora made her way back to the wassail. At the punch bowl, a handsome man with hazel eyes and a neatly trimmed beard refilled her glass. He said something, but Nora turned away to find the pastor. Ever the imp, the priest pulled out his mistletoe and lifted it over a pretty brunette college girl home for the holidays. He pecked her on the cheek. Jealousy set in Nora's jawbone. She loathed his charisma, his jovial charm. ✺ Nora scoffed at the young woman, animated and tittering, taken by the priest's regard. In that moment, Nora detested Father DiMarco—but not as much as she disdained herself. ✺

Nora saw Mrs. Quincy shake her head, but then the pastor approached her with the mistletoe, too. Mrs. Quincy permitted his kiss, then swatted him on the arm. And the rector was off to find his next cheek to kiss. The parishioners allowed it, accepted it, much to Nora's fury. She overheard one man say, "That's just Father Vin being Father Vin."

"Major donors," the pastor said, back at Nora's side in a few minutes. "Now. What's the matter?" he asked in the tone of an indulgent parent appeasing a belligerent child. He took her empty wassail cup. "I know you well enough to know you're troubled," he said. "Santa Claus disillusionment?" She shook her head. "Foreign policy? World hunger? Pantyhose in a wad?"

With that, she cracked a smile. A fissure in her shell. Finally, she came right out with alcohol-induced honesty. "I miss you," she whined. "I can't help it."

"I know, Nora." He squeezed her hand.

"I can't stop thinking about you," she whispered, leaving herself wide open. ✍

He looked around, as if to make certain that nobody was within earshot of their exchange. They stood alone in the corridor. "You have to have some rules. I don't allow birdseed at weddings because it's slippery, and people might fall."

"We're not talking about birdseed. Or weddings," she snarled. "You think everybody else is deserving of love—even Two-Wheel Rich. But what about *you*? What about *us*?"

He turned away from her. She saw the back of his neck go pink. Then he turned toward her, put his hands on her shoulders. "Nora, maybe it's time you started dating."

Ducking from his touch, she backed up two steps. Her eyes throbbed in their sockets. The skin on her cheeks stretched too tightly over the bones.

"Merry Christmas," was the only civil statement she could muster. Her fingernails scraped her palms. She found her coat and headed for the side exit. But just as she yanked the door open, she felt a firm grasp on her arm.

"You're doing marvelous work on the windows."

And upon hearing his words, a gear jammed. "Is that what this is about? You got what you wanted from me; now you can dismiss me and move on to your next manipulation?"

"You're called to do those windows."

"Now you know my calling? I think you may have had too much Christmas cheer," she said. "You just don't get it, do you? I am not doing those windows for you. Or for God. I'm doing this job for myself. It's just a paycheck to me."

"I don't believe that," he said.

"You really don't give up, do you? You're so accustomed to having everything your way in your little fiefdom here. 🕊 You think women—everyone, for that matter—should just jump at your command, cater to your every whim. Well, I am not one of your fawning, groveling groupie Church ladies. I'm not beguiled by the flattery and magnetism bit, so don't expect me to do whatever Father says is best. You use women. Use them up. Just like the Church," she hissed.

"That's a cheap shot," he said. "The Church reveres women. Read John Paul II. Read *Lumen Gentium*, for that matter. It validates the value of women. It says, 'The Father of mercies willed that the Incarnation should be preceded by assent of the part of the predestined mother, so that just as a woman had a share in the coming of death, so also should a woman contribute to the coming of life.' The coming of life, Nora!"

"Oh, spare me." She shook her hair. "Every time you're at a loss for words, you, you go off and quote some lofty thing. It's so pompous. Don't you ever trust your own responses? That's the problem with the seminary: It wipes out every real instinct and replaces it with imprimatur text."

"Oh, really? Is that what you think?"

"That's what I know," she said. "Do you always act out of fear instead of love?"

"You tell me," he said. "You know so much about fear. You tell me."

"I know nothing about you," she said. "And you know nothing about me. Let's just leave it at that." She turned to leave, but he grabbed her wrist.

"I'm well aware that oftentimes for us priests it looks like we're pushing people away," he stammered. "I know that's what it looks like. I know that's how it feels to you. But it doesn't mean I don't love you; it means I do."

He took her by the shoulders, drew her close and kissed her squarely on the mouth. He kissed her deeply, passionately and she kissed him back, her knees knocking. It was a torrid kiss that made her think *Finally!* and *He can't do this!* and *I want more!* and *This is too much!* all at once. Nora was out of breath, out of her body, already anticipating the future, already regretting the consequences.

"I have to go now," he said. "I'm sorry."

"Sorry? Sorry you kissed me?"

"No," he said. "Sorry I can't kiss you more. Sorry I can't offer you more."

Then he left Nora standing there, holding the open door, her eyes closed, wondering who he'd kissed before her.

On her upper lip, a sweat broke, despite whistling wind rushing through her coat, through her velvet dress, through her flesh and directly onto her shivering, shuddering ribcage. His kiss acted like a chemical mickey, surreptitiously arousing her, dissolving any remaining boundary.

Pumping adrenaline, she stomped away from the party. In the parking lot, she looked up at the bell towers. *How dare he?* she asked. *How dare he not?*

I'll resign, Nora thought. *I'll quit and leave him with the broken windows.* And then she remembered one significant detail: The contract she'd signed.

Nora walked across the avenue to an absurdly bright liquor store, grabbed a pint of vodka, a pack of cigarettes.

Back at her car, her hands shook so uncontrollably she could barely stick her key in the lock. She got in the car, lit a cigarette. She pulled up her sleeves and touched the scars on her forearms.

Glass is a brutal taskmaster.  A sculptor gets clay beneath his fingernails. A painter might stain clothes with cadmium red. But a glazier gets hurt. Bleeds.

The next morning, Nora woke up with pounding temples. Tiny angora sweaters seemed to swath her teeth. The phone rang. She saw the vodka bottle more than half empty. A large clam shell was heaped with cigarette butts.

"Hello?" she said, and her voice was raspy and sore.

"I'm sorry, I have the wrong number."

"Mrs. Quincy?"

"Nora? Is that you, dear? Are you ill?"

"Not really," she said. "Just tired."

"I'm ready whenever you are," Mrs. Quincy said. "I like to arrive early. It's bound to be crowded."

"I'll be right out," Nora said, cursing herself for forgetting.

She splashed water on her face, pulled on a ski hat to hide her hair and prevent her cranium from exploding, sunglasses to shade her puffy eyes. Nora racked her brain, taking inventory of whether she did anything to humiliate herself. She heard the priest's voice again: *"It doesn't mean that I don't love you; it means that I do."*

She helped Mrs. Quincy with her luggage and her packages. As Nora opened the car door for her, the old lady asked, "How was the rest of the party?"

Nora bit her lip. "Jolly," she said, stunned at her translucence. Even wearing sunglasses, she couldn't look her in the eye. Mrs. Quincy was no fool. Nora felt blameworthy as Eve, covering up with a measly fig leaf.

"He's a great flirt, but a good man. A good priest," Mrs. Quincy said, folding her hands tightly in her lap. "If women wouldn't play along, he'd have to find another game."

Nora laughed nervously, distressed to her core.

Mrs. Quincy turned her head and looked out her window, her aristocratic features turned toward the fogged glass. "You're not the first," she said. "Don't think you'll be the last."

Nora almost drove off the road. She was ready to cry, but she acted as if it were no big deal. The rest of the way to D.I.A. they didn't speak over the orchestral Christmas music on the radio.

In the cathedral, construction workers hurried to clear out before Christmas services. Everything was repaired except the windows; and Nora's restoration seemed as if it would never end. She spent most of the day painting and wiping down glass, unable to steady her hand. The organist practiced, and to Nora the music sounded like a soundtrack from an old horror movie.

She cleaned up early, unable to tolerate her hangover, and wandered to the sanctuary, leery that she might see the pastor there. At the side altar of Mary, Millie arranged and rearranged the forms of the crèche: the Holy Family, the shepherds and sheep, the oxen and angels, camels, Magi. She looked like a girl playing dolls.

CHRISTMAS EVE (24 December)

Christmas Eve arrived with all the familiar tinsel trimmings, Nora's expectancy bubble-thin as the hand-blown antique glass balls on her tree. She knew Santa couldn't bring what she wished for, even if she *had* been a good girl.

Mrs. Quincy had invited Nora to celebrate the holiday with her son's family in Vail, but she couldn't be convinced. Now she regretted her reclusiveness. On her second Christmas Eve alone, Nora understood why suicide so frequently embroidered this particular night. Exorbitant expectations were rarely realized.

She paced the carriage house, sensing the onslaught of Christmas ghosts past, present and future. She took a bath. She paged through mail-order catalogs. Read the same first paragraph of a novel again and again. She took Pose of the Child, then Corpse Pose, attempting to lull herself. She kept thinking about the yellow jacket sting, about the crushing fright she felt when she couldn't breathe. In a way, Nora wished that she *had* died from the anaphylactic shock. *Wouldn't have been a bad way to go*, she decided.

Nora wasn't too far gone to recognize that her hope had run out. She had no anchor. All she could identify was a vague listlessness, a wretchedness she couldn't put her finger on or label or regulate. Nora stepped outside and stood on the little front porch. She heard in the distance the ringing of bells. Four tons of brass bells at the cathedral clanged out the midnight hour just this one night a year. "*Adeste fideles.*" "O come all ye faithful."

Christmas Eve. Midnight Mass, with all its mystery and majesty, all its community and Catholicity. A force propelled her. Unwilling to chance losing her nerve, Nora bundled up before impulse shriveled.

SOLEMNITY OF THE NATIVITY (25 December)

As she drove past the cathedral, she saw that the imposing front doors were propped open. Nora noticed the archbishop and his entourage convening in the baptistery. Of course, she could not find a parking place. She drove around the block, panicky.

She parked illegally and hustled toward the cathedral. Backlit from inside, the intact windows shone like foil-wrapped Christmas packages. Plywood covered the others, the dull wood unfortunate Band-Aids on the windows' wounds. The cathedral spires pierced the wintery night sky. The building's stone appeared cold and warm, hard and soft. ✎ Nora thought of that little finger play from childhood: "Here's the church; here's the steeple; open the doors, see all the people."

Inside, the faithful gathered. Evergreens formed a forest in the sanctuary. The organ bellowed. The choir sang. Trumpets blared. Juan stood in the vestibule, passing out missalettes. He waved her over.

"Better late than never. Merry Christmas," he said, handing her a song book. "You might find a chair in the back."

Nora moused her way through the vestibule just as Father DiMarco ascended the ambo for his homily. Looking for a place to stand, she heard his congenial voice amplified. People packed the pews, moving closer and closer to one another as ushers directed latecomers to seats. "O come let us adore him."

Nora stood inconspicuously at the back with parents walking fussy babies. She leaned into a corner. From her new vantage point, she appreciated the verticality of the voluminous space. She saw that the cathedral was not so much large as tall. A man offered her his folding chair. She sat.

And then she felt somebody staring at her, looked up and saw Millie. Her piercing stare beleaguered Nora into paying attention. But, try as she might, Nora couldn't translate what Father DiMarco was saying. He might as well have been speaking Aramaic. Nora tried to recapture the sense of herself she'd found at the monastery chapel. ❧ Crossing and uncrossing her ankles, she could not get comfortable, but her unease had nothing to do with the folding chair.

Nora blurred her gaze, looked for the light around him, but could not see it. She closed her eyes and listened. ❧ The priest couldn't know that she was there, but, then again, she could've sworn he spoke only to her as he spoke from the pulpit. His voice was more gravel than honey.

"The gifts the Magi presented to Baby Jesus remind us of the gifts God has given to us, the gifts that we, in turn, return to the Lord. Each of us," Father DiMarco said from the marble pulpit carved with symbols of the evangelists: the bull, the ox, the eagle, the winged man. The priest's voice sounded clear and unrifled like a pond in which to gaze, reflective.

"The presentation of gold, frankincense and myrrh reminds us that failing to present our gifts to the Lord is a rejection of God's gift to us." He paused for effect. His face was almost innocent. The congregation looked to him as if *he* were born the king of angels. Yet what Nora saw was a man. Flesh. Blood. A shepherd beloved by his flock. "Sisters and brothers, at our own peril do we ignore our callings. ॐ Christmas is also about realizing that God has given us many gifts. And these gifts come with strings attached. You see, the string attached is an obligation to glorify God by using our God-given gifts. Our gold is His gold. Our frankincense, His frankincense. Our myrrh, His myrrh. Ourselves, His."

She couldn't help but think he was talking directly to her. She sat up straighter. She looked at all the families and saw that they all formed one family—all the people young and old dressed in velvets and taffetas, suits and holiday sweaters, colorful mufflers wrapped round their necks, arms around one another's shoulders, eyes on their pastor. They belonged: to one another, to the Church, to God.

Nora longed to belong, too. The people in the pews seemed to have a knot tied at the ends of their ropes, and she yenned for something to hang on to, too.

He said, "Advent was about waiting. Anticipation. But the Nativity is about birth. Now is the time for which we have waited. We've anticipated this coming to life, this Incarnation, because we are the 21st century's wise men—and wise women. Now is about searching your own heart to discern and to discover the gift you and you alone have to present to our Lord. Christmas is about realizing the greatest gift ever given—the Son of God, the Son of Man, Master, Teacher, Messiah, Emmanuel, Jesus Christ. Laid in a manger. 🙰

"Christmas is about light, about hope restored and following stars." Father DiMarco said, and he paused before adding, "Follow *your* star." Then he crossed himself.

And Nora crossed herself, too. She declared, along with the priest, "In the name of the Father, and of the Son, and of the Holy Spirit."

The archbishop incensed the altar, circling with the smoking censure. Smoke rose; and with it Nora's thoughts turned to the ghost of her father placidly raking piles of smoldering leaves. She considered the faith of her grandfather. He had never prayed the rosary as far as Nora knew; and when she had seen him in his casket in the living room, the black beads had looked phony wrapped between his fingers calloused from years at his workbench.

The cathedral filled with the dolorous voices of the chorale. Psalms rose and fell in an age-old Latin chant. In his billowing white vestments, Father DiMarco swept to and fro on the altar, the holy man, the high priest. Prophet. King. He wore his crown at a jaunty tilt.

Nora stroked her throat as she looked off in the distance at the crèche she'd watched Millie arrange. She strained to see the Magi, bearing their Epiphany coffers of incense and precious metal. Expanding her focus, she included the pews of worshippers, the populist aisles, the sacrosanct red-carpeted steps leading up to the holy of holies.

Her eyes lit on the androgynous angels perched in the trefoils at the Gothic peaks; their yellow curls, their feathery wings of color and light. And in a lancet—the narrow, vertical windows lined up below the transept—she spotted a slim-necked stag she'd never seen. Her vision blurred. Then sharpened. *How could that be?* she asked herself. *How could I have missed that deer?* And in that instant, she knew that there was much she had overlooked, more mystery than she would ever know. What she did know in that moment was that she possessed the gift of faith, and she claimed it. She couldn't muffle the message. She heard it. And, for once, she listened.

Father DiMarco might call it "conversion."

The celebrant archbishop led the congregation in reciting the Nicene Creed. The words fermented in Nora's mouth: "We believe in one God, the Father Almighty, maker of heaven and earth, of all that is seen and unseen."

She hadn't spoken these lines for years, at least not with any conviction. One part of the liturgy rolled into another.

"Do this in memory of me."

"Holy. Holy. Holy."

"Lamb of God you take away the sins of the world, grant us peace." ✺

"Lord, I am not worthy to receive you, but only say the word and I shall be healed." She felt more lovesick then ever. She wanted the priest to know she was there at Midnight Mass.

The next thing Nora knew, she was standing in the reverential line of people to receive Holy Communion. Organ music blared. "Jesu, Joy of Man's Desiring."

Nora could not deny her desire. She wanted the pastor for her own. And she sensed that was true of many people present. As she closed in on the priest holding the chalice, she saw the women bat their eyes and glimmer adoration his way. ✺ Father DiMarco lifted his chin at them, recognizing his disciples. And the women blushed in his benediction, hugging their hymnals to their breasts.

As she got closer to the altar, Nora kept her eye on the Paschal candles. She couldn't bear to look at the pastor. How she longed for an extension of the intimacy they had shared at Snowmass.

Next to a column, she felt dwarfed. She touched the cool marble base and looked up to the Corinthian capital. Standing on line, as she inched closer to the priest, she looked at the shiny chalice he held and considered the apostolic Church, the institution that dated back to Jesus Christ.

Father DiMarco didn't look beyond the person immediately ahead of him. And when she stood before him, she couldn't look him in the eye.

Father DiMarco held out a consecrated Host. "The Body of Christ, Nora," he said.

"Amen," she stacked her open hands. She received. And as the wafer touched her palm, she remembered their kiss.

Back in her pew, she hovered in the longing for holiness. Wholeness. And then she knelt, entered a trance. ✍ Tranquility. Seas parted. Sweet unleavened bread fell from the sky. Water flowed from igneous rock. Water turned to wedding wine. Prophecies came to pass. The time of fulfillment was at hand.

The archbishop raised his right hand. Nora caught the flash from the large red stone of his bishop's ring as he drew the Sign of the Cross over them, blessing the congregation. "The Mass is ended," he said, "Go in peace to love and serve the Lord."

And with the rest of the congregation, Nora said, "Thanks be to God." ✍

The old pipe organ boomed a triumphant prelude to the recessional song. She moved her spirit—her breath—to her very core. She opened her mouth and along with the choir and the congregation,

Nora sang instinctively deep from her diaphragm, "*Joy to the world...*" ❧

An adorable boy with a mop of dark hair led the recessional, carrying the cross high. Nora watched people bow and cross themselves when the archbishop cast his blessing over the assembly while he made his way out of the cathedral.

Father DiMarco brought up the rear, working the crowd. Nora looked on with jealousy as he joked and shook hands with people, touched the heads of children and the shoulders of seniors as he marched out to the roaring organ music.

He didn't see her. He didn't look for her. Her heart went out to him, to all the people gathered in the cathedral, their Catholic faith steadfast or shaken. Her judgment softened, considering all people everywhere wobbling in the quest to know God any amount through whatever religion or spirituality.

Maybe God really is love; and love, by logic, is God. And maybe that was as close as Nora could come to truth and as close as she dared come to God.

He walked past her, spotted her, touched her hand holding the hymnal. *I love you, Father Vin,* she wanted to tell him, just to hear the words spoken aloud.

Their love was good. Laudable. And the love she felt from him, likewise, beneficent. If only that were enough for her. ❧

In the name of the Father ⊠ and of the Son ⊠ and of the Holy Spirit. ⊠

Are you in your heaven, Lord? ⊠ ⊠ Now is the time of your miracle-working, and I fervently pray for nothing less. ⊠ ⊠ ⊠ ⊠

Dear God, free me from my demons. ⊠ ⊠ Father, remove this thorn from my flesh. You know I am weak with drink. You know I kneel in Gethsemane tonight. Could you take this cup of misery from me? Can you deliver me from evil? ⊠ Could you show me mercy if I were to forsake my vocation? ⊠ ⊠ Would you bless me in a new life?

Father, forgive me, but I cannot recall your grace. ⊠ You leave me floundering, bereft. How can I sacrifice at your altar with a heart filled with guilt and grief? Show me, again, the wonders of your ways, ⊠ O God. ⊠ If you would have me believe, make me believe. ⊠ ⊠ ⊠ You provide me with nothing

but anguish. You humble me, Lord. You refuse me your consolation. ⊠ ⊠ You tempt me. You will not redeem me. I would save myself if I knew how. ⊠ I would save her.

Dear God, I would lay down my life for her. Is that not what you taught from your cross? ⊠ That love conquers death? ⊠ We are people of good will, ⊠ ⊠ Lord. Grant us your salvation here and now. Use us for your glory so that your will be done on earth, in heaven, this day and every day. Father, do not withhold your Holy Spirit's fruits: Courage, meekness, fortitude. ⊠ ⊠

In the name of the Father and of the Son and of the Holy Spirit. ⊠ AMEN.⊠

CHAPTER FOUR

Epiphany

FEAST OF STEPHEN (26 December)

ora wanted, for once, to open her eyes, to see all there was to see: mountains outlining themselves against the sky in the view from her front porch, inconspicuous stags in stained-glass windows. More than that, she wanted eyes to see the unseen.

At work, Juan brought Nora her paycheck. She wanted to ask about his Christmas with his family, but he seemed all business.

"We're closing out the fiscal year," he said. "Is this compensation schedule adequate for you?" he asked.

"You mean paying me in installments? Sure," she said, "if that's how you want to do it." She handed him some receipts from Harry's store. "More materials," she said. "Mostly glass."

Juan pulled on the cuffs of his sweater and gave her a look she couldn't interpret. "We're already over budget, Nora. Father does have a fiduciary responsibility here."

"Father Vin did approve the expenses," Nora said.

"I'm sure he did," Juan said, hands jammed in his khaki pants, his face growing red. ❧

SEVENTH DAY IN THE OCTAVE OF CHRISTMAS
(31 December)

On New Year's Eve, Nora opened her journal and scrawled a list of resolutions:

I will drink more tea and less coffee, eat less sugar and more vegetables. ❧

I will practice yoga three times per week.

I will try to get in touch with old friends.

I will tell them why I seemingly dropped off the planet.

I will try not to be ashamed.

I will try not to claim all the blame for what happened to Liam.

I will be less judgmental and more grateful.

I will keep my house clean. (Cleaner.)

I will take fewer naps.

I will finish this job to the best of my ability and then use it as a springboard to get my studio up and running again.

I will put the past behind me and look to the future. (Or try.)

I will get rid of the stuff in the storage garage.

Nora paused, pen poised above the page with her manifesto. She chewed the end of it; and then she wrote in all capital letters a resolution she feared she was incapable of keeping:

I WILL QUIT TORTURING MYSELF OVER V.D.M.

Nora underlined the last item; and then she closed the book.

SOLEMNITY OF THE EPIPHANY OF THE LORD (4 January)

Heights didn't bother Nora, but scaffolding scared the devil out of her. Always leery that something in the metal Tinker Toy setup could slip or collapse, she ascended the ladder gingerly. The even morning light allowed her to gaze into the glass without flare. Standing 40 feet up and immediately before the glass, the windows took on different proportions and properties, abandoning their big pictures to become pieces of glass: cut, painted, soldered. Church windows are designed to be seen from about 100 feet. Up close, the optic phenomenon evaporated. ✒ Veils fell, revealing glass and brushstrokes that this near made no sense to Nora. Painted lines appeared distorted.

Nora was on the scaffolding when she heard Mrs. Quincy clear her throat. "Don't mean to disturb you," Mrs. Quincy said in a loud whisper. "I just came by to have Mass said for my husband on what would have been our 60th wedding anniversary. Say, I wonder what the traditional gift for 60th anniversary is? Do you happen to know? We never got past gold. Fifty years. Half a century." Nora had never seen her landlady so vulnerable. Her heart went out to the old widow.

Nora climbed down. "I could use a break."

"Seems you're coming along."

Nora sighed.

"Something wrong?" the old woman asked.

Nora wished she could confide in somebody about the priest. She remembered her list of resolutions and promised herself she would call Dinah, her best friend from her married life, her friend who had disdained Liam and knew something was afoul, her friend who had left a dozen messages Nora left unanswered. But how, she asked herself, would she get past the regret of blowing off her best friend? How would she explain what had happened since they last met for lattes? And Nora decided she could not set herself up for more possible rejection.

"Nora? You're a million miles away. What's the trouble?"

She looked at her landlady and knew she was not a replacement for a best friend. She did not want another lecture. She dodged. "Well, there's this glazier's phenomenon called halation. It's an optical illusion that causes light to spread." Mrs. Quincy raised her brows. "Think of a light bulb. Light spreads to fill a room from the thin thread of the filament. In stained glass, what appears from a distance as an opening the size of a dinner plate might be, up close, a hole from a B-B gun."

"You don't say," Mrs. Quincy said.

"Halation eats up trace lines as the light expands, moving away from the window," Nora said, looking up at the windows forming a cove around the sanctuary. "It's tricky because some colors gather light and expand more than others."

"Hmmm." Mrs. Quincy gazed from window to window.

"But painting tempers halation. So does avoiding large, isolated areas of clear glass, which is what they did with these windows. ✒ With glass, it's as much about the light not let in as the light allowed to pass through the panes."

"Sounds like you know what you're doing."

"At least as far as the glass goes."

"Nora, dear, is everything going all right here? I mean aside from the—what did you call it?—halation?"

Nora nodded. The old woman nodded, too, more slowly.

"I'll be going."

Nora slumped in a pew. She wished the priest would happen by. She wished he would vanish from the face of the earth. She wished the job were finished. ✒ She wished she could just fall in love with one of the construction workers, somebody less complicated, more available. Nora felt every bit as fragmented as the broken windows. She started to kneel, stopped herself, unconvinced God would hear her prayer. Her Christmas Eve faith seemed as much an illusion as halation, as if she had fallen under the homilist's numinous spell. She dropped her head back and looked up at the arching ribs of the cathedral. "What's wrong with me?" she asked, not sure whether she posed the question to herself or to God.

She climbed the scaffolding again. Positioned higher and closer on the scaffolding, Nora noticed the clots of solder in the web of lead. Where the storm had twisted lead, pieces of glass jutted out of the vertical plane. With the heel of her hand, Nora tested a mullion dividing panels of glass from the concrete tracery, aware that without the strength of the crossbar the weight of windows would collapse beneath the downward tug of gravity.

The windows' sections averaged three feet high. Eyeballing the windows and lightly running the pads of her fingers against the glass, she checked for buckling panels, but found none. She was amazed, given the tornado's power, that any of the glass had stayed in place. Sometimes fluctuations in cold and heat cause pigments to flake. Drawings fade. Perhaps faulty firing prevented the color from fusing. Fugitive paint. Even up close, Nora saw, the old glass held its own. ❧

Nose to the glass, she observed gradations delicate yet deliberate. The ease of the freehand brush strokes in tracing black and ancient brown and yellowish silver stain gave rise to artistic envy. Though called "tracing," the lines had nothing to do with trying to exactly copy something else. Without the fluidity of the freehand, the windows lacked life.

Saturated color all around her, Nora felt as if she were standing inside a kaleidoscope. For the umpteenth time, she measured a window opening. "Measure a thousand times," she heard her grandfather say, "and cut once." With her tape to the glass, she sensed the scaffolding shake. She looked down and saw the priest on the first ladder rung.

"Want some company?"

"Kind of tight up here," she said.

"I won't stay long, I want to see what you see."

"Not a good idea," she said firmly. Nora didn't want to be rude, nor did she want to be crowded. "I'll come down, and then you can come up." Ignoring her, he started to climb the scaffolding. Nora's whole body went as rigid as the iron saddle bars anchoring the windows. She'd had such a long recovery, she couldn't bear the thought of being injured again. "Don't come up here," she held her hands at arm's length as if to block him. But he continued his climb. "There's not enough room for two," she said, but he was almost to her platform. He took his place next to her. Right next to her. Their hips touched.

"Aah, the view from the top," he said, carefully enunciating each syllable. His breath smelled of mouthwash and bourbon.

She squinted her eyes. Interlaced her fingers.

"Wow, I've never seen the windows this close."

"They're not meant to be seen this close," Nora said through her teeth.

"Wow." He leaned forward to touch the glass, the scaffold shifted. "I'm going down."

"Nora, I wanted to talk to you about the Christmas party. I should not have kissed you like that."

"Could we just pretend it never happened? You're accomplished when it comes to repression and denial, right?"

"I wanted to apologize."

She shook her head. "You're drunk," she said through her clenched teeth.

He blinked, took a step back. "I've had a little wine. A little fruit of the vine."

"It's not a little. It's a lot. And it's causing a lot of problems."

"For whom?"

"For you. For me. Everybody!"

"How would you know?"

"Because I'm here all the time. I see what's going on."

"Correction: You're here a fraction of the time. You have no inkling about what goes on in the confessional. Or the chancery. Or meetings. You have no idea the sort of stressors I face every single day."

"We all have to face stress."

"You really think putting together pieces of glass is the same as ministering to human beings?"

Nora's jaw dropped. "I'm getting down."

"Fine," he said, his voice raised. "*Get down.*" ❧

Bent over my workbench, aligning a pattern on a square of ruby glass, I hear the front door open, slam. Stiffening, I cock an ear, hear his fast footsteps on the hallway wood.

"Nora?" he bellows. I cower. "Where are you?" Liam's voice bounces against the almost finished window commissioned by a bank. The contemporary panel crowds the studio. Propped up in its frame, all the lead soldered, the window waits only for sealant.

Like a protective mother, I cast my gaze toward the poised glass. I will the colors to pale, to secret themselves from him. My husband's malevolence reverberates around the studio, swirling into bins of glass sheets, seeping into the grain of my grandfather's workbench.

Suddenly, his hand on my tailbone. ❧ *Coffee and smoke on his jagged exhalations. A sloppy kiss on my turned neck. The vulgar sound of his zipper unzipped too slowly. A hiss of a whisper in my ear, "Get down."*

My abiding "No," my sick knowing. Outside, an ordinary evening. Inside, glass longs to return to its liquid state. He grabs my arm. We struggle. His hand over my mouth. My shriek checked. My arms flailing. My long hair in his fist. My jeans inside out on the floor next to my head. The blade of a box-cutter at the bridge of my nose.

I am not here, I persuade myself.

His knees on my biceps. Binds my wrists tightly with dull silver tape. A fierce slap. Silver stained stars sprinkle into my vision. Pain pierces my skull.

Liam traces the ridge of my throat with a box cutter. He forces apart my thighs.

Then I rally all my strength and break free. Bolt. To no avail. A kidney punch. A shove. As we both stumble across the room, I look over my shoulder and see that falling through the panel I had designed is inevitable. I fall. In desperation, I grab Liam's shirttail.

We fall together into the glass, the hours spent hunched over my bench: score, snap, position. Solder. Seal. Frame. Hundreds of pieces—all painstakingly chosen—and conscientious to the end, all I can think is that I won't be able to deliver the job on deadline.

Liam goes through first. I hold out my bound arms, as if I can stop myself. 🙖 *I hear but do not actually feel the thud of my body on the floor littered with shards of colored glass scattered like dangerous confetti.*

"Nora!" he shrieked. She looked down and saw the priest, his grip white-knuckled on the scaffolding. She dropped to her knees, clenched his wrists and leaned back with all her weight, dragging him back onto the wobbling platform.

Nora said, "Holy shit."

CANDLEMAS (2 February)

The coldest week of the year, and, sure enough, the old cathedral boiler—a dinosaur original to the 1912 structure—faltered, leaving the Gothic building frigid. The broken windows, though boarded or covered with plastic, admitted frosty drafts. The cold leaked through the chinks, down Nora's neck and up her wrists as she worked. The cathedral may as well have been an ice castle.

Kneeling in the center aisle, she unrolled one of the full-sized cartoons. The unwieldy paper kept curling back up. Nora saw Millie in the sacristy, and almost asked for her help to hold down one end of the cartoon. Millie distributed new candles, gathering up the old, placing them in a box. They exchanged territorial looks.

Cold, numbed, Nora's fingers could barely hold her tools. Nearly a month had passed since the scaffolding incident, and the rector came and went before and after Mass without stopping to speak to her. She longed to unburden herself, but could not share her shame. In her mind, she weighed his distance with her humiliation, aware he was the one person she could tell.

Nora wore her Navy watch cap, layered silk long underwear beneath her clothes. She rubbed her hands together briskly. Every so often, she went to the garage and did handstands against the wall to kick up her body temperature. ✺ In the alley, she saw Father DiMarco hand the box of used candles to Two-Wheel Rich. Rich looked her way, then hung his head. His afro bulged out beneath a too-small cap. The priest hugged him, then turned, saw Nora, and headed the other way.

"God almighty, give me break," she said under her breath. Her nose dripped. Her cheeks went numb. "I could use a little heat here," she said aloud, looking from window to window at the figures of Christ as an infant, a boy, a man, a corpse.

About an hour later, Juan showed up carrying another space heater. "I brought this from home," he said, plugging in the unit. "The boiler should be up and running tomorrow, day after, at the latest. Of course, the repair cost is not in the budget, so I have to do some creative accounting," he said. "Plus, I feel like we should be giving you hazardous-duty pay."

"Glass work is always hazardous," Nora said, fishing, wondering whether the pastor had conveyed his near fall to the staff.

Juan adjusted his eyeglasses, looked up at the stained-glass windows. "I have a down jacket, if that would help."

"Thanks," said Nora. "I'm doing OK."

"You're doing better than that," Juan said. "I'll let you get back to it." ✑

"Juan?"

He turned toward her, his face heavy with concern.

"Why did Father give Rich the old candles?"

Juan's face relaxed. "It's Candlemas; so Father blessed the new candles, and Rich claims the old ones. He uses them for light and heat."

And then, to Nora, the cathedral didn't feel quite so cold. She went back to work; and though she could almost see her breath, she hummed warmly inside, the argon lamps of her creativity heating her through. She completed the intricate soldering on the canopy work of one of the clerestory windows. Stepping back, she shivered, and saw that it was good.

SI *SI* *SI*

Father DiMarco had started coming around again, but perfunctorily, saying hello but never staying long enough for conversation. Nonetheless, in his presence, Nora mellowed. Melted. She saw herself in him. Their regular encounters left her both placated and amped. For the most part, they saw each other in passing at least twice daily: after morning Mass and before evening Mass, which he celebrated in a makeshift area set up in the cathedral basement while the sanctuary windows were under repair.

One day after morning Mass, he showed up with Puccini, and he gallantly offered a cappuccino bowl, steam rising from the rim. "To warm you," he said.

Awkwardly, Nora accepted the fragrant coffee. She wanted to give him the truth in return.

From his pocket he took a check. "Earmarked for glass repair." Flabbergasted, Nora's eyes widened, "A thousand bucks from Millie?"

"She sees what you're doing to her cathedral," he said. "She loves those windows, too."

A silence formed between them. She took a seat in a pew. He sat in the one ahead of her, turned around toward her.

"On the scaffolding, when I pushed you, I overreacted," she said. Her eyes shifted to the altar behind him. "I can explain."

"Only if you want to," he said.

"I think I had a flashback. Have you ever heard of post-traumatic stress disorder?"

He nodded slowly, "Of course."

Usually, tears announce their arrival. There's a warning period, a peppery nose, a screwing up of the face, an attempt to suppress the crying or allow emotion to flow. But Nora's tears gave no advance notice. Like onion tears, they sprang out of her eyes before she knew they had surfaced. Nora cried for Liam, and she cried for Millie and Mrs. Quincy and their dead husbands, for her own dead parents. Nora cried for Two-Wheel Rich. She cried for Vin; she cried for herself. She wept freely, shoulders shaking. Eradicating any self-consciousness, she let everything stream out of her, past that crumbling dam in which she'd poked a finger so long.

He said, "When tears fall, healing happens."

Relieved that he didn't flee from her blubbering, Nora composed herself. When she could finally form a sentence, she said, "I didn't want to cry."

She fidgeted, picked at her ragged cuticles. The priest gently held her hands, smoothing her knuckle bones with the pads of his thumbs.

"I wanted my husband dead," she blurted. She dabbed her eyes, wiped her nose.

Her vault, Nora saw, was locked from the inside. Had been all along. His face showed deadpan empathy. "Liam abused me," she said in a hush. "Not at first. He had this—what?—this rage. This violent temper crept up on him. I could see him change.

"He started doing drugs. Cocaine. Pills. Any chemicals he could lay hands on. And the drugs would affect other things. Namely, his—his—his potency. It got to the point that the only time he could, you know, was when he was violent. And then he'd blame me, saying that if I were a real woman, I could excite him enough. It was a vicious circle. His impotence would make him even more angry—at himself, at me, at the whole world. And I... I craved intimacy." ✍

"That's natural," the priest said in a calming voice.

"But we had none. He'd fly off the handle at the least little thing: if I forgot to enter a check in the register, if I put raisins in the muffins, if I ran a few minutes late or talked on the phone too much, if I gained a few pounds. He made my life miserable. My parents were already dead. I wasn't sure where to turn."

Concern creased the priest's face. For an instant, the lines around his eyes displayed the vestiges of all the pain he had heard all the people articulate in the confines of confessionals. "I'm sorry, Nora," he said.

"I had known the good side of Liam. So I used to just hope and pray that he would return to that princely guy that I'd fallen in love with. But his addiction prevented that."

She closed her eyes, rubbed her neck.

"We used to argue a lot. I used to fight back. Until he started to hit me. It got worse. A lot worse in the last year. We covered it up. I lied. He lied. It was a big conspiracy. I think his family knew, but they didn't really want to know, I could tell; so I never explained directly what was going on. They were in no position to help me, anyway. Nobody wanted to deal with him. Nobody could."

She puffed her cheeks round, then exhaled. "He," she paused, drilled her chin into her chest, whispered, "he raped me. More than once. I know we were married, but I can't honestly call it anything but rape."

"One night, Liam hit me so hard, he knocked me out." She stopped. Bit the inside of her cheek. "I don't remember anything except waking up in a hospital bed the next day. ✑ Liam had sent me flowers. Red roses. When I woke up, the smell of them made me throw up.

"I had a cut on the back of my head. I apparently had hit my head when I fell. They had shaved a patch of my hair to stitch it up. After that was when I started having the migraines. I don't know what Liam told the doctor, but later that day, a counselor from a battered women's shelter showed up. ✒ She tried to get me to leave him, but I was just so stuck.

"She was begging me to leave right then, while Liam wasn't at the hospital. But I couldn't. I couldn't speak my mind. I couldn't cry. I couldn't even move my eyes. I checked myself out against medical advice.

"When Liam got home, he stormed into my studio. He started in on me right away. He had seen those stupid roses in the trash at the hospital. ✒

"He started ranting about how we were meant for each other and couldn't survive without one another. About how he wanted to make love to me and make it all up to me. He pulled me close to him. I tried to pull away, but he wouldn't let me go. He had me by my hair, and he had a box cutter." She pursed her lips, unable to speak. She trembled.

"Oh, Nora, I'm so, so sorry."

"I was trying to get away from him." Nora held her fists to her chest. "And then we fell through the glass. The next thing I knew, I heard sirens. Cops swarmed the studio. Blood everywhere."

"Dear God," the priest said in a monotone.

"I woke up in an ambulance; and then in a hospital bed. I remember a nun was there to tell me Liam was dead. I was glad."

"Oh, beloved one. Oh, Nora." They sat in silence for a few

breaths. A soundlessness seeped in, a gentle breeze, serenity. "God forgives you. Can you forgive yourself?" His voice went lax and lenient.

"For what? For marrying Liam in the first place? For staying too long? Enduring too much? For wanting him dead? You think God loves a woman who wishes her husband dead? Did God answer that prayer?"

"We put limits on God's mercy only because we know limits to our own," he said. "I owe you an apology. I had no idea."

"How could you?" she asked.

"I've been too hard on you," he said. "And the scaffolding: I had no business being up there. That was my fault. Can we get past it? I miss talking with you."

She relented immediately, yielding to his contrition. She forgave him his trespass. *Isn't that what Christians do?* She wanted only to lay her head on his shoulder.

"That tornado changed my life," she said.

And he said, "You've changed mine."

FEAST OF OUR LADY OF LOURDES (11 February)

She made progress and poured herself into tasks, noticing that every time she picked up her badgers and brights, the brushes felt at home in her hands. She stood back and admired her unencumbered strokes on the glass canvas. With ease in her wrist and motion in her forearm, she articulated palm fronds.

The scored glass relaxed between her fingers. And every time she made a clean break, she wondered why she ever had quit. Then, of course, she vividly remembered why. Yet, each piece of glass cut, painted, soldered, sealed took her farther away from her past and closer to a future that mattered.

Her process started with a game, of sorts, trying to decode the job. Eventually, a power struggle escalated, a war. ✍ The glass persecuted her. But if she stayed at it long enough, that fell away. A partnership formed. The process became more like a relationship in which she'd accepted the strengths and limitations of the glass, and the glass had accepted hers. Together Nora and the glass collaborated with light, and the light gave itself generously to the glass. The glass refined and defined the light, transforming the rays into shapes with meaning. In the cathedral's case, Bible stories. Catechism. And in the case of Nora, a glimmer of clarity into her own integrity and the dignity her work bestowed upon her.

As the early darkness fell and Nora's eyes grew fatigued, she turned away from painting and took up the sorting of remnant glass. A row of buckets lined up against a wall in the garage contained scraps of broken glass that had not yet found their places in the windows again. Nora took piece after piece from the buckets; and as if they were pieces of a jigsaw puzzle, she placed the jagged glass shapes on her drafting table. ✑ Shifting pieces here and there, suddenly, she caught her breath and drew together seven small pieces that formed, to her delight, the cipher from Zettler's studio.

✑ ✑ ✑

Almost every day, the priest returned. Often, he quoted Scripture or prayers, the writings of obscure saints or the documents of the Second Vatican Council, reciting the passages in a cadence befitting a Shakespearean actor. He managed not to come off as pedantic or didactic; so Nora listened, intrigued by his theatrics, his devotion. Flattered to have someone of his intellect engaging her, she was an engrossed congregation of one. Since her informal confession she felt closer than ever to the priest.

To Nora, it all seemed safe. And treacherous, too. They were in many ways, she sensed, still perilously perched together on that scaffolding. ✑

"Do you have a favorite?" the rector asked as she was studying color photos of the windows, comparing them to the actual windows.

"I have favorite elements," she said. "I love the poison green of this guy's robe." She pointed.

"St. Augustine," he said, with the slightest slur.

She pointed to the Annunciation window. "I love the way the

leading edge of that angel's wing is lighter than the rest."

"Aah," he said. "Only you would see that. I love the way Jesus has all these different expressions and all these different haloes. It makes me see him as more human, not just staid and static. You see, here he's irritated with the high priests in the temple. Here, he's obedient, bending to his mother's request, making wine from water to keep the wedding feast rolling. Here he's commanding, calming the storm."

"I think that's my favorite," Nora said. "Look at the movement in the waves."

The priest leaned back. "I'm always struck by how, without any mention of Jesus Christ's physical appearance in Scripture, so many faces of Jesus look so much alike even though rendered by so many different artists. I think that owes to a source of divine inspiration."

"Maybe," Nora said. "Then again, the oldest intact stained-glass image of Christ is from 1050 and looks like a jack from a deck of cards. There's a Jesus from 1160 with deep blue hair and a pale purple body and a red cross. But they're severe. Distant. The Jesus here— He's so gentle. So close."

"So palpably suffering."

An elderly couple came in, knelt in prayer, bowed their heads.

"*Lumen gentium*," the priest said in a hushed voice.

"*What?*" she whispered.

"It's Latin for 'light of all nations,'" he said.

"Shhh," she said, indicating the people praying.

His eyes smiled. "I enjoy observing people doing work they love," he said. "You look so intent. Content."

"I was just thinking about all the stained glass that's been destroyed: wars, vandals, fires, religious reform, bad renovations, acid rain," she said, leaning close to him so she could be heard. "Thousands of windows were lost to the Protestant Reformation, all in the name of banishing idolatry."

"Do you always look on the dark side of things?" he asked. "A lot of glorious windows survived, miraculously."

She nodded. "There's this window at King's College Chapel in Cambridge. During World War II, the townspeople wanted to preserve the window. It was already centuries old. Bombs were falling. Germans were invading. And the townsfolk took apart the window; and each person took home a piece of the glass and stashed it. And after the war, they brought the pieces out and put the window back together again. "

"Now *that's* stewardship," he said. "Maybe I can paraphrase it for a homily."

"I admire that sort of devotion. I had it once." She crossed her feet at the ankles. Maybe she could convince herself that talking was enough. Strictly communication instead of fornication. "I desperately wanted to serve Mass. ❧ When I was in Catholic school, I mean. The boys got to; and I considered myself just as worthy."

"Is that so?" he asked, leaning in to her to whisper. "And you resented it because you always wanted to participate at that level but you couldn't. Is that what this is all about? All your standoffishness toward Catholicism?"

"All this—as you call it—is more about you than me. You're the one trying to convert me. I'm perfectly comfortable where I'm at."

"Which is outside of the Church?"

"Well, I'm inside at the moment."

"I'm talking harmony with good old Mother Church." He nudged her. "Did you ever think that all of this—everything that happens—is composed of signs from God?"

She gazed at the acanthus leaves at the top of a rain-stained column in the nave. "Nah," she said. "I think interpreting signs from God is usually rationalization."

"Oh?" His shoulders rolled toward her. "You mean to tell me you're an artist, yet you've never experienced a moment of spiritual synchronicity?" He shook his head. "I'm not buying that. Not for a minute. I thought we agreed that art is one of the most direct bridges between humanity and divinity."

"You're free to believe whatever you want," she said. "I work extremely hard at my craft. It's not something just handed down to me as a gift that I unwrap. It's work. Hard work. And I'm the one showing up to put in the hours. I'm the one with the slivers of glass in my fingerprints."

"But where do you think the talent comes from in the first place? You had to start with some measure of giftedness. We don't just stumble into the world with no hint about what we're good at, where we excel, which aptitudes might be our own. For many people, gifts announce themselves early."

"I've worked at this," she said. "I've spent countless hours stooped over a drafting table. I learned the craft and perfected it by practice. I have the calluses to prove it."

"And you think you're doing it alone?"

She rested her hands on her hip bones. "I don't see any angels floating over my glass cutter."

"You don't see them?"

"I don't believe in them, other than as myth. I believe in me," she said, taking the lie a step further.

"There's a word for that," he said.

"Yeah?" she shrugged.

He pressed way into her bubble. "Blarney," he said. Stale beer breath. He made a sweeping gesture, taking in the windows. "I can see this takes a lot of artistry."

"Some," she said. "Some craft. Some skill. Mostly patience."

"Patience," he drew the word out, "is a gift of the Holy Spirit."

"Well, how do I get on that gift list?"

"You knock," he said. "You seek. You ask. You pray ceaselessly. None of this makes any sense without prayer. If you don't pray, faith doesn't sustain you and isn't sustained."

"I don't know how to pray anymore."

His eyes closed. She noticed his thick, dark lashes. "You pray with confidence. You pray with expectation. But not too much expectation. You pray with specificity—but not too much specificity. You pray the Lord's Prayer, as Jesus taught us. Or pray to your guardian angel."

"I think my guardian angel went on sabbatical," she said, thinking of her dark days with Liam.

"Why would you say such a thing?"

"You know why." She folded her hands in her lap. "Do you really believe in them?" she asked. "Angels?"

"I really do," he said.

"Have you ever seen an angel?"

"I don't need to see them," he said.

"Maybe they're just hallucinations."

"Maybe," he said. "But that's not what my experience tells me."

"You've experienced them, then?"

"Lots of times," he said. "And so have you."

"How would you know?"

"Everyone experiences angels. It's just that most people don't have enough awareness to recognize them," he said. "When I first saw you, that day of the tornado, I sent my guardian angel to your guardian angel and prayed they'd protect us both. And here we are."

Where? she wanted to ask him. *Where, precisely, do we stand, you and I?*

ST. VALENTINE'S DAY (14 February)

Nora woke to deep snow and pearly light. Listening to the radio as she dressed, she heard the litany of closed mountain passes. Chain laws were in effect. All schools canceled. The whole city stalled. And so did Nora's car.

Hearing the sound of her engine struggling to start, Mrs. Quincy opened the door a crack and called out. "Nora, do you want to use my car?"

She waved her off. "It's OK," Nora shouted. "Thanks, though."

Nora realized that she couldn't drive anyway. 🙠 Her car would high center on the drifts in the streets.

Instead, she dressed for Old Man Winter and collected her Nordic ski equipment. She strapped on her backpack and stepped into the wondrous terrain of the blizzard. She set her ski boots in the toe clips of her skis. As she floated the blocks between her place and the cathedral, wind stung her cheeks, but the rest of her body heated up as she glided over the drifted snow, working up a decent pace. 🙠 The snow showed a pastel blue tint, much like the icebergs she and Liam had seen in Alaska. Much like the mysterious light that once emanated from Liam's eyes, long before the man she was married to was no longer the man she married.

All day, she expected to see Father DiMarco, but he didn't show up after the morning Mass. Maybe he'd canceled Masses for the day, she gathered, when she didn't see him after the noon Mass, either.

He didn't stop in as usual with a cappuccino or chai. The hours stumbled and dragged. She was the only one around except for some homeless people sleeping in pews.

Distracted, all day she watched for him, waited, fantasized about him showing up with an armload of calla lilies or a heart-shaped box of Godiva truffles or even a handful of colorful Conversation Hearts. "U R A Q T." "Be mine." "Love me." *Something.* Anything. All the while, she loathed her deviant vamping for a priest. Reluctantly, she let go of the expectation that they could share at least a little time together like would-be lovers in a common celebration of Cupid's aim. He could at the very least give her a history lesson about St. Valentine. ✍ She remembered the first year she'd met Liam; he had delighted her by mailing 14 different valentines.

Afternoon light dimmed, and yet the evening did not altogether darken due to the bleached mantle of snow. The winter storm raged on. Her spirits sank. The glass on the work bench looked dark, fragile, unapproachable. Her fantasy lover's Valentine remained wrapped in tissue paper and tied with red raffia. She had made him a sun catcher: three green glass hearts in the shape of a shamrock inside the eternal circle of a Celtic cross. A reminder, she had intended, of her.

Nora picked up a large color print of the face of the Blessed Virgin Mary and ripped the photograph. She decided she wouldn't give him the gift, after all. She stuffed the unclaimed sun catcher in her backpack and wondered what she had been thinking.

The boiler broke down yet again. Everyone with any sense

stayed home. The cold cathedral numbed Nora to the point that she almost feared frostbite. Her enthusiasm for the restoration of the windows was tepid, at best. She hit a low point, tired of the tedious demands of the glass. If not for her familial work ethic, her ego and her obsession with the rector, she would have walked away. Anyway, it was too cold to go outside.

By four o'clock, the winds picked up again. The temperature plummeted steadily; the snow continued to fall thickly. She worked late, dreading having to ski home. The streetlights flickered on early as night took hold. The sky surrendered not to black, but a peachy pink. Reflective snow set the evening aglow. Her father always said that if the snow hadn't stopped by sundown, it would fall all night.

She finished cleaning her brushes; and just as she reached for her ski pants, she heard the closing of the door from the rectory entrance to the sacristy. "Nora?" she heard him yell. "Nora," he hollered again, his shout thick and hoarse. The sound of his voice pronouncing her name made her stomach drop through the floor.

"Down here," she said. She unbridled her hair from a ponytail, shook it out. Then gathered her hair up again, fastening the elastic band around it tightly. *Just friends,* she told herself.

Father DiMarco stamped his feet, burst in. "Why didn't you take a snow day?" She couldn't tell whether his high color was from cold or Coors. A whiff of alcohol answered her question.

"I was just leaving," she said, embarrassed by her undisclosed sentimental Valentine gift to him, depleted by her desperate waiting for him. ✍

He absolutely glowed, rosy-cheeked and pie-eyed. "Do you have a couple of hours to help me out? I have a truck full of coats and hats and mittens and boots out there." He waved his arms, animated. "I'm taking 'em down to the shelter. I know a lot of the guys from the food line don't even have hats; and the shelter won't fit every-body in tonight. Will you help? I need your help."

"Sure," she said, catching his contagious enthusiasm and eager for his companionship. She started to step into her ski pants, but he tugged at her Aran sweater, knocking her off balance. He caught her, an arm around her waist, steadied her. He handed Nora her shearling mittens and her backpack.

"Hurry," he said. "The guys won't hang around long after the drawing. We have to go!" She dropped her jacket on the floor as he pulled her out the door.

Puccini sat in the pickup truck, riding erect like a person passenger. Nora peeked into the topper. Mounds of winter clothing filled the truck bed.

"Not bad for a day's work, huh?" He rubbed his hands together and opened the door for her. Several empty beer cans rolled around on the floor.

"Are you OK to drive?"

"I'm not exactly blotto," he said. He walked a straight line. And touched his index fingertip to his nose. ✒ And began reciting the Gettysburg Address.

She said, "I thought we were in a hurry."

"Here," he said, tossing her the keys. "You drive."

She climbed in the truck's cab. "Hi, Puccini!" She hugged the dog, who greeted her with a swift lick of her nose. Nora started the truck, turned to the priest, "Where'd you get all that stuff?"

Father DiMarco puffed up. "I went to all the thrift stores to wheel and deal. I got some great bargains. Coats, boots, hats, gloves. All sizes." The priest shifted the truck into 4-wheel drive for her; and they set out steadily over streets drifted waist-high with snow.

Outside Samaritan Center, almost a hundred people huddled. Nora and Father DiMarco hopped out of the warm truck and joined them as a shelter staffer explained the rules of the drawing while shuffling a deck of playing cards. *The hands these men were dealt,* Nora thought, put off by the unfairness of life. She counted her blessings. Wet snow fell, sticking to her sweater and jeans.

"Where's your coat?"

"I dropped it as you dragged me off," she said.

"Here," he said as he helped her into his parka.

"We're full with families," apologized the shelter's director, an earnest young man. ✒ "There's floor room for about 25 more individuals. Men who draw red cards come in. We're awfully sorry about this, guys, but certain laws and fire codes prevent us from taking you all in. Don't chance it outside tonight. It's going to get dangerously cold. Do not stay outside. We're making calls right now to see what might be available elsewhere."

The priest and Nora watched the homeless men draw cards. Nora hopped from foot to foot and wrapped her arms around her chest, trying to stay warm. As the people who had drawn black cards shuffled away into the indifferent Siberian night, Father DiMarco gently gestured them over to his pickup. A lot of the guys were food-line regulars, evidently.

"Evening, Father," they said, "Thank you, kindly," and "God bless you." ✍

She wondered about these men's stories, how they had come to live on the streets, how they would make it through the cruel night. Nora and the priest handed out every last article. Toward the end of the line, Two-Wheel Rich made his way slowly pushing his wobbly shopping cart. ✍ For the first time, Nora took inventory of its contents: Ratty towels, mismatched shoes, a hubcap, an empty burlap rice sack stuffed with God knows what, assorted empty glass bottles and aluminum cans, mismatched gloves of all sizes and colors and styles tied to the cart's handle. He wore a ski mask and a trash bag over his cloth coat. The sleeves of his coat were frozen stiff. His boots had holes in the toes. Puccini barked at him. Rich laughed. From his coat pocket, he took a small, rolled up bag of potato chips. He looked to the priest. The priest nodded. Rich gave the dog a chip.

Nora was shocked that somebody she knew would sleep outside in the cold. "Good to see you, Rich. Well, not good. Not on a night like this. It's really cold," she said, eyes on the ground.

"Colder than a brass toilet seat on the shady side of an iceberg," Rich said.

Nora laughed; and the arctic air seized her nostrils.

When Rich turned to listen to Father DiMarco, she slipped the Valentine package with the sun catcher into his two-wheeled cart.

Puccini dashed through the snow and then lay down, biting snowballs from between his toes.

"Come on, Puccini," the priest said. "Let's get you in the truck. Come on, load up." Puccini jumped in the pickup; and Nora followed, taking the passenger's seat. The priest no longer seemed soused. *A scene like that would sober up anybody,* she realized. The cab filled with the stink of wet dog.

Two-Wheel Rich touched his fist to Father DiMarco's. The priest got in, started the truck. They rode solemnly through the frozen night, the heater on full blast, tires squeaking over snowdrifts.

"Why didn't you offer Two-Wheel Rich a place for the night?" she asked.

"I have in the past. I got busted by the bishop once for opening up the rectory. I was given a lesson in knowing and respecting my limits."

"I can't believe these people will actually sleep outside," she said.

"I can't imagine. I'd never make it."

"But people who are poor develop strong survival instincts. I admire them. Jesus said, 'The poor will be with you always.'"

"Doesn't that depress you?"

"Just because we can't do *everything* doesn't mean we shouldn't do *something*," Father DiMarco said. "We did something."

He drove to City Park and stopped in front of the lake. A flock of Canada geese—hundreds—hushed and huddled on the frozen lagoon, a spectral sight. Nora opened her door slightly and Puccini leapt over her and out of the truck. The dog raced through the snow, barking at the geese, digging his nose into the snowdrifts, rolling and sliding on his back. She couldn't help but laugh, caught up in the dog's exuberance. ✒ She threw a snowball, and Puccini tried to retrieve it, the snow crumbling in his mouth. She threw another. And another. The dog's tail wagged and wagged as he stuck his rump up in the air, growling for more play.

The night was regal—a hibernal winter queen. Few people ventured out and about. Downy snow muffled noise.

"Frost, ice and snow: Nature's winter Trinity," she said.

"Nora, I cherish our time together," Father DiMarco said softly.

She tossed another snowball for Puccini to chase. "Do you ever want more time together?" she asked quiet as snow falling.

He nodded. "If I had known I'd ever meet a woman like you,

there would be one fewer diocesan priest."

"Well," she said, unnerved, "you're a great priest. And the Church needs you. People need you. What about those people tonight?"

"What about you?"

She paused. She rubbed her nose. "I need you, too. I need all the friends I can get." Then, before he could see compunction contort her face, she trudged toward the frozen lake.

"That's all I wanted to hear," he called after her.

In the reflective brightness of the squall, she pondered the geese on the ice. Puccini stalked the big birds, but they remained unruffled, doing the best they could to protect themselves from the storm. The monochromatic vision of all those geese huddled against the snow suddenly chilled her.

"They're just like all of us," he said at her side. Close. "We're all just tucking our heads beneath our wings, futile protection against whatever blizzards blow through us and whatever fanged predators lurk on the shores."

She hugged herself. The cold dug in deeper. Her shoulders crept up to her ears. Her legs went rigid.

"Come on," he said. "You're shivering."

He opened his arms to her, and she closed her heart down a notch. He wrapped his arms around her waist and hugged her so hard he lifted her off the ground. In the twinkling they embraced, suspended between past and future, Nora spun a sterling prophecy:

She wondered about weather patterns, and the patterns of geese in flight. She wondered about living things going out and others coming in to this world. She glimpsed the flux and flow of life on this planet: minerals seeded from big bang dust, peridots in meteorites, the patient formation of canyons and caves, the suddenness of avalanches, a starfish's regenerated points. She saw birth and death, winter and spring, season into season, the fullness of time spilling over and over and over, a cornucopia of mystery filling in from the bottom.

When the priest set her down, Nora's feet found stability on the curve of the earth. Snow waltzed on the wind.

In the car, he aimed all heat vents toward her. She began to shake uncontrollably, her teeth chattering. She realized, of course, that her chills stemmed as much from nervousness as from the elements.

Father DiMarco handed her a flask. "Brandy," he said. "It'll warm you." The leather cover on the flask was well worn, stained dark.

She shook her head and said, "Thanks anyway."

He drank from his flask and then stashed it under the driver's seat. They drove in silence but for the sound of the heater, the thud of snowdrifts beneath the truck and the rhythmic windshield wipers. Father DiMarco slid in a CD; and she tapped her toes to the white man's blues and watched the stalwart snow fluttering in the headlights.

"You missed my turn," she said, thinking he was either distracted or disoriented, knowing full well that he was at least a little bit drunk.

"I know," he said. As they pulled into the rectory driveway, she said nothing. He pressed the garage door opener and drove in, pushing the button again, sealing the storm outside. Her stomach turned over and around and landed upside down. ✺ Puccini placed a paw on her arm.

She climbed down from her seat in the pickup, followed the dog into the rectory without speaking. They stood in the back foyer; and the priest opened the drapes that looked out to the snowy street. "Looks like Millie hightailed it out of here without cooking a casserole," he said in the kitchen. "I could use a drink," he said. "How 'bout you?"

"Nah."

"Coffee and Frangelico? Hot buttered rum?"

"Pass," she said. "I'd better go."

"We just got here. I at least owe you dinner for your help."

"I'm not hungry," she lied.

"Not hungry?" He sighed. "How can you not be hungry after all that?" ✺

She shrugged. "I've got some things I need to do."

"Like what?" he asked.

"I just think I should go," she said, shivering. "That's all."

"It's snowing like mad out there."

"I know. Plus, my clothes are wet, so…"

"There's nobody going anywhere right now, Miss Kelley." He turned on a radio in the kitchen. A DJ ran through his long list of cancellations and broadcast the police advisory to stay off the streets except for an emergency. The entire metro area was on accident alert.

"There," he said, switching off the radio. He poured himself several fingers of brandy. "You don't want me to drive any more in this, do you?"

She flashed her eyes at him and said, "You have 4-wheel drive."

"I've had a bit to drink, too," he said.

"I have my skis."

"I can't let you go out in this weather Nora. You're wet. You're cold." He wrinkled his brow. "Don't leave," he said.

She recoiled at the vulnerability in his voice. "Father..."

He shook his head as if he didn't want her to call him that. "If you want, I can take you home, yes, of course. But I want you to stay. For a while. Please." He bent before her and looked into her eyes. "Please?"

God, I adore him, she admitted in that instant. He summoned his boyish look and tested her eyes even more pleadingly, folded his hands, looked heavenward and said, "Please God, let Nora see that it's perfectly safe to stay and have dinner with me. Open her heart to the memory that table fellowship was important to you, Lord. Let her know that I will feed her well. Amen."

She bit the inside of her cheek. "OK," she said. "If you're sure it's OK."

"Why wouldn't it be? It's all under control, Nora, I assure you."

She knew arguing with him would make him only more determined to have his way. She half resented being all but held hostage, but she also thrilled to the idea of chance conspiring to bring them together—alone—and the allure of spending the entire evening with him. Dinner prepared by his hands. A mostly guileless hospitality tinged with undertones of proscription.

"You'll need to get out of those wet clothes," he said, "and I'll put them in the dryer; and—don't worry—I'll give you my robe," he said. "Do you want to take a hot bath?"

She blushed.

"I mean, do you, you yourself, want to take a bath—alone?"

"No. Thanks." She gnawed her lip and shivered.

He put his hands on her shoulders. "Relax, Nora. Really. I promise you I will never again do anything to compromise you. Or me. OK?"

An old AA maxim came to her mind. *Question: How do you know when a drunk is lying? Answer: His lips are moving.*

"OK," she said too quickly to sound nonchalant.

"You should get out of those damp clothes. You can change down in the guest room. I'll leave my robe on the bed. Drop your stuff outside the door. I'll toss your things in the dryer; they won't take long."

"Don't put my sweater in the dryer," she said. "It's wool. And it was my mother's."

"Gotcha," he said. "Air dry flat."

She couldn't help but grin, surprised by his domesticity.

"I'll go get you my robe," he said, heading for the stairway.

"And socks?" she asked.

"And socks," he bounded up the stairs, taking two at a time.

"Not priests' socks!" she yelled up after him, giggling.

He stopped in his tracks at the top of the stairs. "And what, pray tell, are priests' socks?"

"Those thin, black, silky ones."

His laughter roared down the stairway.

In the guest room, she undressed, shuddering. Her bones felt sharp beneath her goose flesh. As she pulled off her soggy jeans, she took in the nondescript quarters: the beige bedspread, the dun-colored oval rug, the crucifix on the wall. She wrapped herself in his bathrobe and wondered what she was getting herself into.

The robe, striped flannel, smelled of him, naturally; and she pictured him reaching into it after stepping out of the shower, naked, dripping wet. *So what if we're acting a bit reckless?* She tried to reason with herself. *Spontaneity is a virtue, isn't it? Blessed are the cavalier.* But her conscience didn't let her off the hook. *You idiot!* she told herself. *You have no boundaries. You have no shame. This is not just a bit reckless. He is not your friend! This is not just dinner*. And the thought of eating almost made Nora vomit.

Her pink skin stung as her flesh defrosted. Shyly, she walked down the hall and up the stairs. She stood in the doorway of the den a moment, watching him kneeling and blowing on the flames in the fireplace.

Puccini barked and gave her away. The priest turned from his hearth and smiled at her. He, too, had changed clothes. He wore gray corduroys and a charcoal-colored chamois shirt. Men's clothes. Not clerics. In his street clothes, he could be a professor of Romance languages, a dentist, a journalist. He could be a man available for lust—love, even. As he tended the blazing fire, Nora couldn't help but study the breadth of his shoulders, the shape of his rear, his stockinged feet. As he knelt before the hearth, she couldn't help but imagine herself beneath him.

"Better?" he asked, patting a reclining chair by the fire. "Here," he said, "come warm yourself. This should be roaring in no time. Your sweater will dry here. And I took the liberty of pouring you a brandy. It'll help you thaw."

Nora thought, *That's what I'm afraid of,* but said nothing. She curled up in a chair, but couldn't look at him. She sipped the brandy, felt it heat her empty stomach. They sat in bashful silence, staring into licking flames. The liquor soothed her anxiety, dulled her defenses.

"Come on," he said standing, motioning her to him. "How 'bout some dinner? I'm famished, are you?"

She nodded.

In the kitchen, they chatted freely as he cooked. On the counter stood three slender bottles of flavored olive oil. She held them up to the light. The gold: garlic. The chartreuse: basil. The red: roasted red pepper.

He was intent as he steamed an artichoke, prepared linguini with white clam sauce, sliced bread, oiled it, topped it with crumbled goat cheese, chopped roasted red peppers. And, of course, he opened a bottle of wine.

"To gladden our hearts," he said, passing to her a full glass of red.

He fed Puccini treats for tricks. The dog shook hands. Rolled over. Growled, kissed. Preached.

The dryer bell sounded; and she retrieved her warm clothes, changed. When she came back to the kitchen, he was tossing a salad, deftly lifting and dropping greens, chopped avocados, grape tomatoes and shiny black olives in a big wooden bowl. He set down the tongs. "Dinner is served."

"Smells delicious," she said, but her stomach flipped over.

At the table, he reached for her hand. His grip felt electric.

"*Oremus*," he said. "Let us pray." They bowed their heads. He didn't say anything, and she wasn't sure if he was praying silently, or if she was supposed to offer grace. He cleared his throat. "God Almighty, we thank you for this food and all who have had a hand in its preparation, from field to table. We ask your blessing upon this meal; and we ask your blessing upon all those who know hunger this day and cold this night. We thank you for the gift of this chance to break bread together, mindful that as our bodies delight in good food, our souls delight in good works. Amen." And then he raised his wine glass and said, "To the monk in each of us."

And Nora said, "Forgive us our trespasses."

And by the time the clink from their touched glasses cleared the air, he had sucked down half of his wine.

They ate intently, speaking little. They cleared the dishes without saying a word and returned to the lava-red logs of the hearth to drink Irish coffee. "Your cup overflows," he said, affecting a brogue as he gave her the cup piled high with whipped cream. She lapped at the topping.

There was no way she could add whiskey to the brandy and wine she'd drunk. "It's late," she said. He said nothing.

She could see out the windows flanking the fireplace that the snow still hadn't let up. She sat motionless, content. Father DiMarco tilted back in the recliner and dozed, lightly snoring. Nora took the opportunity to memorize the shadowed planes of his face, his squared chin, his deep-set eyes, his oily hairline, the swells of his lips. She would've liked nothing more than to lean over and kiss him. Perhaps he would've blacked it out, anyway, she thought. She looked at his upper lip, shadowed with whiskers.

She sipped at the Irish coffee, after all. The warm whiskey hit her and she tucked her feet underneath her on the couch. Nora yawned and relaxed, inebriated, uninhibited, then stretched out on the couch, borderline sinful. She listened to the priest's even breathing, then got up and covered him with a down throw.

She looked down upon him in his innocence, as touched by the sight of him in slumber as if he were her sleeping child. Maybe it was the alcohol. Maybe the romantic glow of the firelight. Nora's heart expanded. She looked past his shortcomings and toward his largesse. She imagined him wheeling and dealing for the winter clothes. She respected him for being the sort of person who not only had deep compassion, but acted upon it with magnanimity. His tenderness touched her: drying her clothes, loaning her socks, preparing her dinner. She remembered Mrs. Quincy's comment and considered that maybe the old woman was right: Maybe love between a man and a woman does not always need to be expressed sexually.

The fire popped, waking Father DiMarco. They searched one another's faces. The dog circled in his cedar bed, whined, as if to speak for the both of them. He removed the comforter and stood alluringly close to her.

He unbuttoned his shirt. "Hot in here," he said.

She nodded, feeling the heat in her crotch, damp. She looked away, felt as if he had read her mind. The corners of her mouth turned down against her will. She began to shiver.

He kept unbuttoning his shirt. She watched his hands. Priest hands. All digits accounted for. She watched him undo one button after another, slow motion. No hurry. He took off his shirt. Firelight glinted off the Miraculous Medal he wore around his neck.

In just his undershirt, his muscles stood out, collarbones, deltoids, the ellipses of his forearms. Nora sipped the Irish coffee that had grown cool, the fire raging behind him. Her heart beat like a church bell chiming, signaling a gathering. Her reasoning powers dissolved into primal, neurochemical processes. Trip-wired for arousal, her brain lit up, releasing dopamine.

Nora straightened her spine, lifted her chest. She tried to swallow. And then he leaned in and kissed her neck. Twice. So softly. So tentatively. She felt a brush of his beard stubble. A transcendent tenderness enveloped her.

He leaned his forehead against hers. They closed their eyes, then opened them, and all Nora saw was the color of his irises, brown as black coffee. His hands framed her face. They exchanged the look of lovers surrendering to desire, the look of longing and arriving, recognizing one another. And then they were kissing, delicately, at first, but then ferociously, passionately, their mouths open as their hearts, tongues clashing.

They groped and clumsily began undressing one another. When he pulled a wool blanket off the back of the upholstered couch, sparks of static jumped. He spread the blanket on the floor in front of the fire. As Nora pulled her turtleneck over her head, a thread caught on her earring and loosened the clasp on the silver hoop.

They kissed and kissed until there was no turning back. She could not seem to see him, but she could smell him. Taste him. She could feel his sacred hands seeking the profane territory of her.

Nora hadn't been touched intimately for so long. She had forgotten the allure of tenderness, plagued as she was with memories of Liam, the way he held her hand too tightly in public, as if she might escape; his temper playing itself out between the sheets.

A thin line exists between being terrified and being thrilled. So different from Liam's demands and degradations, the priest's touch was gentle and drew her out of the past and into the moment, attuned not only to his hands on her, but her hands on him. The tempo swept her away. All their rationale, all their resistance, all their moral reserve went up the chimney with the smoke; and they became, at last, one. They thrashed at one another, rising and falling together.

She pulled on him. He pushed into her. ✑ They moved like ocean waves until she crested and broke and crashed on a shore, relinquishing a great, long, deep moan; he withdrew and with an impassioned grunt his semen pooled onto her bare stomach.

And the shame set in even before their sweat cooled.

Nora screamed inside. She wriggled out from beneath him and pulled a portion of the scratchy blanket over herself.

They held one another and said nothing. They did not speak of the beautifully steamy build-up, the loss of faculties, the astonishing release, the floating sensation, the oneness they had experienced. They did not caress one another or kiss one another lightly here and there. They knew they had stolen a moment. And that in another moment, it would be over.

He was the first to break their embrace. She got up and dressed. As she gathered her clothes from the floor, she met Puccini's gaze that seemed to hold not so much judgment as sorrow.

The priest dressed. ✒ Nora noticed his shirt was buttoned crookedly. He paced. Clenched and unclenched his hands.

Nora considered telling him about his shirt, but it felt all wrong. She just wanted to leave. Escape. "I need to go," she said. "Home."

"Right." He said. His voice was low, gravelly, pained. "I'll drive you." ✒

They did not look at one another. He held out her jacket for her, gentlemanly, but she yanked it from his hands. She pulled her hat and mittens from her pockets.

He said, "You've got to know that this isn't easy for me, either."

Nora dropped her head and threw up her hands. Words came to mind but coagulated in her throat.

He picked up his keys. Puccini barked and hustled to the door. "Puccini, no!" he said sharply. The dog slumped on the floor, head on front paws, eyes pleading.

The priest held the door open for Nora, and they stepped into the bracing cold. He drove her home at almost four o'clock; and Nora felt that they were the only two people on the planet.

As Nora reached her front step, she saw Mrs. Quincy's porch light go on. Nora quickly stepped inside and locked the door. She pulled off her boots and socks and with measured fury threw them in the corner. A rapping at the door sobered her. Nora stood still. The knocking continued.

She opened the door never expecting that the old woman would venture out in the middle of a blizzard, in the middle of the night.

"Still think he's harmless?" Mrs. Quincy asked. Over her flannel nightgown, the old woman wore a long fur coat.

"Nothing happened," Nora lied.

"Nothing until 4 a.m.? I may be old, but I'm not senile. Did you realize you're missing an earring?" she asked.

Nora's fingers shot to her earlobes, and sure enough, she felt only one hoop. Her heart filled with anguish.

"How can you be so quick to judge? Isn't that what happened to Jesus?"

"Jesus was innocent!" Mrs. Quincy snapped.

"What crime has Vin committed?" Nora asked in a hushed voice, trying to muffle her shrill tone.

"'Vin' is it now? That's familiar, isn't it?" The old woman stabbed her cane into the floor. "It's one thing for him to lie to you. It's another thing for him to lie to his parishioners. But he's lying to himself, as well."

"It's not like he's molested kids!" Nora waved her arms. "It's not like he's embezzled from the collection basket!"

"Now you're reaching. It's hardly the same. He's made a mess of things."

"Haven't we all?" Nora asked.

"We're not in charge of the well being of an entire community of faith. He's making a mockery of the priesthood."

"He's not the only one. You can't tell me you believe this sort of thing never happens."

She looked Nora in the eye. "He's way out of line now, and he needs to step down."

"And who will stand in his place?" Nora asked.

"The archbishop will appoint another rector."

"Nobody will replace him."

"Not in your mind," Mrs. Quincy said. "You've allowed yourself to fall in love with the man."

"*Allowed* myself?"

"Don't act as if you have no choices."

"Then tell me what to do."

"I'm not your grandmother, but if I were, I'd tell you you're as much an addict as he is."

◈ ◈ ◈

The St. Valentine's Day storm draped Colorado, raging, dumping three feet of snow on the metro area, seven in the high county. Winds whitened the landscape, howled through cracks in the weather-stripping, buffeted the doors. Denver shut down. The power flicked off and on. The phone was dead.

Nora slept a lot, too much. Woke tired. Her throat burned. She took echinacea tincture and drank hot tea with honey. She gargled with hot salt water, to no avail. She looked in the mirror, opened wide and saw her disgusting tonsils raw red and white-spotted.

Delirious, she went back to bed, intermittently sweating and shivering. She took a hot bath, turned the electric blanket to "high." Still, chills shook her until the fever turned a corner. She grew hot again, feeling as if the wires in the blanket might at any minute burst into flames. She slept on and off all day and through the night. Dreaming. Delirious.

She woke up the next morning to the telephone ring; and immediately upon opening her eyes Nora knew she was sick, dreadfully sick. A cough came on, a phlegmy bark.

The phone rang again. ✒ She snapped out of the remnants of a panicky dream.

"Hullo?" Her voice was groggy. "Hang on," she said through her hacking. She blew her nose. She said "Sorry," but it came out "Thorry." ✒

"You caught a cold."

It's him! She sneezed.

"You sound awful," the priest said.

"I'm fine."

"I shouldn't have had you out in that weather."

"It wasn't that," she said. "Actually, you catch cold from a virus, not from getting wet and chilled."

"Nevertheless," he said. "Are you taking anything?"

"Nah." She sneezed again. Her chest rattled. Her eyes burned and watered. "I've been drinking lots of hot tea with honey. And juice." The truth was she hadn't been taking care of herself.

"Did you call your doctor?"

"No, really, I'm fine."

"You don't sound fine. How 'bout I make you some soup and bring it over?"

Her throat burned. Even the roof of her mouth itched. She hurt from the part in her hair to the soles of her feet. "You don't have to do that."

"Do you have a fever?"

"I don't know," she said. "I don't have a thermometer."

"Have you had chills? Or sweats?"

"Both," she said.

"Get decent, I'm on my way," and he hung up the phone just before she dropped back into bed.

When the doorbell rang, Nora was sleeping again, huddled under an afghan. She had no indication of which end of the bed her head was on or what time it was or even which day of the week. Lethargy dashed her entire aching body. Clammy, she shivered and sweated. She couldn't muster energy enough to get up. "Come in," she said, her own voice an unrecognizable croak.

The door opened; Puccini burst in, barked his greeting. Father

DiMarco carried several containers, a plastic grocery sack dangled from his wrist. The priest kicked the door closed behind him.

Half delirious, Nora got out of bed and made her way down the stairs from the loft. She paused, unsure of how to greet him. The nape of her neck was damp with perspiration. She slumped on the couch, amazed that he was actually there in reality, that she wasn't dreaming.

He held the back of his hand to her forehead, her cheeks. "Holy Mother of God. You're feverish."

Self-consciousness returned when she realized she was wearing long underwear printed with polar bears, plaid flannel pajamas, a fleece ski band, wool socks and a terry cloth robe. She wished he could see her, instead, in lacy lingerie.

"Who's your doctor?" he asked, pouring soup into a pan on the stove.

She hugged a heating pad and curled under her Hudson Bay blanket. She couldn't control her shivers. Before long, he tried to spoon minestrone into her mouth. She moaned. "I can't swallow." She coughed and held her hands to her throat.

"You must have strep," he said.

"Or tonsillitis," she squeaked. "I'm so tired."

"I know, I know," he said, smoothing her hair. He pulled a box of cough drops from his coat pocket. "You need something stronger than this."

"I don't want to call my doctor," she said.

"And I don't want to give you Last Rites." He squeezed her wrist. "You're sick. You need medicine. Where's your doctor's number?"

"It's in the book," she muttered. "It's Doctor Finesilver. Ira Finesilver."

"Everything's OK," he said. "You'll be fine. Let's see if the doctor's office is open."

She gently felt the swollen glands in her neck as he walked into the kitchen, dialed the phone number. Her neck went floppy. She drifted, unable to keep her eyes open.

Father DiMarco said, "I actually got through to him. I mean, he took the call. It's a slow day in his office, he said. A lot of cancellations, no shows. Anyway, he phoned in a prescription for you. He said you have a history of tonsillitis?"

She nodded. She closed her eyes and whimpered, "I haven't had it for a long time. ✖ Maybe this is God's wrath because we..."

"No, No. I don't think God punishes us. We punish ourselves. You're run down; plus, you've been working in that cold cathedral," he said. "How 'bout that soup now?" She turned away. He opened the grocery sack he'd brought. "I know you like pudding—it's vanilla!"

"We shouldn't have done that," she said.

"Shh," he touched her chin. "Not now. You're ill. I'm going to make you a hot toddy." ✖ He lifted up a bottle of whiskey he'd brought. She made a mental note of how much booze was in the bottle. He mixed whiskey, honey, lemon juice, boiling water from the kettle. "It'll make you sleep well."

She coughed and held her palm on her sandy throat. "That's all I've been doing. I don't ever sleep well; but I've been asleep for days. Dreaming like a mad woman! I don't want to sleep. I want to talk."

"We will," he said, "but I'm going to go pick up your prescription."

Nora couldn't help but smile. "I'm glad you're here."

"Rest," he said.

And she did.

When he sat on the edge of the couch, Nora woke up again.

"Your medicine." She sat up and took the pills. Father DiMarco balanced a ramekin on his knee. He blew steam off the small bowl. "An old Italian mama cure. And it works." He held up a spoonful of something purplish.

"What is it?" she asked, wrinkling her nose.

"Apples cooked in red wine and sugar."

"You think booze cures everything."

"Eat." He waved a spoon in front of her mouth.

"Aah," she fanned her mouth. "Hot, hot, hot."

"Sorry. Has to be hot, though. It helps you sweat out the cold. It helps you sleep. And it gives you some nourishment. Here," he held out another spoonful.

She finished the concoction; and before she knew it broke a sweat and started to doze.

"Why don't you go back to bed," he said, handing her a box of tissues. ✑

She pulled several, blew her nose. With zero resistance, she slowly climbed the stairs to the loft. Puccini followed her. The dog jumped up on her bed, snuggled in with her.

The priest called, "Puccini, come!" several times, but the dog stayed with Nora. And with one hand on the dog's rising and falling back, Nora tumbled into a fevered sleep.

✑ ✑ ✑

When the zealous sun poured through the slats of the Venetian blinds the next morning, Nora plunged into wakefulness. When she walked out to the living room, she saw Father DiMarco wrapped in the Hudson Bay blanket on the window seat. He stared at the ceiling. A wine glass, empty, balanced on his prayer book on the ottoman, which he'd pulled alongside the window seat.

"Good morning," she said. Puccini wiggled and whined.

"Good morning yourself," he said drowsily. "Welcome back." He yawned.

"You stayed?"

"I couldn't just leave my dog here," he said with a smirk.

"Mrs. Quincy will see your truck!"

"Mrs. Quincy has her own secrets."

"What do you mean?" she asked.

"You look like you've rounded the bend. See? That old Italian mama cure. What did I tell you?"

"I guess it worked. Or the drugs did. Something."

Pasty in her pajamas still damp from sweating, she longed for a shower and clean clothes. "Thanks for everything," she said. "You must think I'm a case. I mean, first anaphylactic shock, and now tonsillitis—but I hardly ever get sick, really." She realized she hadn't had a full-blown migraine in months.

"We all need a little help from time to time. Listen. I have to tell you," he sat up, "because I think these sorts of things too often go unsaid. I want you to know that it has meant a great deal to me to be able to," he paused, "care for you."

She sneezed. He held out the box of tissues for her. "As a pastor, I've been loved by a lot of people. ❧ I've eaten in their homes; I've participated in the lives of their families during turnstile moments like baptisms and weddings and funerals. ❧ First Communion, Confirmation parties. I've counseled them; I've cared for them spiritually. I've been gifted by them at Christmas, even remembered in a few wills.

"But, Nora, there's something very powerful, very profound about giving concrete care. What I mean is, I don't know how to express it, except to say that I enjoyed taking care of you. Sometimes, I'm so intent on taking away people's pain in a Godly way that I forget I might do so in a human way."

She wanted to sit in his lap. She wanted to rest her head on his shoulder and feel the warm press of his holy hands molding her played-out muscles. She wanted to welcome him between the layers of eiderdown with her.

But she could barely keep her eyes focused. Her head nodded. Dimwitted, she worried that she might say something inappropriate. She worked the tip of her tongue around her eye teeth.

"You need to climb back into bed," he said. "I'll bring you a pill; and then I'm going to let myself out."

When she woke up again, she felt considerably better. She noticed that not much whiskey was gone from the bottle he'd brought. ✍ She took a long shower, put on fresh pjs, towel-dried her hair, all the while remembering him feeding her wine-soaked apples. In some ways, she realized, she was sicker than ever. If she'd had a white flag, she would've waved it.

FEAST OF THE CHAIR OF ST. PETER (22 February)

To Nora's astonishment, she itched to get back to the glass. And, if she were honest with herself, back to Father DiMarco.

"I can't thank you enough for coming over and taking care of me," she said as soon as she saw him in the rectory kitchen.

"I told you. It was my pleasure," he undid his Roman collar.

"I don't know how to thank you, but I did think of one thing."

The little strip of white plastic jutted out of his clerical shirt. "Yes?"

"I'd like to start walking Puccini for you. In the morning before I start and either on my lunch break or after work. I know he loves to go for a walk. And I know you're busy."

"That's considerate," he reached out for her hands. "I'm so glad you're OK."

And just then, Millie walked in. They quickly pulled back their hands. Nora's face went red. Her back to them, Millie banged some pots and pans on the stove.

Nora started to snake out of the room with Puccini on his leash.

"Oh, by the way, Father," Millie said, reaching into her apron pocket. "I found this while I was vacuuming." She opened her palm to reveal a silver hoop with a dangling pearl.

☙ ☙ ☙

Nora couldn't help but notice the cold and spiteful stares from some of the parishioners. She walked to the alley one pleasant morning, and the food line volunteers would not look her in the eye. Juan stopped bringing by her paycheck and started mailing it.

Determined to make the windows so wonderful people would

have to acknowledge her, she soldiered valiantly on. She called upon her ancestors, the tellers of stories long buried deep in the moist Olde Sod. She begged the intercession of the one who first had taken up the glass.

Ever since they made love in the rectory, Nora avoided the house. Father DiMarco didn't seem to notice. Feeling shunned led Nora deeper into emotional entanglement with the pastor, yet never did they mention the truckload of winter wear, the candor of the Canada geese on the ice, that night in front of the fireplace, the lost earring, the lost innocence. They didn't mention Millie or Juan or Mrs. Quincy or anybody else.

They created a vacuum for themselves. They talked, instead, about theology, Christeology, ecclesiology—subjects safe for their loftiness, as if intellectual conversation could quell heart's desire.

Nora walked the dog at least twice a day. She observed Puccini, curious about his habits: the way he sniffed at trees and rolled in the grass and bolted after squirrels. Puccini curled up beneath her table as she worked.

One afternoon, as Nora was sharpening her cutting wheel, she heard a whistle. Puccini dashed out the door.

"Not only have you taken over my parking space, you've taken over my dog," the priest said.

Nora couldn't be certain whether he was genuinely annoyed or just joking. Or both.

Puccini panted. Nora took a dog biscuit from her pocket. "Puccini, catch!" she said. She tossed the treat high in the air and he caught it.

"Oh," the priest said. "Bribery. I see."

"I've never had a dog."

"The archbishop wants the windows ready by Easter," the priest said abruptly.

"Easter?" Her face fell. "Are you serious?"

Puccini turned circles, plopped down with a sneeze.

"He wants Easter vigil in the cathedral."

Nora planted her hands on her hip bones. "He wants me out of here," she said. "Somebody said something."

"I know; I know," he said.

"What will he do?" she asked. "He can't fire you, can he?"

"He can reassign me."

Shame swallowed Nora. She turned her back on him.

"What do I tell Archbishop?"

She turned to face him again. She noticed how haggard he looked. "About the windows or about us?"

"Please, Nora," he whispered. "I don't want any trouble. For me or for you. Can we finish by Easter?"

"Yes," she said, fully aware that the end of the job would mean the end of their relationship.

He pressed his hands together and bowed slightly toward her, "Thank you." The priest left, but the pooch stayed.

"You're a good dog, Puccini," Nora told the dog. 🙰 "And I'm a bad girl."

MARDI GRAS (24 February)

To keep her promise to the priest, Nora abandoned her own hopes and worked later and later into the evenings. During the days, she noted the people who came in to light candles or place flowers before statues. They prayed with heads bowed or eyes fixed on the crucifix above the altar. Nora preferred the solitude and relative silence after everyone had left. Unless Father DiMarco and Puccini kept her company.

On the night of Mardi Gras, while she was leading glass, the priest showed up with a six-pack. She could tell from his loose carriage that he'd already had a few.

"Behold, I bring you tidings of Fat Tuesday," he said, presenting the beer as if gold or frankincense or myrrh.

"No, thanks," Nora said.

He opened a beer and handed it to her, "No one's around."

With his hand so near her body, Nora's breath accelerated. "I've got an Easter deadline."

"But Lent begins tomorrow. We have 40 more days." She couldn't resist him. She accepted the beer. He opened a second can and raised it to meet hers. "Tonight's the night to eat, drink, make merry."

"I'm merry enough," she said, taking a sip, recalling Irish coffee by the fire.

"You don't strike me as merry. Musing, reflective, ruminative, yes. But merry? No."

She hated herself for going along with him, for pretending nothing was wrong with drinking beer with him and wishing they'd find themselves in bed. ✍ She knew from her dreadful days in group therapy—back when she was trying to redeem Liam—that she was enabling the priest. She knew she couldn't make him stop drinking. And if he did stop, she had to wonder, would he still feel as wanton about spending so much time with her?

He said, "I think you'd be more merry if you let God back into your life."

Nora tried to remember Midnight Mass. Communion. Smelling the wine at the monastery. The opening of herself. But she would not march with the Magisterium that kept him away from her. "Just accept that I don't count myself a member of your Church anymore. I'm pagan."

"You can't be pagan," he said.

"I am."

"You were baptized."

"Technically speaking, I'm a born-again pagan," she said. "Instead of getting religion, I got nature. And art."

"You can't come to a dead halt at nature and art. You have to follow them to their source. You're Catholic."

"Not anymore," she said.

"Once a Catholic, always a Catholic."

"Isn't that what they say about alcoholics?" His grimace was barely perceptible, but as soon as it was fired she regretted her shot across the bow. To change the subject she asked, "When did you decide to become a priest, anyway?"

He crushed an empty beer can. "I was in 5th grade. I heard that Gospel asking 'What good does it for a man to gain the world, but lose his soul?' I thought, 'Well, what's the best way to save my soul? I'll become a priest.' So to begin with, it was very narcissistic, very self-serving. But it grew from there. I love people. Like you. I would never have met you if I hadn't been a priest."

"You don't know that. We might have met in a bar," she said. He scowled. "So you love people. And you want to save them."

"I like to help, if I am able, particularly in spiritual matters. I like to think of myself as someone with an outstretched hand, inviting people into the Kingdom. I'm inviting *you*."

"You're proselytizing."

"Is that what you think?" he asked, his face going sour.

With her grozier, she ground away a last bit of rough edge. She rapped the jaws of the pliers on her workbench for emphasis. "Look," she said, shaking her head, "what do I have to do to convince you?"

"Give God one more shot: Keep a holy Lent."

"Oh. That's good," she said. "And, by the way, quick. Have you, by any chance, rehearsed this?"

"You asked," he turned his beer bottoms up. He had drunk three to her one. "Tomorrow is Ash Wednesday. The timing is right."

It occurred to Nora that some men wanted their women wearing flashy fashions, exhibiting sex appeal, and other men needed their women to be nurturing homemakers, but maybe what Vin needed was a woman of faith. "I always liked Ash Wednesday," she said. "I think the whole thing is humbling: walking around with a black blotch right in the middle of your forehead."

" 'Remember, woman, that you are dust,' " he said, paraphrasing the rite. " 'And unto dust you shall return.' "

"Nothing," said Nora, "is more accomplished than smoke and ash."

"So what have you got to lose?"

"Forty days," she said.

"Forty days doesn't account for much in the face of eternity." He stifled a belch, "I beg your pardon," he reached out and touched her wrist. She squiggled in her skin. "Nora, I work with people. You think I can't tell you harbor an abiding unhappiness?"

"And you know why."

"Liam wasn't your fault."

"That's not what I'm talking about," she said, wanting to fling her glass cutter at him.

"I know," he said. "I was thinking that this might wipe the slate clean, if you're feeling as guilt-ridden as I am."

And she could see in the moment that heartache burdened him, too. She wasn't sure whether she was the source of his pain or the antidote, but she knew his drinking couldn't be part of the equation. She wanted him, but she wanted him sober.

"I am," she said. "One year in junior high, I gave up chocolate for Lent. And when Easter finally rolled around, I bit the ears off my chocolate bunny; and I'd never tasted anything so sweet."

"See?" he said. "What do you say?"

"OK, I'm in, under one condition."

"Name it," he said.

"I get to decide what you give up for Lent." The mood swerved. The air in the room altered. She gathered her nerve and said, "Booze."

He paused, stunned. "I have to drink wine," he said, picking up his harlequin act, animated. "It's part of my job description."

She said, "Nothing but sacramental wine during Mass."

"For 40 days?"

"And nights."

He said, "All I can do is try." ✒

In the name of the Father ⊠ and of the Son ⊠ and of the Holy Spirit.⊠

Dust unto dust. You take away the sin of the world, but you leave me with temptation at every turn. Will you not turn stones to bread? ⊠ I want to follow you, ⊠ Master; but I am weak and weary and wondering: If you are the God of mercy and forgiveness, could you forgive my change of heart? I ask for patience, Lord, and discernment. If there is another path for me, reveal it. ⊠ I ask to pilgrimage through one more Lent, one more span of 40 days toward death and dying that come before—God willing—resurrection. ⊠ I would make my way to the City of Grace.⊠ ⊠ ⊠ ⊠

Messiah, you know all too well betrayal; yet did you ever betray yourself? In your humanity, did you ever know self-loathing? Did your palms ever sweat at the sight of a woman? ⊠ Did your body give in to worldliness? ⊠ ⊠ How can you mandate

the gift of celibacy, Father, any more than you can mandate the gift of prophecy or the gift of healing? ⊠ ⊠ ⊠

Lord, I would, if I could, make the blind see. ⊠ I would call up the lame, liberate their limbs. I would forgive sins, as you forgave. ⊠ ⊠ ⊠ I would forgive my own. ⊠ When you healed, were you, too, healed? If I am to lead your people of covenant, strengthen me. ⊠ ⊠ If I am to serve you, God, and the people of God, I beseech Thee, grant me saving grace. ⊠ ⊠ ⊠

In the name of the Father and of the Son and of the Holy Spirit. ⊠ AMEN. ⊠

CHAPTER FIVE

Lent

ASH WEDNESDAY (25 February)

ora wanted to see whether he would hold up his heavy end of the deal if she held up hers. She wished she could interact with him sober, entirely sober. He occupied her thoughts almost constantly. If she could not have commitment, she would settle for companionship. She'd take him in any form. She'd settle. She wanted to show him the mammoth oak tree she passed every day on the way to the cathedral. She wanted to pack a winter picnic and sit in the stone shelter at Daniel's Park, overlooking the foothills. Of course, she wanted him carnally, as well. The lure of losing herself to him again thrilled her. Orgasm echoed in her body. She remembered his chain with the oval depicting Mary dangling from his neck, like a pendulum between her thighs, hypnotizing her.

She foolishly gambled that drawing closer to the Church would draw him closer to her. Before work, she opened her mother's Lane cedar chest—repository of sentimental personal history. She dug out an old, white leather-bound devotional prayer book. The little volume bore an inscription from her parents on the occasion of her First Holy Communion. She flipped through the traditional prayers: the Acts of Faith, Hope, Love and Contrition. Phrases unwound in her memory. She heard the lowered voice of her mother praying *The Memorare* laden with mysticism: "...inspired by this confidence, I fly unto you...."

Nora saw herself as that girl in the starched Campbell plaid pleated jumper of Saint Oliver Plunkett School basking in the glow of another gold foil star bestowed for another prayer memorized. Such small rewards she cherished then. Such clear-cut expectations of her. Not that she had understood the prayers—not intellectually, anyhow. Nonetheless, she had recited those words with purity and piety, a soul questing for sainthood, or at least the convent.

From her cordoned-off work area, Nora had kept an eye on the life of the cathedral. Just the day before, she had looked up from her work to observe a funeral. Only a few mourners were present. Junior high students in their acolyte garb reverently carried the processional cross, the lectionary, the thurible smoking with nose-tickling incense.

Going a step further than Universal Church norms, Nora fasted all day in the strictest sense of the word, taking nothing but water, wanting to start strong. She thought long and hard about what to "give up" for Lent. She was playing by the rules, and decided that for 40 days she would clean up her act and stop cursing.

At Mass that Ash Wednesday morning, she watched the priest position his hands as he blessed last year's burned palm branches: "Father in heaven," he prayed, eyes closed, "the light of your truth bestows sight to the darkness of sinful eyes. May this season of repentance bring us the blessing of your forgiveness and the gift of your light. Grant this through Christ our Lord."

And Nora responded, "Amen."

❦ ❦ ❦

Together with devout Catholics the world round, during Lent Nora abstained from meat on Fridays. Above and beyond the Lenten obligation, she fasted by Catholic standards each Wednesday, allowing herself only one full meal or sometimes ate virtually nothing all day. ❦ Fasting slowly, she liked to call it, because in her half-starved state, time seemed to pleat. But every time a ravenous pang clamped her gut, she considered the people in the cathedral's food line, people who filtered through Dumpsters behind fast-food restaurants, hoping to find a few bites to eat. People like Two-Wheel Rich. Her stomach gripped and griped, but every time hunger broke her concentration, she offered up her one measly act of solidarity that it might diminish in some small way the global injustice of basic human needs gone unmet.

The major difference was, of course, that any time she chose she could open the refrigerator or order Chinese or walk into a restaurant and stuff herself, satiating her appetite and caving in to the temptation toward gluttony. She came to realize that she had choices that many people couldn't fathom.

And she became acutely aware of just how much she cursed.

Nora was desperate for transformation; and the familiarity of ritual comforted her. So she fasted. She gave alms. And she prayed. Morning and evening she got down on her knees and prayed. She prayed the old prayers. The ones she had memorized as a girl in Catholic school. And she prayed extemporaneously, talking to God as granddad, as therapist, as genie.

Some afternoons after she finished for the day, she lined up her tools on her bench and prayed the Stations of the Cross at 5:15. The liturgy drew regulars: young mothers, business people in suits, mostly elderly parishioners. Nuns. Millie, invariably, was there in her chapel veil. And, occasionally, Millie shot nasty looks Nora did her best to ignore.

Above all, Nora poured herself into her work. She lavished care and craft upon every detail. *God, after all, is in the details. Or is the devil in the details?* Nora could never remember. ❧ She felt like a hypocritical sap at times, but, in earnest, she made of every effort a prayer. She had no intention of taking Lent so seriously, yet something bound her. Buoyed up, she forged ahead. And the work slid into a flow of relative effortlessness. She practically disappeared into the grand form of the windows taking shape.

At the cathedral, she worked maniacally toward the goal of completing the job in time for Easter. Momentum built. Her work took on a piercing focus as she closed in on the deadline. Her ambition ran high. Physically, mentally, spiritually, she felt better than she had in years. Engaged. Energized. Sure-handed. Work days filled with ease. Time skipped like a stone on a lake.

Each day, as they came together, the windows revealed more of themselves: colors, patterns, intricacies. As the work took shape, elation zinged her. Process was one thing. Progress another. And Nora knew she was succeeding on both counts. Even after a long day, she didn't want to put down her tools. She didn't want to leave the glass, attempting to channel lust into creativity, lead into gold.

ๆ *ๆ* *ๆ*

One evening, as Nora rode home after work, for the first time she noticed the cherry tree at the corner of Mrs. Quincy's large lot. She remembered her mother's Easter tradition: Each Lent, Nora's mother had cut branches from the back yard cherry tree and arranged them in a heavy vase of water and sand. *ๆ* From the branches she hung blown eggs, dyed and decorated. She added tiny straw hats with thin satin ribbons and silk flowers. Petite porcelain birds nested here and there in her mother's Easter tree. And before Lent ended every year, the white cherry blossoms opened, just in time.

What would Mother make of all this? she asked herself, knowing full well. ❧

Nora reluctantly pressed the doorbell and the Westminster chimes sounded inside Mrs. Quincy's foyer. The evening was so quiet that Nora could hear the old woman's heels clicking on the parquet floor as she made her way to the front door. She hoped that time had cooled Mrs. Quincy's temper.

"What is it?" Mrs. Quincy asked curtly.

Nora bumbled through an explanation of her mother's Easter tradition. "Would you mind if I lop off a few branches?"

"Be my guest," the old lady said, "if you think that will make you feel better."

"I know I'm acting like a fool."

"I can't argue with that." Mrs. Quincy looked Nora in the eye. She handed over her cigarette case.

They took seats in the wing chairs that flanked the fireplace in Mrs. Quincy's living room. ❧ The old woman's collection of glass paperweights caught Nora's eye. She noted the prominently displayed portraits of family members who rarely came to call. Her eyes came to rest on a sepia photo of Mr. and Mrs. Quincy on their wedding day.

Nora held Mrs. Quincy's wrist to steady her hand as she lit the cigarette for her. The old lady's nails were freshly manicured. Her stacks of platinum and diamond rings nearly reached her knuckles. She breathed in the smoke as if it were salvation. "A vice, I admit," she exhaled. "And probably a sin, as well."

To avoid a conversation about sin Nora reported, "I finished sealing the rose window today."

Mrs. Quincy's hand covered her heart. "My favorite. That band of angels," she said. "Rumor has it there's a bell named St. Cecilia in the tower. The inscription says that she's the angel at the organ. La-di-da."

Nora grinned. "Looks like everything will be installed in time for Holy Week."

"And the parish mission—are you planning to attend? A lot of these speakers are for the birds, if you ask me, but we're having the abbot from the Trappist monastery in Old Snowmass. He's the real thing. St. Benedict's is a marvelous place. The monks bake cookies and…"

"I've been there," Nora said, instantly regretting her admission.

"Really? When?"

Nora looked away. "I wanted to see their grisaille window. *Grisaille* means 'painted gray,'" she said.

Mrs. Quincy raised an eyebrow. "Oh?"

"The Cistercians had a mandate for austerity. In 1134, they had a decree ordering that windows be clear glass and without images. Not even crosses. And then about 50 years later, they had another decree that forced the monks to fast on bread and water if the windows weren't replaced. So the Cistercians—to comply with the rule, but still have lovely glass—created these quietly beautiful windows."

"You sound like a docent." Mrs. Quincy snuffed out her cigarette. "When did you go up?"

"Last fall," Nora said, vague as fog.

"When Father DiMarco was on retreat?"

Nora said nothing, which said it all.

Mrs. Quincy got up from her chair, grabbed her cane, walked to the foyer. "Don't you read the papers?" she asked over her shoulder. "Don't you get the 10 o'clock news?"

"No," Nora said, honestly. She got up from her chair and went to the foyer, where Mrs. Quincy held open the front door.

"Just because these sexual misconduct cases are focused on pedophilia now doesn't mean that the heat hasn't been turned up across the board," she said. "Soon the women will come forward, too. In droves."

Nora took a step toward the open door. She bit her tongue, but then couldn't prevent herself from asking, "Will you be one of them?"

The old woman dropped her rosewood cane on the parquet floor. For an instant, neither woman moved, their eyes locked. Nora bent, picked up the cane, held it level across her open hands and extended it as if a peace offering.

Mrs. Quincy snatched the cane and rapped its tip on the floor several times. She closed the door, pointed back to the living room. "Sit," she said. ✒

And Nora did, crossing her legs tightly.

The old woman lowered herself slowly to the seat of her chair, adjusted her house dress over her lap, folded her hands across her narrow chest. "I know what it is to love a priest."

"You do?" Relief rushed over Nora, her intuition affirmed.

She shook her white-haired head and continued: "After Mr. Quincy died so suddenly, I was fit to be tied. Once the kids went back to their lives, once people stopped calling or stopping by, I was lost. I had relied on my husband for so much. That I knew, but I had never realized what a companion he was. We had braided our lives. We had traveled together, played bridge together, entertained together. We had raised our family together, yes, but then we'd gone on to have a wonderful life as a couple again. Once he was gone, all that was gone, too."

"I'm sorry," Nora said. "I…"

But Mrs. Quincy held a finger to her wrinkled lips to quiet Nora. "Naturally, I turned to God. ✒ I started going to daily Mass, volunteering for everything under the sun. At the time, there was a retired priest assigned to the cathedral. He joined the pinochle group and became my partner. Back then, I didn't have the heart to play bridge without Mr. Quincy.

"Well, pretty soon this priest and I started to spend more time together, just involved in ministry, at first. We sorted the donated clothing for the shelter. We counted the collection on Sunday. He was the chaplain for the seniors' club, and he went along on all our outings. We were sweet on one another. And before I knew it, we were more than pinochle partners."

Nora stared at the old woman as she lit her own cigarette and smiled at the memory of the man. She tried to dampen the eager curiosity in her tone when she asked, "But what about his vow of celibacy?"

"You're confusing celibacy with chastity. All Catholic priests take the vow of celibacy, which forbids them from marrying. Whereas, technically, chastity is not a vow, but a virtue that tempers sexuality. ✺ It's a common confusion—almost as common as the confusion about the Immaculate Conception and the virgin birth," On the rim of a crystal ashtray, Mrs. Quincy rolled her cigarette ash into a point. "In our case, we weren't sexual partners, but make no mistake: It was an affair. We didn't make love, but we were in love. We fooled around a bit, but in those days we maintained a sense of decorum. We kept it venial."

Nora leaned forward, elbows on her knees. "And what happened?"

"More like what didn't happen. ✺ I assumed he might seek laicization—you know, that's where the fellow leaves and gets a sort of pardon. He would have lost his priestly faculties, but he would have gained me. Pshaw!"

"He didn't leave?"

"He did leave. He left the parish. He got reassigned, just pulled up his stakes and left."

"And you never heard from him again?"

"Oh, from time to time. A Christmas card or two. And then I saw his obituary in the newspaper a few years back." She clucked her tongue. "They're like boys, Nora. They never have a chance to mature. They don't marry. They never come into sexual maturity. They have a lot of women in the parish who want to mother them. They have Big Daddy Archbishop. They never really grow up, most of them. And yet they're expected to be leaders." She wrung her hands. "Regardless, it goes without saying that I felt my share of punishment: guilt, regret, loneliness." ॐ

"God didn't punish you. You go to daily Mass. You give money to charity. You volunteer. You raised three children. Why would God punish you?"

"Because I strayed too far off His path."

"You really believe that? What about your God of love? What about His everlasting mercy? And the idea that we're under grace— not under the law?"

Mrs. Quincy took a long drag on her cigarette, exhaled slowly. "Perhaps I've punished myself."

ST. JOHN OF GOD (8 March)

Ever since Mrs. Quincy confessed about her affair with a priest, Nora's thoughts turned torturous. As Nora painted glass, she shifted into an artistic trance that allowed her hand and eye to work while her mind roamed among the ruins of her consciousness. Nora imagined every possible scenario from forging a friendship with him to muttering her first name with his surname: Nora DiMarco. She imagined them living in Evergreen, on the sunny side of a creek, with a big kitchen where he could cook, and a barn for her studio. One minute, Nora stood firmly in trust that Vin was different from Mrs. Quincy's priest. He had made love to her, after all. Mrs. Quincy had proffered that her affair was not sexual. They couldn't have had the same connection, she told herself.

Yet, Nora couldn't shake the shock that she and Vin had actually had sex. She'd grown up knowing many priests, and she'd always assumed they were chaste. *How common is this?* she wondered. She speculated what he might want, what he was thinking. On one hand, she felt rage, maddened that he could go on acting as if nothing had transpired. On the other hand, she felt compassion, knowing he was trying to be a good priest, which only made her feel bad about herself, tempting him. ✍ Eve with her shiny, tart apple.

But in the next breath, Nora fell into a downward spiral, clinging to a firm conviction that Mrs. Quincy was right. Nora remembered the old woman pointing a finger and saying, "Some priests prey on women with flat spots on their wheels." Nora knew exactly what that meant; and she resented that Vin knew all about her flat spot. *A* Nora could plainly see that the pastor flirted with lots of women—not just her.

She tried not to think about their carnal encounter. Then she worked to recall every detail: the breadth of his shoulders, the heat of his breath as he had nestled her. She wondered whether they'd ever find their way to a bed together.

Nora was at a breaking point, feeling fragile as glass. She wished she could find a space for retreat and dispensation. She could no longer cope. She wanted only to relax into verdant green pastures of catatonia. The departure, she knew, could be easy, swallowing a handful of pills, merely a slipping out.

The return trip? Reparation? Not such a lark.

ST. PATRICK (17 March)

The sanctuary light burned. Members of the Perpetual Adoration Society kept vigil. More and more, as the restoration wound down, Millie inhabited the cathedral space, preparing for Holy Week and Easter. Wearing her chapel veil and surgical gloves, she polished the monstrance, a well-buffed silver and gold starburst on a pedestal ringed with sparkling precious stones. Nora watched

Millie gaze into the little round glass housing the Host. They didn't speak. But Nora caught Millie from time to time with her eyes lifted to the windows, softly smiling at the glass.

Nora's work seemed only burdensome and tedious. Blasphemous. She burned out on the mundane aspects, the brain-damaging details, setback after setback: fractured glass, unsuccessful firings in the kiln, chips, cracks, breaks, shatters. Slivers and shards in her fingers. ✒ The glass was temperamental as she was. Unforgiving.

She waxed up the window of Jesus in the Garden of Gethsemane, preparing to paint. To hold the pieces in place temporarily, she dabbed thumb wax on the shapes of the rock on which Christ leaned.

Her Lenten discipline of "giving up" had worn off considerably. Crankiness ruled. She was tired of hunger pangs on Wednesdays. She wanted to take all the change she'd saved and rush out to buy new yoga togs. ✒ On Fridays, she wanted a T-bone steak grilled medium rare; and she wanted to pick up that steak with her bare hands and with her teeth rip the meat from the bone.

But that was the least of it. She couldn't keep the pastor out of her mind. Far more than meat or money to spend frivolously, she wanted love. Real love. Not a fantasy, not forbidden love. She wanted somebody who loved her unabashedly. In return, she would risk her heart. She pined for someone to kiss in public, hold hands with in movies, somebody who cared about the details of her days. Somebody who showed up sober. Somebody available.

Don't I deserve that much? And in asking the question, she began to discern her answer.

ST. ENDA (21 March)

Nora stood in the center of the nave. In her peripheral vision, she saw light from an open door. She expected the priest, but a layman entered the cathedral, a guy in his late 30s. Tall. Ruggedly handsome. Refined in his dress and his manner.

He didn't genuflect and kneel in a pew. He didn't drop money into a metal box and light a candle before a side altar. He didn't open the book of prayer petitions and add an entry.

He made a bee-line to Nora. The report of his heels on the marble echoed. "Are you Nora?" he asked. He reached out his hand. She looked down at hers, grimy from dust. "I'm Will Taylor." His eyes flickered. She realized they were hazel, almost the color of the autumnal foliage in the background of the east transept windows.

"Hello," she said, showing him her gritty palms apologetically. She rearranged her ponytail. "Nora Kelley."

"Yes, I know your work," he said. Southern accent. Well-trimmed beard. "I tried to introduce myself to you at the Christmas party, but you were... distracted."

"Oh," she remembered the punchbowl. "Well, this has been a huge project."

"Extraordinary!" he said, surveying the progress on the restoration. "They're wonderfully lively." His voice was a mint julep on a verandah. 🙰

"They are special," she said, as if the windows were her children. "The men who made them really knew what they were doing." She beamed almost as brightly as the fully lit windows. She enjoyed him enjoying the glass, impressed with the way the windows stirred wonder, invited awe.

"I'm an architect," he said, drawing out the word, dropping the "r" a bit: "Ah-chitect." She tried not to smirk. From the inside pocket of his tweed sport coat he took out a small leather case. "My firm took the job on as a pro bono project. We have a site supervisor, but I wanted to weigh in on the installation." As she admired the Le Corbusier pattern of his necktie, he extended his business card, which she took from his hand—no ring. Yet she didn't read the card because she couldn't take her eyes from his Adam's apple working up and down his throat. "It's the best ecclesiastical French Gothic building in the region, so I volunteered my firm's assistance," he said again, jingling change in his pocket.

She could see that she made him nervous, which gave her a little thrill. 🙰 Then *she* got nervous. "I'll archive my materials and maintenance requirements with the cathedral. I've arranged for the scaffolding and the lift for the actual installation. We need to talk about framing. And you need to make sure there's an inch of space between the stained glass panels and the outer glass. Thermal breakage is the biggest threat."

"Yes," Will said with a bashful smile. "I want you to know I've designed with glass before. In fact, I'm working on a project you might be interested in. Or at least I hope you'll be interested in."

"Oh?" She felt a tickle in her nose as a surprise sneeze seized her. She tried to repress it, but out came a raucous "Achooooo!"

"God bless you," he said. "I'm, as I say, working on a project that might appeal to you. It's a hospice downtown. The president of the board sits on the Colorado Council for the Arts. I'm working with elements of sacred geometry; and the design incorporates a lot of native stone and a lot of glass. I've been so impressed with your work here—"

"Cool," she said, interrupting him, wishing she'd responded with something a tad more suave. "A lot of glass?" she asked, her arms akimbo. "Are you offering me a job?"

"I am."

"My designs are considerably less romantic than these," she said, looking up at the Wedding Feast at Cana window, the young bride and groom with their goblets of miraculous wine raised, beribboned laurel wreaths in their curls.

"Good," he said. "I'm talking contemporary."

"Sacred geometry. The Fibonacci series?"

"You know the Fibonacci sequence," he said—a statement, not

a question. 🙟

"The pine cone numbers," she said. "I know a smidgeon. I know the numbers work in sunflower seeds and nautilus shells."

"And spiral galaxies," he said. "Cresting waves. Plato thought the Fibonacci numbers ordered the cosmos. There's a priest in California who heads the Fibonacci Society. He goes so far as to claim that the Fibonacci series is a gift from God. Divine proportion."

"Well, Will, I'd like to know more," Nora said, not sure whether she meant more about higher mathematics or more about this man. She paused, trying to decide if his visit was strictly business. She withdrew, turned her attention to the glass. Then she asked, "Are you a 'form follows function' kind of guy?"

"Of course, first and foremost. However slick their design, I don't like leaky roofs." Will smiled, and Nora, despite herself, did, too. "I'll let you get back to it. 🙟 I know you're trying to nail a deadline here, and I know you have a reputation for coming in on time. And under budget. Let me just leave you my card," he said. "If that's all right."

"You gave me one," she said, waving the little rectangle of impressively weighty embossed paper. Picking up her glass snips, she got back to work.

"Do you have a card?" he asked.

Pulling the pencil from behind her ear, she jotted her phone number on a leftover piece from a cardboard pattern.

"Great, I'll be in touch." They shook hands.

To Nora, his felt slightly rough. *A hands-on man*, she thought. She said, "I look forward to it." Which was true.

The architect bowed ever so slightly, nothing mawkish. "Good luck with the rest of the installation." They looked at one another sideways, eyebrows lifted. Nora looked away as immediately as possible, examining his business card, a toothy stock engraved with his name and title: William Lyle Tyler. Principal. His tag line was a Dostoevsky quote: "Beauty will save the world." His logo, a pine cone.

"Great card," Nora said. "I love pine trees. And aspens. I love the mountains." She smiled.

He smiled. "Do you ski?"

She said, "I do."

"Nice," he said, "I better get back to my office." He took his leave, she presumed, to don his shining armor and saddle up his white steed. Just before he opened the door to exit the cathedral, he looked over his shoulder, back at her.

Outside the cathedral doors, crocus petals unwrapped themselves and faced the sun. A pair of squirrels chased one another around the trunk of a tree. Without fanfare, the Spring Equinox occurred— the celestial moment around which the entire Catholic church calendar orbits.

‰ ‰ ‰

As the cathedral bells rang at 8 a.m., she found herself on the priest's doorstep. Nora had in her head an argument, a line of reasoning based on the priest's own logic. And as dreadful as instigating a direct conversation with him seemed, she couldn't face her future never knowing what might have been between them.

He opened the door. His eyes were puffy and red. He evidently had slept in his clothes. Clerics. "Nora?"

"I know it's early, but I have to ask you something." She searched his eyes, "How can you tell God is present?"

He screwed up his face. "I haven't even had coffee yet and you want to talk theophany? Come in, then." He filled the kettle with water, set it on the stove burner. He turned up the heat.

They sat in painful silence. "How do you *know* God is present?"

"Agitation. Exuberance and energy. A wrenching of the gut. Tears. When it happens you know, but then you can't find words to describe it."

"Try," she said.

He spooned coffee beans into the grinder. "It's between joy and ecstasy and bewilderment and confusion. It's all of that."

"Sounds like falling in love," she said.

"John the Evangelist, of course, said 'God *is* love.'"

The kettle whistled.

She decided to plow ahead before he shut down and sealed her out with somebody else's words. "Then I don't understand why priests aren't allowed to fall in love. To *be* love."

"It's complicated, celibacy. It's a gift."

"Then you can't force it," she said.

He poured himself a cup of coffee, walked to the kitchen window. "But it is mandated. Christ was celibate."

"Do we know that?"

The priest sat down next to her at the table, his elbows on his knees, his head in his hands. "I won't argue with you that celibacy has taken on an essential, divine character I don't believe it was ever entitled to. There's no Biblical support for it."

"Then why do you do it?"

"For the sake of the Kingdom, I suppose." He stood. He ran his thumb along the spines of cookbooks on a shelf. "And because I took that vow."

"But you broke that vow."

His face reddened. He removed the white tab from his Roman collar. "Nora, when a man is ordained, the sacrament of Holy Orders doesn't evaporate all his testosterone. But it would be wrong for you. It would be wrong for me. It would destroy our friendship, and, most likely, my vocation."

"But you're talking about an affair," Nora said, trying rationale to force his hand. "What if we had a publicly acknowledged relationship?"

"It would scandalize many, many people. It would bring disgrace to you, to me, my family, my brother priests, my bishop, the Church."

"They're starting to allow some married priests, I thought."

"Converts. Priests who were married in other denominations," he said. "Nora, I could never be present to you in the way you deserve. My life is so chaotic; the demands of the priesthood are so many and so constant and—"

"But that's if you stay a priest. What if you leave?"

"It's not like resigning from a corporation." He tucked the medal back into his shirt. "We're talking about the sacrament of Holy Orders here."

"But what about the priests who were blind and then they changed the rule?" Grasping at proverbial straws.

"The rule," he said, "has not changed, Nora." He shook his head. "You're asking too much of me."

She swallowed contempt. "But it's OK for you to ask so much of me? What did you expect? That this flirtation could go on forever and I'd never hold you to it?"

"I am not thinking of leaving the priesthood. What would I do?" He pointed toward the dining room. "How would I put bread on the table? I have no marketable skills."

"That's pathetic," she said. "If that's the reason why you stay a priest, that is *pathetic*."

"Maybe so," he said. "But I vowed. Before God and many witnesses,

I vowed. If I'm not good for that, what good am I?"

"I thought you told me that God's happy when we're happy. You think it's all suffering? What about redemption?" Nora turned and braced herself against the counter. "What about love and lovemaking as grace?"

"I'm a priest. I think I will die a priest. What I really want is to live as one. For me, it's the instant of transubstantiation, the moment I lift the Host, the chalice, and cast the miracle with the words of Jesus. I've been celebrating the Eucharist day after day for years, and every time I elevate the bread and wine, I fight tears."

The wall clock ticked.

"I can't expect you to understand my ministry nor could I ever replace it. I can't even give it a name. I can't put it to music, even though that would come closer than words. It's the miraculous, privileged mingling of the human and the divine; and nobody can bottle that and advertise it. That's how I know it's really real."

"What's between us is real, too."

"I can't deny that. But I *can* deny myself. I have to."

"You're denying both of us."

He pressed his forehead to the cupboard. "I never meant to hurt you."

"Hurt *me?*" Nora picked up a paring knife and stabbed its point into the wooden cutting board. "You've got nails pounded through your palms, and you don't even know it."

ANNUNCIATION OF THE LORD (25 March)

Nora didn't regret her harsh words; what she regretted was that the hope was gone. The buoyant infatuation had turned to a dense disappointment. As much as she had fantasized about a future with him, she had to admit there would be none. Could be none. She felt sorrow in her marrow. She wavered between hating herself and hating him. She had played the fool. He had let her. A bitter pride took hold, and Nora cleaved to a determination to save face, to never let on to him or to Millie or to Mrs. Quincy or even to herself how hurt she was. ✍ Despite her devastation, Nora tapped in to her integrity and focused on finishing the commission. Long days passed without seeing the priest.

One night, at about midnight, her doorbell rang several times. She woke up, unsure, but the ringing went on. She dragged herself out of bed and into her robe. Sleepily, she peeked through the window and saw Father DiMarco. Her first thought was that the archbishop had reassigned him. Her next thought was that he had reconsidered. Her expectation rose like a delicate cake, only to fall.

"I can't find Puccini!" he said, whiskey on his breath. Outside, a light snow softly fell.

"Can't find him?"

"I—I fell asleep in the den. And when I woke up, he was gone."

"Gone? But you don't have a dog door, do you?"

He shook his head. His hands shook, too. "I looked all over the house. Everywhere outside."

"Let me get dressed." She pulled on jeans, a turtleneck, a down jacket, grabbed a stocking hat and gloves.

They drove to the rectory in silence. Rushing to the front door, he fumbled with his keys, his hands trembling. "You're sure he's not inside?" she asked.

He shrugged, wrung his hands.

Inside the rectory, she called out, "Puccini! Here, Puccini!" Nora moved through the house, switching on all the lights. In the den, she noticed a fifth of whiskey, almost drained. She looked in closets. Under beds. "Puccini!" she called. The priest followed her. "Maybe if he hears food," she said.

They headed for the kitchen. She rattled the dog food tin, poured kibble into a bowl. "Puccini, come!" he said, his voice cracking.

"He can't just be gone," she said, touching his arm. "Let's check outside." She walked around the cathedral. "Puccini! Come on, Puccini!" she called. She looked in the alley where the people lined up for food. She looked near the front entrance. She looked near the prayer garden, calling, "Puccini!"

At the side entrance, near the garage, she picked up tracks. She pointed. Paw prints. She followed them, rushing, the priest on her heels. The tracks led to the garage. The side door was ajar.

"He's in the garage!" she said, relieved. "Maybe he was trying to come to my studio."

But Father DiMarco gave her a grave look, pushed past her. In the garage, she heard him moan. "No!" he shouted. "Oh, no!"

He knelt by the dog, stroking his brown and black fur. The dog's mouth hung open, his pink tongue limp and lolling out the side of his slack jaw.

"Puccini?" she said.

He pulled the dog's body to his. He wailed and wept.

At first she didn't understand. "What?" she asked. "What is it?" She came closer, and then she saw the green fluid around the dog's muzzle. She smelled the vomit on the garage floor and saw the pan of antifreeze near the old MGB.

"Oh, no."

"Oh, God. Oh, my God. Oh, Puccini," he moaned. His shoulders shook. "I drained the antifreeze. I left it on the garage floor."

She sucked in her breath, took a few unsteady steps. "We have to get him to the vet."

He looked at her. "It's my fault," he mewled. "I'm so sorry, Puccini."

"Come on!" Nora said, pulling his arm. "Let's go!" She jumped in the truck. "I'll hold him." The priest placed the dog in her lap. "Hurry!" ✒

"There's an animal ER on Colfax," he said.

As they sped off, Nora held her head against Puccini's. *Oh, please God,* she prayed. ✒ *Please spare the life of this beautiful creature of yours. Please, God. Please don't take him. Please, Dear God. Please make him well. Please let him live. Please heal him.*

At the veterinarian's office, the priest rushed in with the dog. "Antifreeze," he said.

Attendants rushed the dog through swinging doors.

"How serious is it?" Nora asked one of the aides.

"Very," the bearded young man said. "But sometimes, if we catch it quickly enough, there's hope. I'll let you know as soon as I know anything."

Nora and the priest stood at the reception desk, trying to fill out paperwork.

"I'm so sorry." The priest looked at the ceiling.

"Me too," she said, as if agreement could trump lamentation. And before her own tears began to fall, Nora opened her arms to Vin, and he stepped into her enveloping embrace of charity and mercy, and she held him. His Madonna.

"I don't know what to do," he said.

"Well," she said. "I guess pray."

"Will you join me?" he asked. And she nodded. They found a quiet corner in a hallway, and they got down on their knees. "I have no words," he said.

So they prayed in a fervent silence. Nora felt the linoleum hard beneath her knees. Her fingers intertwined tightly, forming one large fist. She shut her eyes tightly and fought back the urge to imagine the worst.

She felt a warm light fill her chest and move up and down at once, flooding her forehead and her belly. She felt airy. She opened her arms, palms up, taking the orante pose of prayer. She begged and pleaded, bargained.

And then she heard his name called: "Vincent DiMarco?"

"We're here," he said, getting to his feet. "Is he OK?"

Nora stood, whoozy. "Is he going to make it?"

The veterinarian paused. "You're dog has what we call ethylene glycol toxicosis. It causes severe kidney failure. About 80 percent of the time it's fatal if not treated within four to eight hours. Do you know when the dog got into the antifreeze?"

They shook their heads no.

"The fact that he was down suggests he ingested it some hours ago, at least, because it looks like it affected the brain and spinal fluid," the vet said. "We induced vomiting and gave him charcoal and an antidote. We're running some tests. We've got him on IV fluids to ward off dehydration, but he'll be here a few days. At least."

"But he'll live?" Nora asked.

"We won't know for sure," the vet said, "but we'll do everything we can." ✍

At her bench, Nora's back ached, but no more than her heart. That Puccini and Vin were both lost to her cast a pall. Holy Week approached. Nora felt anything but. Holiness loomed distant, denied to her. Holiness, she assumed, was not of the earth, but a state reserved for saints. She swore she heard the angels imprisoned in the windows singing, *"Kyrie eleison."* Lord have mercy.

Desperate, Nora even considered the Sacrament of Reconciliation, which she knew to be part and parcel of keeping a holy Lent. She gave serious thought to finding another priest in another parish and stepping into the dark closet to make a confession that might assuage her guilt. Guilt over sex with a priest. Guilt over Vin's increased drinking. Guilt over Puccini's possible death. Guilt over the havoc she'd wreaked in the cathedral parish when she was supposed to be making repairs, not making trouble. On the other hand, Nora felt as if God should be apologizing to *her*.

She channeled her remorse into the glass, making her work a penance, an act of contrition. She wanted to do one thing, at least, right. She wanted to finish on time and to leave behind restored beauty.

Most of all, she wanted Puccini to walk through the door, Lazarus dog, alive and well, resurrected, tail wagging.

When Juan showed up in the garage, Nora knew it was not to discuss the budget. "I heard about Puccini," he said.

Nora nodded, sighed, and searched for an evasion. She slumped, her elbows propped on a tall stool. "It was an accident," she said, straightening up.

"It was negligent."

"I don't want to judge him. It could happen to anyone."

"Especially if they were drunk."

"He's inconsolable."

"He's…" Juan rubbed his hands on the suede elbow patches of his sweater. He took a pen from his pocket, clicked it again and again. "Nora, I think you should know that Father DiMarco is a recovering alcoholic."

"Recovering?"

"It's an ongoing process," Juan said, "but we're all aware that he's drinking. To excess."

Nora met his level gaze. "And that's my responsibility?"

"We can't afford to lose him."

Neither can I, she thought. "What are you getting at?"

"You need to end your relationship with him outside of work."

"Father DiMarco and I are just friends," she said, letting the sad truth of it sink in.

"The bishop called me in to the chancery last week. I was in his office for a good hour. He's taking no prisoners. Not with what's transpiring in the media. Archbishop asked me if I felt Father DiMarco needed to be reassigned."

"What did you say?"

He fell silent. "I can't lie to the archbishop."

"Haven't you ever heard of *agapé*? Christian love, Juan. Isn't that what it's all about?"

"Based on what I've heard, this isn't *agapé*."

"It's none of your business. Or the archbishop's."

"That's where you're wrong," Juan said. "In the end, the Church is a business. The archbishop is the corporation sole."

"What are you telling me, Juan?"

"I'm telling you that it's not just Puccini in trouble; and I'm not about to stand by and watch you two topple this institution. The cathedral means so much to so many. If we end up in some sort of scandal, followed by litigation, we won't survive. You two carry on as if nobody cares. I care!" Juan pointed to his chest. "Father thinks he can conduct himself as unprofessionally as possible and get away with it because there's a priest shortage and he thinks he won't be reprimanded. He's wrong! Dead wrong!"

Nora's toes curled. She looked up at the ceiling.

Juan looked down at the floor. He crumbled the invoice, pitched it against a wall. "You think the windows are the most important thing about the cathedral?" He pointed out the window at the spires. "It's not about pieces of pretty glass, Nora. It's about people—people who would come here to meet God if we kept the *plywood* on those windows!"

And with that, he left her alone with her shock and her culpability.

ST. FRANCES OF PAOLA, HERMIT (2 April)

After an excruciating week, Nora was working in the garage when she heard Puccini bark. She hustled to the driveway, where the dog stood, thinner, and with a shaved spot on his haunch. He wagged his tail weakly when he saw her. Nora knelt and hugged the dog, stroked his ears, and said only two words: "Thank God."

HOLY TUESDAY (6 April)

The priest did not darken Nora's doorway. Since the night Puccini almost died, Nora had seen little of the pastor. And when she did, he reeled with contrition, never even making eye contact with her.

Generous days warmed and lengthened, melting the last of winter's final snow. The sun felt nearer, lighting the windows longer into the evening. ❧ The season of psychological sinkholes drew to a close again, yet Nora could not find the usual joy that returned with the migratory birds.

She knocked off early one night. Mrs. Quincy pulled up as Nora locked her bike to the railing on the front steps of the carriage house. Nora tried to scurry inside, but Mrs. Quincy beeped her horn.

"Would you mind?" she asked, pointing to sacks of groceries in her trunk.

"Not at all," Nora said, walking toward her.

Mrs. Quincy opened the front door for her and said, "He's beside himself, as he should be: He almost killed his dog."

Nora walked to her pantry, set the groceries down on a counter.

She pulled her shoulder blades up to the nape of her neck. "I know."

"He's as broken as those windows, but if you think you're going to fix him, you're sorely mistaken." Mrs. Quincy began unpacking groceries. "You seem to think you're the flirtation to end all flirtations. Yes, he makes you feel special.  He makes us all feel special."

"That's why we all love him," Nora said.

"He's got his cross to bear," the old woman said as she piled artichokes in a colander. "You're not the problem, Nora. But you're not the solution, either." She put her sunglasses in her ivory clutch purse. "Are you going to the Chrism Mass tomorrow?"

"I don't even know what the Chrism Mass is."

"All the priests of the archdiocese come to the cathedral," Mrs. Quincy said. "They celebrate Mass together. They renew their priestly vows. They get the holy oils, blessed by the archbishop, and they take them back to their parishes."

"They renew their vows?"

"Every year," Mrs. Quincy said. "It's a beautiful liturgy. You might want to attend."

"I won't have time. I'm trying to finish," Nora said, flustered, clinging to her own vow, resentful of his other woman, the Church.

❧ ❧ ❧

HOLY THURSDAY (8 April)

She looked at the last window on her bench. The final one. Nora boxed up the cullet. Even unset, the leftover bits of cut glass possessed their own alchemy. She rolled up the enormous cartoons and labeled the cardboard tubes and left them on the workbench.

In the window Nora was sealing, Jesus extended his curative hand over a man on a stretcher. She rubbed some oxidation from the lead, swishing fine gauge steel wool back and forth over the soldered joints. ✒ For the last step, she rubbed on car wax to make the glass easy to dust.

She cleaned her brushes for the last time and collected her tools. Nora took one last look around the garage as if she were a home-owner about to turn over her keys.

She wandered over to the cathedral, where Harry and his crew wrestled with a panel of glass. The last phase of the installation went smoothly. ✒ She watched the men on the scaffolding and held her breath as they hoisted the panel on a lift. She observed them as they set the final section into the T-bar. The armature accepted the glass; the glass rested on the metal. Two-Wheel Rich worked diligently, responding to Harry as if he were a general.

The noise of drills and lifts pulsed at her temples. Exhausted, Nora's feet were anvils. She walked through the cathedral in an arc of ache, double-checking the windows—each soldered corner, each millimeter of glass. Every gaffe jumped out at her. Every minute chip, every infinitesimal variation in coloration, every wayward stroke of a paintbrush.

"You did one hell of a job here," Harry said.

"Hell," Nora said, "being the operative word."

"I can almost hear your granddad bragging on you." He put his big hands on her shoulders. "You're a talent, kid. Always were. See you around?"

"Yeah, you will. Thanks, Harry," she said and hugged him, noticing the comfort in their embrace.

The cathedral seemed especially tranquil. With her barely dry coat of paint and her windows restored, her roof fixed and her statuary repaired, the cathedral was like a *grande dame* fresh from the beauty parlor, looking fine and feeling a little proud.

Nora left the cathedral, but she could not leave the grounds. She didn't want to go home alone. ✍ She sat in the prayer garden. She looked up at the gargoyles and considered the cathedral's nature: by day, alive inside with color; by night, with light from within, alive outside, windows shining like giant gemstone brooches.

Torn between darkness and light, Nora went back in the cathedral and snuck down the back stairway to the Bride's Room, where it all began. ✍ She remembered Vin and Puccini comforting her as the storm peaked. The door was unlocked. She stepped inside and looked at herself in the three-way mirror. She folded the hinged mirrors in so that when she leaned forward she saw a row of infinite images of herself growing smaller and smaller in perspective, more and more distant. Nora granted herself a moment of self-congratulations: She had given form to the indefinable. She had made perceptible the long gone world of Jesus Christ, the invisible arena of angels.

But she was unknown to herself. The windows were finished, yet so much felt undone. Unsaid. Unresolved. ✍

FATHER VINCENT DiMARCO

In the name of the Father ⊠ and of the Son ⊠ and of the Holy Spirit. ⊠

Your mercy endures forever. ⊠ Your ways are everlasting. Your miracles numberless. ⊠ ⊠ ⊠ My hands and feet are pierced; my bones numbered. I die with you on a hill of skulls. I offer you my sorrows, God; in exchange, grant me faith or hope or love. ⊠ ⊠ ⊠ I have lost my path, Good Shepherd. O God, lead me in a life in which my actions glorify your name. ⊠ Cleanse me of my iniquities; wash away my hypocrisy, my transgressions. I know what you ask of me, Lord. ⊠ Give me the fortitude to accept the answer to my prayer, not according to my will, but to yours. ⊠ ⊠ ⊠ Bless the good people of your parish; especially bless Nora Kelley, your artist servant. ⊠ In this time of renewal, grant salvation to the poor, freedom to all who are imprisoned, joy to the sorrowful, as you promised. ⊠ And to me, Father, prudence. Give me eyes of faith to envision a future of hope. ⊠ ⊠ ⊠

In the name of the Father and of the Son and of the Holy Spirit. ⊠ AMEN. ⊠

CHAPTER SIX

Triduum

GOOD FRIDAY (9 April)

In a curious pagan twist, the liturgical calendar of the Universal Catholic Church schedules Easter on the First Sunday after the first full moon after the Vernal Equinox. Love, too, is linked to the moon by poets and songwriters across cultures and ages.

Nora woke up before dawn and peeked out a window. The waning moon glowed like an ancient, worn coin; and she could not decide which would be more lunacy: to see the priest one more time or to see him never again.

She went back to bed, but when she closed her eyes, she saw only broken glass, a kaleidoscope shifting. Nora hugged herself, yearning for his embrace.

In the space between waking and sleep, another realm opened. Nora fell into reverie, felt as if she were floating above her bed, looking down at herself. Her flannel pajamas, the twisted cross made by her sprawled body. An astonishing music filled her ears.

Nora observed herself sitting up in bed below, tilting her head to listen. Was she dreaming? Was it the echo of the chorale practicing in the cathedral? Nora would never be sure, but something shifted. Something revelatory and hyper-real. An intimation. A confirmation.

Now that the work was completed, she felt like an imposter, a criminal returning to the scene of the crime. Now that she had no literal business in the cathedral, she approached it not as a worker, but as a worshipper. ✑ She slipped in a side door, dipped the fingers of her right hand in the holy water fount, only to find it dry. The lack of water shocked her, saddened her, as if she were being denied. Then she looked up and saw all the statues swathed in purple—the color of royalty, the color of passion—and she realized that Good Friday ritual calls for emptying the holy water fonts.

The altar was stripped bare. Nora peeked into the sacristy, wondering whether the pastor might be hanging up his vestments. The room was crowded with potted Easter lilies, and they gave off an acrid smell almost like urine.

Outside, between the cathedral and the rectory, Nora spotted him. With a small shovel, the priest dug a hole in the ground. She approached quietly, gazed up at the window where the wasps' nest had been.

"What are you doing?" she said.

He dropped the spade. "Nora. You scared the devil out of me."

"What are you planting?"

He shook his head. "I'm burying the holy oils. We do it every Good Friday."

"So I guess you got your new oils. And renewed your vows."

He nodded.

Nora felt the earth beneath her clogs, as if the holy oils had seeped through Colorado's clay soil to anoint her feet.

"Vin," she said, secure for the first time in speaking his name, as if by speaking it aloud to him, she had named him, and the word held no allure. By speaking his name with no attachment, she had incarnated him. Christened him. Taken him from mythic to real, cracking love's unspoken spell that had rendered him closer to angel than man. He was a man, Nora plainly saw. A man for her unlike any other, but a man, nonetheless. Human. Flawed. Yet lovable. No more, no less than her. ❧ Ordained, yet a person with a name and a DNA profile and a path of his own, yet shared by all humanity. Nora knew that there was no accident in their meeting and no coincidence in their parting. She felt destiny's tug. She sensed the eternal, the numinous.

"Nora."

"Vin," she said again and held her hands up as if to hold him back, to shield herself from the energy he emanated. The last thing she wanted was to see him flail.

And he didn't. He gathered himself; and in his scholarly tone, he gently said, "To answer your earlier question: 'How do we know God's near?'" He cleared his throat. "I think theophany comes at times when we need to be reinforced—whether as confirmation after we've been through a trial, or to prepare us for tribulations to come."

For Nora, the miracle was not that she had repaired the windows, but that a broken priest had helped her repair something in herself. ✍ She had not gone back to the Church, but she had returned to the mystery. She had resumed her craft, and her craft had given her purpose. Having purpose had allowed her to love herself again. Self-love, in turn, had inspired higher love. When Nora looked at the priest, she felt not concupiscence, but compassion. And the emotion felt right, good, just.

Like lovers everywhere across eons, they had lived for their love. They had cast caution and rationality to the winds and put everything on the thin line. Their love had driven them to the brink of destruction, yet also had affected reparation.

Nora had not seen love coming, but she definitely saw it going. She knew it was over. The spell broken, infatuation dissipated; and Nora saw Father Vincent DiMarco as a man who needed his vocation and whose vocation was much needed.

Nora knew she needed her own vocation, too.

As if taking in one another's soul, they stared without a lick of malice, a long, lingering, last look. Nora saw in his eyes that she would never have him, and she hoped he saw in hers that she would always love him. Love him without desperation, without expectation. The pain of love no longer felt tantamount. ✒ The entanglement untwined, and Nora no longer felt hemmed in by destiny. She had free will, after all. She had choices, and she made one. She took heart. And in doing so, an intangible triumph welled up in her. Call it conscience. Call it courage. Interior knowing. Fruit of the Holy Spirit. Call it calling. Call it love.

She knew it was good-bye; and she knew it was for good.

"I'm finally finished." The look on his face told Nora that Vin knew she meant more than the restoration of the glass.

He looked like a lost boy. The priest pinched the bridge of his nose. "I wish you didn't have to go," he said, his voice pained.

Nora nodded. She touched her fingertips to her own heart as she said, "It doesn't mean I don't love you," she said, "it means that I do." ✒

FATHER VINCENT DiMARCO

"My God, my God, why have you abandoned me?"

⊠ ⊠ ⊠

Eastertide

ora knew she would hazard her heart again. Just over a year later, a few days before the Feast of the Ascension, Nora and Will wandered to the farmer's market. All about the landscape, nature displayed evidence of a new season. The warm days had devoured most of the snow on Mount Evans, proud in the distance. The deciduous trees had not yet concealed their nests.

As they walked, Will pointed out architectural details in the buildings of his historic neighborhood: wrought-iron scrolls and stone cartouches and gabled rooflines. A gentleman, he maneuvered to make sure he always walked nearest the street. At the corner, he took her hand, smooched her knuckles. Their love was fresh and bright as the forsythia glowing like fireflies.

Nora swung her canvas shopping bags. "I want to get some euphoria-inducing asparagus. And I want some pansies, but not to eat. I'll plant those urns outside your front door."

"I'd like that," Will said.

Nora veered off toward a grower's striped tent filled with flowers. "I'll meet you by the goat cheese guy."

"There's a goat cheese guy?"

She pointed across the parking lot. "Right over there."

Greeted by the cheery faces of the colorful pansies, Nora couldn't help but smile. She made her way along the tables, trying to decide upon colors. And then she overheard somebody speak his name: *Father DiMarco.*

She froze. Her belly seized. Sheepishly, Nora looked across the table crowded with culinary herbs. At the checkout stand, a cashier spoke with a middle-aged woman. To position herself for easier eavesdropping, Nora feigned interest in rosemary.

"Of course, we knew Father Vin when we were in the cathedral parish. He baptized all my grandkids. I used to see him here pretty regularly," the cashier said as he weighed snow peas. "But not for a while. Yes, Father DiMarco. Such a good guy."

"I hear he's doing better," the woman said, taking bills from her wallet. "I don't know if you heard: He's in New Mexico."

Nora's chest tightened. ✺ Her head flooded with memories, questions. She kept her gaze down. Her pulse pounded.

"I did hear," the cashier said. "I heard he'd be there for at least 90 days." ✺

"It's a shame, but I've heard it's a good facility."

The man lowered his voice a bit and said, "Especially for priests. I heard they even take dogs. Puccini is there with him."

Nora edged closer, alert. ✑ Her head whirled. She picked up a bedding plant and read the label: Dianthus. Sweet William.

"We sure miss Father. It's not the same without him." The woman stuffed her produce into a colorful vinyl tote.

"He's a good priest," the cashier said, "He'll make it."

The woman said, "I hope."

And the man said, "That's all any of us can do."

Nora made her way out of the tent, shocked by the reminder of Father Vincent DiMarco's existence. Her heart felt thick with loss and the taunt of what might have been. From the farmer's market, she could see the tips of the cathedral's spires. Nora's mouth filled with ash, the taste of his taboo kisses.

"What? No pansies?" Will asked.

She turned toward him, then away. Nora shook her head, unable to speak, lost in the past. She recollected the day the priest first took her to lunch, the way the wind had combed her hair as they drove in his convertible, the way his forearm had grazed her chest. And how they had run out of road. Nora wondered whether Vin ever confessed or ever would confess their tryst.

"Nora?

And with a squeeze of Will's hand on her wrist, Nora snapped back into the present moment. She considered for an instant trying to explain to Will. But she thought better of it, knowing there's no explaining love any more than there is explaining God. Maybe, in the end, St. John had it right all along: They are one and the same, God and love.

"Did you know there's a flower named after you?" Nora asked, leading Will by the arm, handing him the plastic spike from the bedding plant.

"Sweet William," he said, reading the label. And he looked as if Nora had given him a blue ribbon.

And she said, "Let's go home."

As they walked slowly through the neighborhood, striding in syncopation, Nora took in the details of gardens. Flowering crab apple trees frothed pink and white. Redbud trees flaunted exotic purple limbs. Against all likelihood, knobby bulbs buried deep last fall pushed pointy green shoots through the winter-thawed earth, staging their own blossoming resurrection. Crocus. Daffodils. Tulips. Perfumed hyacinths would overlap with honeysuckle, the wheel of time ever turning. Hand in hand at a corner, waiting for a green light, Nora noticed new leaves unfurling on the twigs of shrubs. The lilacs would bloom early that Eastertide, an off year for miller moths.

THE END

ACKNOWLEDGEMENTS

You know that saying—"It takes a village"—about raising children? In my case, the maxim held true while writing this book. I owe 100,000 thanks to at least as many people: all those who read versions of the manuscript, wrote advance reviews or blurbs for the book, provided design feedback, or supplied spiritual succor in any way along the long way.

I've collaborated for 20 years with James Baca, the photographer of the cover images, and Nancy Benton, who helped design *Glass Halo*. Lori Spencer Smith copyedited *Glass Halo*.

THE FRIDAY JONES PLAYERS
In-house interns staffing Friday Jones Publishing, in order of appearance: Josie Bouchier ⊠ Maggie Ragatz ⊠ Jesse Krieger ⊠ Quincy Benton ⊠ Andrea Collatz ⊠

My profound appreciation goes to Joel Cooperman, the good doctor who helps me heal.

Thank you all for helping me wag this tale.

Please visit www.GlassHaloNovel.com
for the long list of collaborators, contributors and friends of
Friday Jones Publishing.

READERS GUIDE

1. Which character do you most identify with? Nora Kelley? Father Vin?

2. What are the underling character flaws in Nora and Father Vin?

3. What attracts the two main character to one another? What repels them?

4. Why is stained glass an appropriate medium and metaphor for the relationship between Nora and Father Vin?

5. How do Nora and Father Vin break one another? How do they heal one another?

6. How do you feel about Nora and Father Vin consummating their relationship?

READERS GUIDE (Continued)

7. What are the moments of conversion for Nora and Father Vin?

8. What role did the vocations of Nora and Father Vin play in their redemption?

9. What do the secondary characters bring to this novel? Mrs. Quincy? Puccini? Millie? Juan? Two-Wheel Rich?

10. What does the title *Glass Halo* mean to you?

FRIDAY JONES PUBLISHING &
THE ARTS & CRAFTS MOVEMENT

Glass Halo's cover and page layouts, and Friday Jones Publishing's logo and philosophy draw inspiration from the Arts & Crafts Movement, in particular William Morris and Kelmscott Press, and also the Roycrofters. A movement that valued the beauty of nature, the importance of books, hands-on craft, joy in work, and women's creative contributions, the Arts & Crafts influence also is reflected in the fonts, dingbats, graphics and patterns found in *Glass Halo.*

Cover photo illustration and page design by Colleen Smith and Nancy Benton ⊠ Cover and front flap stained-glass photographs: James Baca ⊠ Cover and interior pattern, illuminated capital letters and angel bookplate: William Morris Designs, Dover Publications, Inc. ⊠ Woodcuts: Quaint Cuts in the Chap Book Style of Joseph Crawhall, Selected and Arranged by Theodore Menten, Dover Publications, Inc. ⊠ Typography: book text set in Goudy Old Style, initial caps for chapter beginnings in Morris Ornaments, other headings and book title set in Rochambeau from the Arts & Crafts type collection. ✎

ABOUT THE AUTHOR

COLLEEN SMITH earned her B.A. in English at the University of Iowa, which awarded her the E.P. Kuhl Shakespeare Prize for Literary Criticism. Smith studied the writing of fiction and poetry in the Iowa Writers' Workshop, which named her the Fairall Scholar of Creative Writing, then the highest award for undergraduates. For the last 20 years, Smith has written for several Catholic archdioceses across the nation, and garnered numerous awards from the Catholic Press Association. A freelance writer, editor and creative director, she contributes regularly to secular magazines and newspapers. Smith lives in a Denver, Colorado, historic district and is an avid alpine skier and gardener. *Glass Halo* is Smith's first novel, to be followed by *Only Wild Plums*, another work of fiction.

Photo by James Baca

Yes! I want to order *Glass Halo* by Colleen Smith.

GLASS HALO

First Name

☐ Check
☐ Money Order

(   )

Last Name   Telephone

Number of Books _____

Address   Apartment / Unit #

Price $ 24.95

City   State   Zip Code

Shipping per copy $ 2.00

Signature

Total $ _____

Your e-mail address (please print clearly)

Thank you for your order. Please make your check payable to
FRIDAY JONES PUBLISHING

Send to Friday Jones Publishing ▪ 600 Cook Street ▪ Denver, CO 80206-3591
FridayJonesPublishing.com

FRIDAY JONES
:: PUBLISHING ::

FRIDAY JONES
:: PUBLISHING ::
WAG YOUR TALE.™

Denver, Colorado ▪ FridayJonesPublishing.com ▪ GlassHaloNovel.com

Only Wild Plums

ᏭᎲᎲᎩ

by Colleen Smith

Only Wild Plums introduces readers to the Larkins, a large, quirky, Irish-Catholic family living in Colorado. Narrated from the points-of-view of seven well drawn characters, the novel details intimate and memorable portraits of a mother, five of her children, and one of her grandchildren—each walking through one of life's major turnstiles. Rich with detailed description; complex relationships; and witty, true-to-life dialogue, *Only Wild Plums* examines clannish bonds and the truth that sometimes family has nothing to do with blood.

FRIDAY JONES
:: PUBLISHING ::
WAG YOUR TALE.™

www.FridayJonesPublishing.com
www.GlassHaloNovel.com